MW01600393

FEMALE SHARPSHOOTER
IN THE CIVIL WAR

KENNETH ALDER

Copyright © 2024
KENNETH ALDER
Female Sharpshooter in the Civil War
All rights reserved.

No part of this publication may be reproduced, distributed, or transmitted in any form or by any means, including photocopying, recording, or other electronic or mechanical methods, without the prior written permission of the author, except in the case of brief quotations embodied in critical reviews and certain other non-commercial uses permitted by copyright law.

KENNETH ALDER

Printed Worldwide
First Printing 2024
First Edition 2024

ISBN: 979-8301073342

10 9 8 7 6 5 4 3 2 1

This is a work of fiction. Names, characters, places, and incidents either are the product of the author's imagination or are used fictitiously. Any resemblance to actual persons, living or dead, events, or locales is entirely coincidental.

FEMALE SHARPSHOOTER
IN THE CIVIL WAR

FOREWORD

This is a story of love, passion, and the Civil War. A present-day lesbian couple discovers a group of letters written by two young lesbian lovers during the Civil War Era. They came into possession of these letters through an unexpected inheritance.

The two main characters are seventeen-year-old girls who fell in love with each other when social norms had no tolerance for same sex unions. The primary setting is in Pennsylvania during the Civil War era. Both lovers hate slavery and the looming Confederacy totally. Out of a sense of duty one of the girls (Rachel = Ray) enlists in the Union Army disguised as a man.

A sizeable number of women did serve as men during that horrific war. Rachel (Ray) serves as a sharpshooter throughout that conflict. The heart of the story is two small groups of letters. Rachel's parents use letters to describe the political and economic factors that led to the Civil War. The remaining bulk of the letter collection is between Mary and her lover Rachel. Rachel's experiences during many battles are timeless. Mary in turn reflects on the confusion of civilian life during this conflict. The Civil War was the most tragic war in American history.

Rachel Summerfield comes from a wealthy family and Mary comes from a bottom class dirt poor family. Mary is trying to survive an abusive father in a crushing household. Rachel has sworn to somehow extract Mary from this violent home. Both Rachel and Mary are intellectually gifted.

Rachel's battle history is truly history as an enlisted officer would experience it. All the battles reflect a soldier's emotions and fear as many experienced it. Rachel's views on Union, slavery, death and the war itself are relevant to this very day. Rachel's struggle to hide her gender was constantly challenging. All these factors are compounded by their lesbian love. A situation that was far more difficult in their day than ours. You are the judge of this story. I hope you will enjoy this saga.

CHAPTER ONE

April 21, 2006

New Haven, Connecticut

I will never forget that spring day in April. It was a beautiful day far removed from our last harsh winter which had been barely endurable. The scent was of promising plants and fresh cut green grass was uplifting. Life was exploding with hope. Last winter's cold bitter claws were fading in our memories. The Elm trees were in full bloom. Its leaves reaching toward the sun..

The lightly swaying limbs left shadows that danced across the manicured lawn. The sky was of the deepest cobalt and the clouds were of the voluptuous pearl variety. The clouds seemed to be tinted with the faintest gold at the edges and they floated across the sky like a leisure ship.

It was truly gorgeous. I felt so glad to be alive and I was so grateful for my good health. The blood in one's body was rushing with momentum. The picturesque grounds at Yale University were covered with resting students reclining or gathered as groups amid this oasis of greenery and shade.

I watched a pair of students engrossed in throwing a Frisbee. Another couple of lovers were kissing slowly and ardently while laying supine on the green in the warming air. Clearly they were alone in their world of passion.

I can remember thinking how wonderful it was to be so young, healthy and hopeful. I was reminded of young love and the flames that burned so hot in my youth. It was magnificent to see this affirmation of love. Life on that spring day was reasserting itself with all its pulsing vibrancy. I saw my reflection in the one-piece plate-glass window, and I was satisfied that I had aged well. The image of a tall slender woman reflected toward me.

Undoubtedly I am vain, but I still have curves in all the right places. I wear my hair tastefully in a short style. My blue eyes often received compliments and fortunately I have never needed glasses. I am sixty-three. The years had been kind to me, and I could still draw the attention of much younger men and even younger women who are much more attractive to me.

I exercise with a personal trainer and watch my diet carefully. All in all, I was content and fulfilled. With these pleasant thoughts in mind, I returned to my desk to grade papers from one of my English classes.

Then, I noted a thin shouldered quite tall special delivery man franticly trying to read the names on the doors of the English department. I rose just as he rapidly approached my door. He stopped so abruptly I thought he was going to fall. He apparently was looking for me. He asked in a quick manner whether I was Professor Joyce Summerfield. I replied that I was her and accepted his small package.

This type of delivery is common in academia. There were always messages and announcements of various types. There were always meetings and conferences that beckoned with glossy petitions for one's time. Most of the older professors hoped for rest rather than status. At the end of their careers the drive to excel was somewhat tempered.

Most professor desks were covered with these unwanted packets. As was so often the case I didn't find time to open it until late in the day. I had no idea of the massive change this slim document would make in my life.

Before this strange narrative can be told I must mention a little about myself. My name is Joyce Summerfield, and I am a writer and English Professor at Yale University of Connecticut. I have been fortunate to have lived here in New Haven for decades.

As a tenured facility member, I teach English Composition and Advanced Writing at Yale. I have written over seven historical novels and in general my writing has been well received. I have held my university position for over 23 years. I have been an open lesbian for over forty years. I had recently married my lifetime partner Ann.

My sexual orientation became ironic as later details will show. I have been fortunate to live in New Haven where the tolerance for gay people has been good for many years. Of course, at the age of 63 I can easily remember when lesbian relationships were not accepted by general society.

This information will be useful as you read the rest of my strange account. The history of the past often has a strange ability to pierce the years and confront us with surprises. Of all my life surprises, that thin plain envelope contained a surprise that was by far the greatest.

I looked at the return address and was perplexed. This packet had the return address that stated simply "George Hansal Attorney of Law, 237 Hager St. Red Cloud NE. Using an ancient letter opener that had belonged to my father I broke the seal. Upon careful perusal I was astonished to read that the letters claimed that I appeared to be the last living relative of a Rachel Summerfield who died in 1927 in Titusville PA. Ms. Summerfield died the age of 84. I was told that the estate was substantial.

Apparently the deceased owned twelve sections of prime farmland in Nebraska. The property had a small home, a small caretaker cottage, a barn, a single car garage and three bank accounts. One checking account of 1,250, 067.74 dollars and one savings account held Forty-Nine million dollars and another checking account of 1.5 million dollars set aside for caretaking and maintenance.

In addition, it was mentioned there were miscellaneous personal effects held in a trunk at the house, A few other personal items were stored in a safe located at her lawyer's office. It was listed that there was a firearm. The firearm had been cared for and stored by three generations of Hansal lawyers.

Apparently these items were meaningful to Rachel Summerfield. The value of the firearm was not listed. Without the real estate the cash remainder was apparently worth more than forty-nine million dollars at current market value.

Even though it was late in the day I wanted to get some answers. I called the number that was on the legal letterhead. A male attorney answered the call with a surprising uplift voice. This was alleged to be a Mr. Hansal who apparently worked long hours. I explained to

Mr. Hansal that I had no knowledge of a Rachel Summerfield and had no doubt that he had the wrong person. Mr. Hansal became more serious. He insisted his firm had made all diligent efforts to locate the last heir. I was the result of these efforts.

He further stated his firm had been searching for over 8 months. After public and professional private searches, the firm was sure this research would meet the legal approval of the State of Nebraska. Naturally, I was skeptical. I was certain this was a prank or more likely a scam. I cut the conversation short after I gave him my personal mailing address. I simply requested the detailed paperwork. That seemed to be the logical move. Mr. Hansal assured me that all particulars would come shortly.

Naturally, I did not expect to hear from Mr. Hansal again. However, in three days I received a bulky packet of mostly legal papers. Among the paperwork was a copy of a will and the various accounts that held the cash assets of the deceased's estate. Since I am not a lawyer there was much I didn't understand. Within a week I took the documents to my cultured and expensive lawyer.

I asked her to examine the papers and determine if the claims were true. I confess by this time I was bewildered. Was it likely this might be a legitimate situation? After nearly three weeks I had nearly forgotten the papers that I delivered to my lawyer. When I received a phone call from her everything in my world changed. My hands sweated and I confess my hands became shaky. This was not at all normal behavior of a woman of my age and education.

She requested a meeting as soon as reasonably possible. My lawyer said that she had studied all the paperwork, state records, bank records, death registers and had called Mr. Hansal many times. She had also hired professional researchers who had expertise in this field. She felt that an office visit was necessary. Of course I was in a daze by this time. My former life had been normal and except for four decades of work on feminists' issues I was just a normal citizen with average aspirations. I looked forward to my retirement and the writing I would do with more leisure time

Later that week I was able to have a teaching assistant stand in for me while I went to my well-known attorney. When I entered the attorney's office suite I spoke to the brightly toned secretary. With her poise and her bearing she projected power and established money.

CHAPTER TWO

May 15, 2016

As I entered the posh law office I spoke to the receptionist, "My name is Joyce Summerfield, and I believe I have an appointment with Ms. Salsist. "Yes Ms. Summerfield I will tell Ms. Salsist you have arrived."

I was shown to the office. I was greeted by an older woman whose age was near 55 who was refined and professionally proper. She came around the desk to help seat me. This was the first time I had been in her office properly, and it was opulent. As I carefully glanced around I saw that this office dripped wealth in its furnishings.

From the carpet to the ornate lights all were of the highest quality and arranged by a professional of flawless taste. Upon the walls were the documents of a well-born successful attorney who had graduated with honors from Harvard law school 35 years ago. She was clearly aware of her accomplishments and her distinguished career.

Every thread on her Giorgio Armani suit was perfect and carefully tailored to show her excellent figure. Her gaze with gray eyes was level and her handshake was firm but tasteful. On her left arm she wore a Reverso watch. Her shoes were Christian Louboutin. Around her neck was a stunning B.ZERO1 necklace.

I knew she was wearing well over $30,000.00 on her well-toned and sculptured body. Of course, the average client would know these facts instantly. That is why she wore them. Unfortunately, I noted these facts myself. I tried to chastise myself. Perhaps we are all too vain. This was not a store front law office with a painted shingle. I reminded myself that I was here for a legal opinion.

"Please seat yourself Ms. Summerfield. This has been an unusual assignment, but I am now able to give you a reasoned legal opinion. As I mentioned over the phone I have reviewed the documents, and I have carefully checked the legal validity of all the paperwork. I have worked carefully and thoroughly with Mr. Hansal.

I have also worked hand in hand with the State of Nebraska through all applicable offices. She paused for a pregnant moment. I felt strained but I knew the bottom line was coming shortly. True to my instincts Ms. Salsist spoke smoothly and directly.

"The will and all the particulars are correct as Mr. Hansal stated in his original documents. Since the estate was somewhat large we ran our legal combs through it. Most unusual the estate has fulfilled all the requirements of probate and has been sitting in abeyance until the issue of the legal heir could be determined. You are the final legal heir, and you can assume ownership of all the items listed in the will."

"As I mentioned this was a most unusual case. Since the death of Rachel Summerfield all her real property and her savings was placed in an irrevocable trust. Whoever was the legal heir since the day of her death could only draw on the interest of her assets. They could not sell any real property nor use the principle on any liquid funds or savings. The liquid assets were accessible but only with the approval of Mr. Hansal the trustee.

We also researched the actions of Mr. Hansal to see if there were any red flags. It is now clear that Mr. Hansal was careful and prudent with his decisions. However, none of these restrictions apply to you."

"For whatever reason Rachel Summerfield allowed the legal heir living on or after January 1, 2016, the right to use or sell any real or liquid assets in any manner that the legal heir chooses. Basically, the estate was held in trust since the day Rachel Summerfield died.

Even more unusual the house and all its items have been maintained just as it was in 1927. No one lived in the home, but a cottage was provided for a caretaker to oversee his duties. Sizeable funds were provided to keep the house, and the outbuildings repaired and maintained."

I have always prided myself as having a calm rational mind. However, on this subject I was stunned.

I asked the attorney.

"How large is this estate?"

The attorney smiled slowly and then said

"Not counting the value of the real estate, the liquid assets are over forty-nine million dollars."

It took a few moments to take in this information. I seldom lose my composure, but this was so new I did not know how to respond.

"What do I do now? I have not a clue as to how I should proceed. I realize what you have just told me but is it possible such a thing can happen to an ordinary person like me?"

The attorney smiled again.

"I assure you that such things happen. This firm has handled estates much larger than this one and we have handled estates that have had many unusual requirements. We will be able to assist you with all the paperwork to change titles and to fill out the forms to claim your liquid assets. At this point it is all straightforward. I suggest that you go to Nebraska to inspect your holdings and work with Mr. Hansel.

Our office will also work closely with Mr. Hansel and we will convey all the transfers of real property, liquid assets and personal effects. Of course, you are to sign nothing until our firm has carefully reviewed the documents."

"We will assure you that all things are in legal order. These are normal details, and they can be fulfilled at the normal pace of legal transactions. We live in the computer age and documents can go around the world in seconds. I suggest being thankful for your good fortune and I hope you enjoy your new assets."

"Do you have any further questions?"

I felt as if a fog had dropped over my mind.

"No. It appears I am to be rather passive until you tell me what papers to sign."

Ms. Salsist, rose from her desk and it was clear the session was over. I was politely ushered out the door into the spring air. For a while, I just walked aimlessly. I was numbed by this turn in my life. I finally entered a coffee shop and ordered my normal strong black coffee.

As I sat sipping my cup I pondered about my current finances. Over the years I have been paid well by the college. Ann and I owned our townhouse equally and we owed nothing on our home. My retirement funds were adequate with normal prudence.

Ann also had reasonable funds. She had worked for several decades as a records person in a large accounting office and had been able to save a large percentage of her income. Ann and I had always lived modestly and within our means. We had no expensive habits or vices. Our normal evening was sipping a glass of wine and reading our books. One luxury we indulged in was books. We owned an extensive library. Ann had been raised poor and she knew the value of money.

I suddenly stopped in the middle of the sidewalk and asked myself what would I do with forty-nine million dollars? It was even stranger that a large part of the estate was liquid. The only thing I could think of was to go home and talk to Ann. I rode the subway home in deep thought. Frankly, I walked like a person in a confusing dream. I believed I would wake up any second to my normal life and reality. This did not happen.

When I arrived at our townhouse, the city's daylight was fading fast and the shadows were lengthening. I walked up the same stairs that I have ascended for years. The treads still protested as they had for many decades. Yet nothing seemed the same. Mentally I was wading in deep water in the slowest motion. Yet my thoughts were racing. I reached our expensive steel-clad door and said the same thing that I have said for many years.

"Ann, I am home."

Ann in turn would establish through the peephole whether it was me. After that, the modern cold chains and latchets were released and I could enter. This had been our stable ritual for many years.

Now I must tell you of my wonderful Ann. Ann is a 5'8' woman of slender built with a vitality that I had never seen in anyone else. Her hair is a beautiful silver gray, and she always wore her hair short. Her eyes were a mystery; they seemed to shift from brown to green. When she was amorous or excited the eyes shifted to a shining green.

She has always been physically active, and she goes to the gym several times a week. She has a figure most twenty-year-olds would love to possess. She loves the English language in all its facets and her knowledge of the classics exceeded most of my professional fellows.

Her eyes are always so filled with joy that she is a delight to be with. She radiated life in all its positive forms. She is a wonderful and gentle lover, and I honestly don't know if I could live without her. Thankfully, Ann is my junior by eight years, and I pray daily that I pass away first.

She has been my wonderful companion and soul mate all my adult life. She is such a positive person it is nearly impossible to be sad or depressed around her. During my writing endeavors she is my muse. Her writing insight was infallible, and her comments were always constructive and kind. She was divorced as an eighteen-year-old girl in a marriage that could not survive. The man turned out to be a brutal alcoholic who beat her often. On top of that she discovered she was gay.

Once she came "out" the disgusted husband went out the front door. Ann in turn was happy to leave through the back door. Ann and I were students together at MIT and we fell in love. We are more in love today than when we were love drenched undergrads.

We were kids then and the world has matured us into a solid placid romantic partnership. We are the type of couple who always walk hand in hand no matter what the circumstances. When I walked through the door Ann was shocked at my confused demeanor.

"Joyce what in the world is wrong with you? You look like you have been mugged on the street."

I could only reply,

"Ann, the world that we have known has been turned upside down."

"My God, are you ill?

"No, my love, I am quite well. I am just stunned and bewildered.

"Please Joyce you must sit down and slowly tell me what is wrong."

She brought me a glass of iced tea as I sat in my favorite chair. Reflecting idly that my chair is now out of fashion, yet I still love it. I carefully explained the entire situation to her. She had not been aware of the original letter because I didn't believe there was anything to it. Ann responded exactly as I had, skeptical and somewhat frightened.

She could not believe that we were in this strange situation. I explained that my attorney had suggested that I go to Nebraska and establish ownership of my assets. Naturally, I don't go anywhere without Ann. Ann mentioned that she had built up many days for vacation. I in turn knew that college would break for the summer in three weeks. We decided we would go to Nebraska at that time.

Chapter Three

June 10, 2016

The days seemed to fly by as any older person can attest. Our flight to Nebraska was not eventful. We had to change flights three times and finally landed in Omaha Nebraska. Omaha seemed to be a normal city. In Omaha we took a cab which took us to the car rental where we had made arrangements.

Red Cloud Nebraska appeared to be a 3-to-4-hour drive. We had reservations for a bed and breakfast for a week with the option of staying longer if necessary. We drove though the countryside that was green with corn, wheat, and alfalfa. We drove on a two-lane highway that seemed restricted compared to our multilane freeways in the East.

We were thankful for modern devices like a GPS which directed us through lands that seemed empty. About every mile or two we would see a farmhouse but beyond that the land seemed void of human life. However, we had no difficulty finding our bed and breakfast. The owner of the lodging met us as we pulled onto a graveled road. He was what one might call a tidy man. He was friendly and polite. He made conversation in a friendly non-intrusive manner.

He welcomed us to Red Cloud and he answered all our questions. He took us to a small but clean cottage. He did not take our offered tip and kindly told us that it was not necessary in Red Cloud. After we unloaded our baggage and freshened up we thought we would drive around this tiny community. Most of the population seemed white. There were a few people of color but nothing like the racial mix that is found throughout the East Coast.

The next day we drove our car rental to a prearranged appointment with Mr. Hansel the local attorney that we were to work with. The contrast between this firm and the one I did business in New York was nearly unbelievable.

Mr. Hansel ran a modest firm that consisted of him and one older solid secretary. The secretary was probably around sixty-five years old. She had that eastern European body type. She was square as a brick. She was about 5'7". I would say she was nearly 180 pounds. Yet there did not seem to be too much fat on her. Her hair was steel gray. Her hands were large and appeared robust enough to strangle a bear. Later we gleaned she was German in heritage. She radiated competency and unflappability. The relationship between her and Mr. Hansel was nearly symbiotic. Each person seemed to know exactly what each person needed next.

CHAPTER FOUR

June 11,2016

Likewise, Mr. Hansel was a short portly man who wore heavy black glasses. He was professional without any pretense. He moved gracefully for a large man. His suit was clean and well pressed but certainly not up to date in big city fashion. The only adornment that he wore was a well-worn wedding ring. His dancing blue eyes seemed to hold constant humor as if he just heard a charming joke.

He greeted us warmly and helped Ann and I to a pair of well-worn comfortable chairs. I have read of people who were as plain as a glass of water. That hackney phrase for once was appropriate. Mr. Hansel was the first person who filled that unlikely personality completely.

It was clear that this man treated everyone the same. The cut of clothes or the age of the cars his clients might drive meant nothing to him. I noted as we entered that the only car in the back was a modest car in spotless condition. When I commented on the contrast between his practice and my firm back East he took it with a chuckle.

He explained that he worked with people of all social positions from laborers to bankers and beyond. I liked and trusted him immediately.

He explained that his grandfather was the original attorney that handled the legal needs of Rachel Summerfield. With the passing of both his grandfather and his father he continued the legal services of the estate. He explained that this situation was most unusual, but the original will stated that Hansel lawyers to be used if any remained living and in practice.

He also mentioned one firearm that had been stored in the Hansel office safe since the death of Rachel Summerfield. That meant 89 years of oversight. The original will provided funds to maintain the rifle every six months by a firearm expert. I mentioned that my urban background did not prepare me for a firearm. I openly said I knew nothing about firearms and was in fact quite terrified by them.

He said that the decision to keep or sell the firearm could certainly wait until larger details could be settled. I felt I should address these items after I and Ann had gotten a handle on the bigger assets. He smiled while he told us that these items had been in the same safe for 89 years.

He again said that these smaller possessions could be handled later in any way I desired. The rifle had a specific place to donate it to If the person who inherited the estate did not want to keep it. With a smile he said he now stood ready to serve us in any capacity.

I thought to myself what an original and modest man he was. In the East we are surrounded by people who want to impress you and charm you. Certainly, the East Coast could have used more attorneys of this demeanor. Mr. Hansel faxed several items to my attorney in New Haven and within minutes I had the necessary paperwork to inspect the property. We asked Mr. Hansel if he knew anyone who could take us to the farm and fill us in on the local culture. He recommended his son, and we agreed to retain him.

We waited for the young man in a nearby café. Within the hour we had met the young man, and we were on our way to view this farmland and home. The young man was named Robert, and he was a stocky version of his father, short with broad shoulders, dark hair and a radiant smile.

He projected the friendly demeanor of a person who had never taken life too seriously. In our general conversation Robert freely answered any question. It became clear that Robert knew this area down to the square inch for a fifty-mile radius around Red Cloud.

He was a fount of state and local history. He spoke in awe of the strength of the original immigrants that settled this area. As we drove past the flat lands he pointed out a crumpling sod house of one of the original settlers. It was not hard to see that these original settlers must have been made of steel.

It was explained to us that the property that he was to show us was on good soil, but he did not know the land prices. He said this father could get someone for that knowledge. I had to be honest and say that I knew nothing about farming. That did not disturb Robert. He seemed to assume that anyone with grit could master anything. Robert said the landholding and the house were about 11 miles from Red Cloud.

As Robert drove, Ann and I were looking at the countryside. The land was mostly flat interrupted with farmhouses every mile or so. The countryside seemed to convey a scale of time that I had never appreciated. The land seemed indifferent to the humans that lived here. It was as if the land was merely tolerating this new human species that was scratching on its timeless surface.

It was not hard to imagine that this land would revert to an empty prairie in a few hundred years if man disappeared. Seemingly man was just a fleeting species and a failed experiment at best. We were struck with the impression of neatness. Although the local structures seemed modest they were laid out carefully with nearly a military precision. The lack of weeds was striking. When we brought this up to Robert he merely laughed.

He said. "The residents of this area dislike any type of disorder, and they appear to live for nothing more than to keep things tidy. "

He said most of the people were Lutheran who felt that dust and fun were the ultimate sins. When we asked about the political tenor of the area he mentioned that the state was very conservative in their politics and their lifestyle."

As we approached our destination Robert pointed out our land holding with a simple white clapboard house. The white home was quite small and there were several outbuildings that were painted red. As far as Ann and I could see red and white were the primary colors of the area. When one considered the amount of money Rachel Summerfield possessed she was certainly modest with her expenses.

The house was surrounded by hedges and Robert mentioned it was to break the wind which could be very harsh in the winter. He mentioned that 30 below zero was common during their winters. He went on to explain that nature did not give much away in this area. There were many tornados, droughts, blizzards, and at times unremitting wind.

We were introduced to the ground's caretaker a Mr. Samuel Hartman. Samuel lived in a smaller structure and his duties were to maintain the structures and to keep the grounds clean and in good order. Samuel was a small quiet man in his sixties with balding hair who clearly knew his job. His wiry body seemed fit, and he appeared to be in perfect health. He had strong regular white teeth. There were probably few sweets in his life. He was friendly and polite.

His hands showed the scars of a lifetime of toil. The structures and grounds were immaculate. The small lawn was perfectly maintained. Lawn hoses were hung up in perfect concentric circles. There was a woven wire fence around the house itself with a rustic metal gate. When I questioned the fence Mr. Hartman explained that cattle gleaned the fields after the crops were harvested and the fence was to keep them out of the yard.

Everything was freshly painted and there did not seem to be anything out of place. He mentioned that his father was the care keeper before his death. Then he stepped into his father's shoes. One got the feeling that the Summerfield holding was a well-oiled clock.

Robert explained to us that the land was farmed by a neighbor under his father's oversight. The accounting books were open for her inspection anytime at his father's office. He mentioned that my attorney had already inspected the books and found nothing lacking.

Ann and I were given the keys to the house, and we walked on a narrow concrete path to the dwelling. Robert mentioned that the area was total mud for brief parts of the year. Thus, most drives and walks were concrete to overcome this liability. With Robert in tow, I opened the front door which swung easily and soundlessly from well-oiled maintenance.

We remarked on the even temperature of the home. Robert explained that the home was heated at all times paid by the trust for all those years since her death. A housekeeper kept a schedule to keep everything spotless.

Thus, the house was the same as the day that Rachel Summerfield died and left this earth. As noted a cleaning lady was retained to come in bi-weekly to make sure nothing was remiss and to ensure that dust did not gain a foothold. Everything was small.

The home had two small bedrooms, a small kitchen, and a small living room. On the outside was a screened off porch with a quaint swing that appeared to have had a long history of use. One had the sense that all this was a doll house owned by a loving child.

The silverware was clean and neatly aligned in its drawers. The floor was true wood and polished to a high sheen. Kitchen towels were hanging properly. The entire house had simple furniture. All the furniture seemed to be built by hand and seemed to be as solid as the day they were made. All wood surfaces were well oiled and waxed. The small bed was neatly made with fresh linen. Everything seemed simple, strong, and utilitarian. Rachel Summerfield seemed to be a person of simple tastes.

When we entered the living room we received our first major surprise. On the living room walls from floor to ceiling stood shelf after shelf of books. Clearly Rachel Summerfield was a serious reader. Ann ran her fingers over the titles with awe.

Dozens of classic books were included. I have always felt one could know the owner by the books that she owned. In the end this was true of Rachel Summerfield. We were mesmerized by this library.

"By God look at these titles! The Illiad and the Odyssey by Homer. Beowulf and The Epic of Gilgamesh. Aeschylus and The Theban Plays by Sophocles, Euripides and his masterpiece The Oresteia."

I also ran my fingers over another row.

"Herodotus and his history, the histories by Thueydides, Livy, Tacitus, and Caesar with his 'The War in Gaul" Gibbon and his Rise and Fall of the Roman Empire. Marco Polo and his The Travels of Polo. I kept moving my hand. Socrates, Aristotle, Thales, Empedocles, Democritus Heraclitus and Pythagorras.

More recent thinkers were represented including Kant, Hegel, Marx, Descartes, Spinoza, and Locke. The books went on and on. Row after row of books in total the number had to be in hundreds of volumes. I was speechless. The subject matter went from agriculture to Shakespeare. There were volumes of poetry.

The titles seemed endless: Frost, Whitman, Dickinson, Yeats, Blake, and Byron. Economics was supported by Smith, Keynes, Hayek, and Marx. Political science was not lacking: Locke, Paine, and Hobbes. Erotic titles were well represented: The Lover, Memoirs of a Woman of Pleasure, Tropic of Cancer, Fanny Hill and The Story of My Life.

On and on ran the titles. There were dozens of history books. There was a large collection of Civil War history. The library contained many books that were rare and expensive. Some were leather bound. One got the impression that in these rooms lived a secret wealthy scholar. I could hardly believe my eyes.

"My God Ann it will take a lot of time to catalog these books.

"I swear to God I have never seen such a private library. Who dreamed that this world of scholarship would be in a simple farmhouse in Nebraska?"

We carefully examined some volumes. Each volume showed many dog ears showing where the reader had to set a book aside. Many sections of any given volume were underlined. This was clearly not a show library owned by a wealthy person who wanted to pretend vast learning. No, this was a well-used library where every single book we examined showed signs of heavy usage.

Then I saw a small flat wooden box in an alcove in an interior wall. It appeared so strange sitting in solitary splendor. The alcove was polished maple; the workmanship was complex and flawless. It appeared to be some sort of shrine. It clearly was the size to hold a book. I remember wondering: A shrine for a book?

The box was beautifully crafted. It was made from burled walnut. All the joints were finger jointed with perfect symmetry and the small hinges were of brass of the highest quality. Ann and I felt drawn to this box as if we were iron filings drawn to a magnet. We both looked at each other and I carefully eased the box open. Inside wrapped in red velvet was a leather-bound volume of 'The Poems and Fragments of Sappho."

This nearly took our breath away. Any English scholar would know about Sappho. Sappho was an ancient Greek female poet. The best guess was she was born 630 B.C. and died around 570 B.C. We knew that she was born on the island of Lesbos. Lesbos in later years was turned into the modern term of Lesbian.

Most scholars felt lesbianism was simply sex between two women. Most of her poems were lost but despite that she was known as one of the greatest lyric poets to ever live.

In early Greece, most love poems were homosexual in nature. Sappho loves were clearly between females. This volume was made to the highest level. The binding was a masterpiece made of the highest quality leather. The book used gold leaf in all the right places. It was a stupendous book. Clearly the book was a masterpiece. We felt afraid just touching it.

"What in the world is this?" I asked Ann.

"Here are walls of masterful books. Yet, this solitary book was a total mystery. How did a person of such learning end up in this modest community? We both felt we had to do our best to understand Rachel Summerfield. All of this seemed so strange. Her personal possessions pulled us deeper into this vortex of questions. So far no-one could explain anything about this quiet and learned woman.

Ann ventured an opinion.

"Whoever Rachel was it is clear she was well read. Perhaps a few scholars have a library of this quality, but they must be few."

She continued, "I don't have a clue, but she clearly set the works of Sappho apart from all the others. I have no idea what we had stumbled upon."

We decided we needed to see the rest of this strange house. In the pantry the house cleaner had cycled new items as old items expired. A can of beans on the shelf in 1927 were continually recycled. Eventually there appeared a can of beans made in 2015.

There were some pictures on the ledges and walls. The pictures were covered with cloth. Apparently this was to prevent the pictures from fading.

These photographs would soon be a part of our studies. Everything was as it was when Rachel Summerfield died. I was astonished as to the level of care that had maintained this house after so many years. I asked Robert if he would leave Ann and me so that we could speak privately. He quickly retired.

"Ann I want work on this mystery. Clearly Rachel Summerfield was much more than money."

"I am in total agreement. There are things here to be found and I certainly want to find them."

We looked in the small bedroom and in one room there was a large steamer chest of the type commonly used in the 18th century. Mister Hartman had the keys. Inside the chest was a simple box of yellowing letters, a series of leather-bound books which were the financial records of this farm holding dating from 1876 and many invoices showing the purchase of books from all over the United States and many from other countries. Here the secrets of Rachel Summerfield began to unfold.

This might be a good time to describe the sense of the place. It was not at all spooky as empty homes often are. It seemed comfortable to be in. We learned that electricity was added when that became available. The home and everything about it felt positive.

Neither of us could deny that it felt as if we should be here and that it was here to study. We felt compelled to unwrap the history of this house. However, we wanted to go slow like experienced lovers.

Mr. Hartman the caretaker came to show us the barn and the car garage. Everything was maintained in a flawless manner. Without prompting, I told Mr. Hartman that his employment and that of the house cleaner would continue unchanged. If we had all this money we felt assuring the employment of the faithful caretakers was the right thing to do.

We asked Robert to take us back to our cottage. This vast land intrigued us. We speculated what stories it could tell of its millions of years of existence. Robert had that rare gift of knowing when to talk and knowing when to be silent. He was able to answer any question I had or could tell us about a source for that question.

After we arrived we thanked him for his services and told him we would retain him until we knew what we needed. I asked him quietly "Is there any place that might have more information about Rachel Summerfield?" Robert thought a few moments and said, "I really don't know anyone and beyond my dad I doubt if there would be another. Of course, it was a long time ago.

There was a lot to think about. A modest farmhouse full of hundreds of books worth tens of thousands of dollars was intriguing. When Ann and I reached our room then the thoughts began to develop between us.

I stated:

"We should go to the bank that holds these liquid assets and find out where we stand on any cash. Assuming that there are funds I suggest we carefully go over Rachel's books and every physical item in the place. Then we must sit down and make plans for how we are going to adjust our lives to what the farmhouse may contain.

Ann said

"I totally agree." There is something important to learn from Rachel's effects. How do we proceed? Going to the bank should be the first step."

That evening Ann and I had a wonderful meal at a place called the Silver Spur Restaurant. The cuisine leaned heavily toward beef. The "Silver Spur Restaurant" to us was a strange name but I assumed it related to the state culture. Most of the menu contained large helpings of beef, bread and potatoes. We decided to dine on trout and rice since we seldom eat beef. We relaxed by drinking some excellent White Oaked Chardonnay.

Thank God, wherever there is good wine there is civilization. When we returned to our room the atmosphere was more relaxing. It had been a long day but also an eventful time. After showers we enjoyed ourselves by making slow love to each other. Our lovemaking had always been good.

CHAPTER FIVE

June 12,2016

In the morning, we had a visit with the President of the Red Cloud Citizens Bank. Mr. Howard was a man who seemed to be in his sixties. He was about 5'8' tall with interesting brown speckled eyes. He was slightly overweight with the broad shoulders of a football player but walked gracefully and he seemed in good health. After all the introductions he escorted us to his modest office and began to talk.

"Well, I will explain the current situation on the Summerfield estate. We have been working with your attorney in New Haven. Your attorney has taken care of all the arrangements. I can tell you that all of Rachel Summerfield assets have been converted to the name of Joyce Summerfield.

All you need is to sign the papers that your attorney has pre-approved. He pulled up the account on his computer screen. Not counting the real estate, the current balance is over forty-nine million in savings." Your checking is over 1,250,067.00. There is also a maintenance account of 1.5 million dollars. I will have a printout shortly showing the assets to the penny.

He seemed to lean back and wait for my comments.

"So, the funds are free and clear? Can I access them at any time?

"That's correct. You are free to use, convert or withdraw the funds in all or part at any time. I would like to add that the Summerfield account is our oldest account. It was opened when my grandfather owned the bank. I would like to assure you that we are as capable of meeting your needs as any bank in America. This is a small town with small banks but in the computer age large and small banks are in the same basket. We would like to retain your business. We are here to give you service."

"Well, I want to keep doing business with your bank. My checking account has more than enough funds. I will need check blanks to go with the account.

"This is no problem at all. I can have the paperwork ready for your signature within ten minutes. He picked up his phone and talked to someone to make these transactions. Ms. Summerfield, I am pleased we can continue to have your business. Do you have any questions that I might be able to answer?"

"I am most interested in any information that you may have about Rachel Summerfield. I would appreciate any information about her life. She gave me a lot of money and I feel I owe it to her to know and understand how this situation came about."

Mr. Howard leaned back in his chair and formed his fingers into a steeple. "Of course, there is no one living that you could speak to. 1927 is a long time ago. Did she leave any notes, letters, or personal items with anyone?

Joyce replied, "We have found some letters in a trunk that might be interesting. As you noted it was a long time ago."

Joyce shifted in her hard chair to be more comfortable. "Ann and I would just like to understand more about her life. I am sure if we can find the right details that it was an interesting life and one I would like to know."

Mr. Howard pondered, "Again, I can't think of anything or anyone I could suggest. However, I can quietly put out feelers to find any other sources. Lives here are often interwoven. Sometimes information can come from the oddest sources. There are some old timers out there who might have some information. If I can find anything I will surely get in touch with you."

"Thank you very much. We appreciate your helpfulness and do keep your nose into the wind."

At that moment, the necessary paperwork arrived, and I signed the papers. I walked out of that bank in a fog. I was now the owner of a new checking account and a savings account. Between the two of them I had well over fifty million dollars. Ann was ecstatic about my good fortune.

I was ecstatic because I could take better care of Ann and her financial needs. I have never downplayed the importance of money, nor have I ever mocked money. I realized that money was wonderful and indispensable. Neither Ann nor I are flippant about money. Money can certainly smooth many bumps in life. Yet being in love and happy was difficult to put a price tag on.

The best of both worlds was to be in love and have enough money to meet one's needs. That seemed to describe us on this unlikely day. As we walked, we paused to see the beauty of the day.

The sun was shining, the air was fresh, and it felt glorious. The air was so clear. Not at all like New Haven. I felt I was floating on a cloud.

We had no special place to go so we walked a few blocks and just chatted. I reminded Ann that I had no family. Through time, accidents and health I have lost everyone over the years. I had no children and the same was true of Ann. This made our lives much simpler. It also meant we had only each other between us and a lonely world.

I conveyed to her that all this estate would belong to her if I preceded her in death. As soon as the dust settled I would write up a new will. My existing will already named Ann my sole heir but I want to update it and make sure everything stated the new situation. Ann cried and I hugged her.

Ann was my entire world. She has always my deepest friend and my only love. She had been a perfect companion and a wonderful lover all these years. We have grown closer over the years. We have learned and observed that maturity helps a good relationship.

I wanted so much to assure her a more secure financial future. We had been lesbians far enough back that we could have gone to prison for the simple act of making love. Now we were both blessed with healthy libidos and our lovemaking was frequent and wonderful. We still held hands wherever we went. This simple statement of love could now be openly expressed. Even here in this tiny community no one paid the slightest attention to us.

The freedom was uplifting and refreshing. We walked into a small café and looked at the menus. It seemed that the state was run by a tribe of red meat eaters. It was difficult to find healthy or light meals. We both had fish sandwiches and ignored the mountain of fries that seemed obituary in this area.

The day was still young. I called Mr. Hansal for some more hometown advice. I explained that I needed two girls/women who were well suited to inventory a private library. They had to be meticulous and able to put this data on a computer. I gave him my cell phone number. He said he would see what he could come up with. I assured him that anything he did for us was billable time. In addition, we told him that our help would be paid well. He laughed and said that was a good thing.

We decided we would return to the farm. Upon arrival we touched in with the caretaker and we entered the house. We sat down on the living room sofa and planned our assault on the mysteries of Rachel's home. It was agreed that we would spend our summer if necessary trying to get a grasp of the assets and most importantly the facts of her life.

We both felt we were on the right path by starting with the books. Hopefully, we might have a team for the library accounting starting tomorrow. We decided we would move into the farmhouse to really get into its secrets. We personally would uncover all the pictures on the shelves and walls. This was a big step because it was here that we began to understand Rachel Summerfield.

There were three pictures on shelves and two pictures hung on the walls. Three of the pictures on the shelves were tintypes. These were popular around the Civil War because they could be produced cheaply and rapidly. One depicted what was probably a family group. This seemed to be a standard group picture of a well to do family. The father seemed to be around fifty years old, whose features were gaunt, and it seems he was a solid citizen. He was dressed formally in a dark tailcoat with matching trousers, Linen shirt with a light-colored cravat. The mother was slender who seemed to buck convention with a faint smile. She appeared to be in her forties. She had the appearance of being a strong woman.

Her gaze was straight and penetrating. Her jaw was firm. She clearly dressed as a refined lady with the fashions of that era. It was an evening gown with a large voluminous skirt, low neckline, and short sleeves. She also wore short gloves. Upon her head was a lace covering with embellishments.

She gave the impression of a strong woman in a time that did not support her nor others of her gender. From her appearance she did not seem to care what society thought.

Behind them were three teenagers. The teenagers seemed the hardest to place with ages. They all seemed to be nearly the same in height and weight. The teenagers seemed happy and smiling. Their facial features were fine and delicate. However, their bodies seemed wiry and fit. A written legend on the photo said Papa, Mama, Rachel, Johnny and Max. The year was noted 1858.

The second picture was also a tintype. It only showed the three teenagers. All it said was Rachel, Johnny, and Max 1859. It was still hard to discern ages. Only a year had lapsed but young people do grow rapidly. Luckily, the young people were in the same order, so it was easier to compare one to the other. Little change, if any change.

The third tintype was dated 1867 and it was markedly different. Only Rachel and Max were photographed. There were no more teenage smiles. It appeared that Rachel was probably the oldest and

Max might have been the youngest. Once again that is only a guess. Both seemed the same height and weight.

They looked into the camera with steady even eyes. There appeared to be a sense of stiffness in these young people. Rachel had her hat pulled lower to her eyes. Strangely her eyes appeared to have a glitter or a spark. They were black and deep. They spoke of steady strength. One could drown in those eyes.

Max's eyes were also dark as if his eyes were obsidian. Max gave the impression of a man growing into a solid citizen. Both people gave the impression of tenseness. As if they expected something dangerous to happen. This picture was taken with a well-maintained white house in the background.

Beautiful shade trees flourished, and the yard had a classic white picket fence. The house had an enclosed shaded porch and was supported by beautiful circular wooden columns.

Everything was maintained well and smacked of solid prosperity. Both young men wore the styles of that era. Linen shirts with high standing collars, neck ties looped in a loose knot, single breasted frocked coats which extended to mid-knee. These garments placed their owners in the well to do classes.

As mentioned there were two pictures on the wall. The first was in 1859. It showed just four people. The father was standing behind his three teenagers. They were kneeling and the father proudly holding what appeared to be a shooting target against his chest. The kneeling teenagers each held a rifle. With strong magnification we were able to see wording on the target. Williamsport long range Shooting Club, Pennsylvania October 13-1859. Three-man teams. Five shots each.

The winning team Ray, Johnny and Max Summerfield who lived in Titusberg PA.

Joyce and Ann looked at each other in surprise. The faces of the kneeling matched the young teenagers in the earlier pictures. However, there was one huge difference. Rachel was changed to Ray. Height, weight, hair length was still the same. With this new bit of information, we looked at Rachel/Ray closely. Rachel could easily be taken as a boy. This fact figured strongly in the story we finally uncovered.

Without the name change from Rachel to Ray they were impossible to separate. Although we studied carefully it was clear that it was nearly impossible to tell gender. Later we would find experts to validate our opinions.

There were also firearms, perhaps a gun expert might figure out something from gun markings: what type of guns and perhaps what they meant. We also wondered if the firearm in Hansal's safe had anything to do with the pictures. Later this proved true. That was to be another piece in our puzzle.

The second wall photograph was different than the others. Dated 1868 it appeared to show only the father, mother and Ray/Rachel. The mother still wore fashionable clothes but one got a sense of age and sadness. There were worry lines on her forehead and slight crow lines at the edges of her eyes.

The father seemed to have aged sharply from his earlier picture. He wore the fashions of his era. Also, the same house stood in the background. At least Ann and I had some solid dates and images of Rachel Summerfield.

I then received a phone call on my cell phone. It was from our good man Mr. Hansal. He said that he was able to find two people that were qualified to do the library. One was a retired high school librarian who would take on the job for some extra spending money. The second person was a High School senior who was an avid reader and highly qualified with computer use and record keeping. He asked if I approved of his selections. If so they would be at the farmhouse at 10:00 a.m. I told Mr. Hensal that his choices sounded fine, and we would look forward to getting started.

Ann and I felt we were making real progress. With modern technology the titles for the real property had been successfully transferred to my name. In addition, the liquid assets were also transferred. What we thought would take months in fact had been resolved within hours. I now own cash assets worth over fifty million dollars. The land itself had vast value as I learned in time. Although I knew this was real I was still having trouble wrapping my head around it.

We returned to Red Cloud excited and eager to follow the evidence until there was nothing more to be learned. Since we quit early we had time to leisurely explore Red Cloud. Red Cloud seemed to have two cafes. And one evening club. With some effort we found the evening club served more than steaks and hamburgers. The food was excellent and there was a lot of it. Prices were far lower than citizens paid in Eastern states.

CHAPTER SIX

June 13, 2016

The next morning, we rose to a bright new day. We had an excellent breakfast and were completely refreshed. We were ready to follow any new leads in the Rachel Summerfield mystery. Although we were at the farmhouse thirty minutes early our new assistants were already there ready to go to work. We discovered being late was a serious offense in Nebraska. The Protestant work ethic in Nebraska was still strong.

The older lady looked exactly what one would expect from a professional librarian. She seemed to be in her seventies. She was at least twenty pounds overweight, but she soon showed us she really knew her work. Her white hair was pulled back in a bun without a hair misplaced. She spoke quietly but it was clear she was used to being in charge.

Her assistant was quite different. She was a girl about nineteen with hair that was a deep brunette and silky. Her hair was long and nearly reached her waist. She had blue eyes. She was short and slender. I doubt if she weighed 105 pounds. She wore heavy frame black eyeglasses.

She had the most beautiful hands. The hands flowed gracefully as she used them. Her skin was flawless. When she smiled it was joyful and the smile lit up her facial features. She was also quick and active. Her face seems to change its appearance as she worked. Her face was expressive, and she seemed to bring light to any room.

I explained that I wanted a complete and formal inventory. Whenever possible I wanted the books separated into categories by topic. For example, all philosophy books together and all political books together. Once this was accomplished I wanted all books to be given a permanent library number to aid in searching and restacking. Finding the total number of books was necessary and how many books in whatever category.

I explained to the elder lady that I wanted a manual card system as well as several computer systems. She was surprised that a manual card file was desired, and she completely agreed with my practical request. I explained that speed was not the issue and that I would usually be here to answer questions. I told the people there was one book in the alcove, but they need not trouble with that.

I placed the older lady in charge and that was that. I trusted her judgments and experience completely. Later results showed my judgment in her was well grounded. Beyond that I would try to be out of their way. That said I turned to Alice. It was time to explore the chest in the bedroom.

I left our library people alone. Ann and I took our tablets for notes and a good magnifier if needed for closer work. I opened the trunk with apprehension. It did not feel frightening, but it did place a responsibly upon my shoulders that felt heavy. It felt like I was looking through a keyhole watching someone undress. Upon opening the trunk there were a number of letters and a single folded package.

We opened the large package with care. Within the package was a soldier uniform of the Civil War era. The uniform itself was filthy and seemed so out of place in this home setting where everything was neat Strangely the jacket had a ragged hole through the right shoulder and a much larger hole on the back. The jacket seemed to be stained with black residue. Ann spoke quickly. "This appears to be old blood stains".

They set this mystery aside while Joyce removed letters from a bygone era. The pages were yellow, and they were fragile. The letters were bound with a satin ribbon and were lay upon the uniform with care. There were not that many letters, but Ann and I felt sure they were important enough to be preserved.

A picture was also lying upon the uniform. It was a tintype and it showed a slight Union soldier standing next to another soldier who appeared to be in his thirties. On the back it stated Ray and Joe 1865.

The older soldier seemed tired, and his face was deeply lined. The eyes of the older soldier looked sad, and it seemed clear that he did not want to be in the picture. The smaller soldier looked directly into the camera with dark steady eyes and with a boldness that seemed unusual. We withdrew the letters and the photo and carefully laid them on the bed.

We noted a stack of letters were arranged by date and recipient. Some letters were written between a Mary Summerfield and Ray Summerfield in care of Staff Command of the Army of the Potomac. They were clearly dated. There were also some letters between a Senator Frank Summerfield apparently to his wife Vergia. The letters drew us like parched humans toward a water hole. We had no idea how important the letters were. In truth the letters told a remarkable saga. Starting letter one:

CHAPTER SEVEN

April 11, 1859

To Vargia Summerfield

From Republican Senator Summerfield

My Dearest Wife Vargia,

I can't tell you how much I miss you and our family. I would give almost anything to have you in my arms with our beloved children gathered around us. When will the Summerfield family be released from our long line of public service? I am expected to remain in our capital to do the impossible. Yes, it is true that our family has been wealthy for generations. Yet what is wealth if I am forced to be absent from my wife and my children?

These last months have been the most trying of my life. As always, the cursed issue of slavery has again risen to threaten the existence of our country. The slave states are again threatening to leave the Union unless we give them even more protections to slavery. I despise slavery but like many I am willing to bend as far as possible to save our United States Union.

How long must the horror of slavery vex us? Secession is the threat that the Southern slave states hold over our heads. I am sorely pressed. I truly do not know what to do. The Federal Government has made compromise after compromise and the pro-slavery states are still not satisfied. Many of my party are angry and losing patience. Members of our party are refusing to compromise any longer. I constantly urge restraint, but I am losing influence. Even my closest friends are drifting to extremism.

Where will this end? Is it possible that both sides of the issue want war? Why are old politicians so quick to send young men to war? I tremble before the prospect of a Civil War. I try to explain to both sides that a Civil War would bleed our social body white and would empty our national wealth for generations.

The cost in blood and gold would be impossible to reckon. Do they truly wish to see their sons' lifeless and prostate in blood on the ground? I fear time will tell and I tremble for our future.

How are our children doing in their studies? The world is growing so fast and complex I fear I will fail the children in their race of life. It is essential that the children learn French. The French hold the power in Western Europe and commerce always drifts toward power.

I want our children to be able to converse in Europe as in England. Vergia, I fear that my absence from you will form a gap between us. It is hard for me to tell you how much I hold you in my heart. Do not skimp on purchasing the things that you need or fancy. I love to see you in the latest fashions.

When I see you at social functions I swell with pride to see you so beautiful in your finery and your jewels. Do not hold back on anything that you desire. I am aware of your thrift but truly it is not necessary. Our farms and assets are doing very well. The recently discovered oil on our properties is filling our coffers to overflowing.

Your oversight of our foreman Samuel gives me full confidence with our finances. Tell the children how much I love them and long to see them. How can I tell you how much I love you? Please write and hold me dear in your heart.

All my Love,

Frank

Chapter Eight

June 3, 1859

From Your Wife Vargia

To Senator Frank Summerfield

My love do not carry unnecessary burdens. I have always known that you must serve our country as your father and grandfather did before you. I enjoy the daily study of our finances. Of course, our foreman Samuel is priceless. I sincerely believe he runs our farms as he would his own. You have been wise to pay him well. With his careful management of our farms Samuel is becoming wealthy himself.

Your belief in sharing wealth has borne beautiful fruits for all of us. I too hear rumbles of war. I often overhear people in our valley discussing the health of our Union. It is with some foreboding that I often notice their voices becoming louder and louder. It is not healthy that people are so intense.

Sometimes I think I can see a coming war in my mind's eye. Like sheet lightning across black roiling clouds before the deep rumblings of a looming storm. I pray that peace continues across our Union. The very thought of war is chilling.

I look at the young men who work on our farms and I see their joy in their youth. If war comes it will devour many of these fine men. I often see one or the other young men courting some country girl in the cool of the evening. Their love is so new, and I marvel at their innocence. Their future appears fresh and limitless to their eyes.

I wish all of them the joys of a hearth, family and home. The realities of war would kill many and mentally crush others. Frank, I admit I am afraid.

The boys are doing well in their studies. Our French teacher says they are proceeding well and are mastering the language. Once a week I take one of the boys to the veranda so we can visit in French so I can assess their progress. John and Max are doing all that one could desire. They are dutiful in their lessons. Rachel seems to outstrip me in the language. She speaks fluently and within two years I believe she could pass as a native of that cultured land.

We can be proud of our children because they study with earnest all their subjects. Max seems to conquer mathematics effortlessly. John is the steady quiet child. He masters all his lessons with solid performance. All this war talk frightens me very much. I really need to know the issues with depth and clarity. I know you are horribly busy but if you find the time please put down your thoughts and opinions on paper.

Frank, I miss you so very much. I know of your duties. But we must remember the cool evenings when we would drive a fine team through our lands and watch the growing beauty of fruitful nature. Our private lives give me such satisfaction and priceless memories. We are not as young as we were, but we still enjoy solid passions. When I lay in our bed I can feel your hands touching my body in the most sensitive places. I eagerly await your visits. Praise God for his kindness and mercy upon us.

With All My Love,

Your wife Vargia

CHAPTER NINE

June 27, 1859

To Vargia

From Senator Summerfield.

Dear Vargia

I will be home for a month vacation starting April 27. What a joy that is to me! So far the weather has been fair, and we seem to have a beautiful spring. What a privilege it is to have a beautiful wife who is also intelligent! I plan to be with you and the children every minute. I want to breathe the fresh air of our farms.

Of course, one cannot escape all labor. As you are aware I make a point to meet our workers one at a time to assess any problems they may be having. Often our workers come up with excellent suggestions for our farms.

There is no comparison between free men and slaves. Slaves do their work as slowly as possible and with as few words as possible. A man who labors under the lash is not likely to care for the man who holds the lash.

You have asked me in the past to give some clarity on the slavery issue. I hesitate to trouble you with the Georgian knot. It is getting harder to even discuss slavery in Congress or in public. It is even getting hard to discuss the issue with members of my own party.

Everyone is becoming so rigid in their views and that hardness is deadly to a democracy. When a branch does not bend it will surely break. Democracy depends on compromise. Usually, each side gives up some of what they want and in turn the other side gives up some points that they wanted. The South has hardened its stance as have the Northern states.

When I get home I want to just enjoy your company and hope that we can have our quiet times. I can't bear the complexity of the slavery. However, I am happy to use letters to discuss this growing monster with you. Strangely writing does help me in organizing my thoughts as to the why and how of this looming storm that threatens all of us. So, in that sense, writing letters to you on slavery helps me. When one must write his thoughts on paper it forces one to be clear.

I will send some thoughts with this letter and let me know if you want more of this type. On this problem I believe I have as much insight as any man in the world. I don't want to lecture you.

Again, when I return home all I want to see is you and the children. I need time with you my love. The nights are lonely here and I so miss your touch and our lovemaking.

I am so blessed in having you as my wife. When I am home I will politely say to any visitors that I do not discuss affairs of state when I am with my family. I am writing this in the evening in my office because this is the only time I am not surrounded by loud angry men. The problems of the South are political, emotional, financial, religious and cultural.

The South wants to have a mythical kingdom. The wealthy Planters wish to be a new aristocracy in the South. They currently propose that all labor is done for them with slaves. Like the Greeks of ancient times, they do not consider a slave a human. Labor of all types is felt to be disdainful and beneath the Planter class.

In the South, a slave is property pure and simple. A slave seldom takes pride in his work. This also means that few in the South have any ambition to advance. This covers the hard truth that the South is a financial slave of the North.

The South has little industry. Thus, the South buys machinery from the North. Clothing is bought from the North. Tools come from the North. Fine clothes come from the North. The North sells nearly everything to the South. Even the last nail used for caskets is purchased from the North. The South has little industry because of a lack of capital and ambition. Labor in the North can be hard, but one has the priceless advantage of freedom. The worker can move on to try better opportunities. Due to Southern debt (owed to the North) the master's themselves might envy this power.

The economic base of this fantasy consists of two assets: land and slaves. Most Planters don't own the slaves or the land. In truth most Planters are heavily indebted but all of them pretend that financial matters are of no concern to them. It is interesting to realize that most of the banks that support them are in the North. Compared with the North the South has little lendable capital. Of course, I know many of the leading bankers and they are quite free with the information.

As noted, the South is mostly agricultural, and they have almost no industry. This means that the South is going backward and not forward toward a modern nation. The South is on the wrong side of history. Slaves are most profitable if they are used in row crops. The most profitable row crop is cotton. The main customer is the British. Once the cotton is in England it feeds their vast textile industry.

On Northern farms the land has a diversity of crops. Therefore, all income does not come from one crop. This diversity allows the fields to rotate one different crop after another. Often land lays fallow for a year for it to rest and regenerate. Since they usually have livestock, the manure is collected to fertilize their ground. With crop rotation and daily care, the land is not worn out in a few years. In fact, the land often becomes richer by the year. The husbandry on Northern farms is much better than in the South.

The Northern farmers love their land, and they nurture every foot. The South, with much lower populations, exploits their land and would rather buy new acreage than take care of what they already own. The difference between the North and the South is noted by every visitor who has traveled to both regions. In the North farmers truly live to work and they find joy in it. In the South, work is considered odious, and the goal of the Planters is to live a life of leisure.

Love,

Your Husband

CHAPTER TEN

July 14, 1859

To my Dear Husband,

I very much desire to receive your letters. I truly want your opinions and insights. Like you I read all the newspapers both South and North. Sometimes I really don't understand what the South truly wants. As you know I have often gone to Richmond, Atlanta or Charleston for social functions among the most elevated women from the best families.

It is sobering to see how the slaves are looked upon by the wealthy. They will discuss the most private of subjects when the servants are in the same room. It is as if the Negro servants are not in the room at all. It is so easy to discern that Southerners feel the Negro are objects, The Negros are felt to be less than human.

When I carefully ask a question about slaves the ladies all were shocked that I would even think of Negros. It was simply unheard of. The entire question is greeted with surprise as if they had never thought about the subject. I have learned to be circumvented, or one will lose their company. On some evenings I am asked to take a causal ride in a carriage about their large plantations. On one evening recently I was surprised that the Negros were still working in the fields even though it was late in the evening and darkness was close on hand.

When I mentioned this issue to my host she explained that the "darkies" worked from first light until it was too dark to see the cotton pods. At this time of year, it meant the workers labored for around 14/16 hours a day and they did this day after day.

A Northern draft horse would receive far better care than these slaves. When the slave reaches the age where he cannot do the field work he is often sold to rid the plantation of a worthless item. It is one thing to read these things but seeing it firsthand is far worse. I was repulsed.

Love,

Virgia

CHAPTER ELEVEN

August 3-59

Dear Wife

Thank you very much for your letter. I look for your letters like a parched man seeks water. I have read your accounts of life among the Southern barons. Yes, the poor Negro slaves in the South work under horrible conditions. It is easy to push the Slave Question away when the idea is just an abstract thought.

When one sees the overseer upon his horse standing over the laboring slaves with a shotgun it is suddenly very real. The master requires every pound he can extract from the slave's body. Young children must work with the adults in the fields regardless of age.

I have seen six-year-old children sweating under the blazing southern sun pulling their child size sacks filled with cotton.

As you are aware we own large assets in the South. However, I have never invested directly in slaves. I don't want to be that close to the slave industry. Yet the slaves in the South are entwined with almost everything. We own many banks in the South, and it is impossible to lend money without the money supporting some part of the slave economy. However, our banks take only land or fixed assets for collateral. Our banks do not take slaves for collateral. In this sense our banks are a rarity.

As you are aware we make large sums of money from the buying and selling of cotton. In turn, we own several ships that move that cotton to British markets. During good weather our ships are in constant motion going to and from England. Of course, our risks are high due to possible losses to the sea. I try not to deceive myself. We make money in the Southern economy.

No matter how one parses the issue the Southern economy is built upon slavery. One cannot be in business within the United States without dealing with the South as well as the North. For the present time the South is supported by cotton. I want to speak about cotton because that is critical when trying to understand the South.

Cotton is hard on the soil. If the land gets planted with cotton year after year the soil will wear out. Each year the land will bear less and less cotton until it is not profitable to plant. This forces the Planter to keep buying new land to obtain new soil. More land demands more slaves to work it because every acre demands hard labor. The slaves must work even harder to make the tired old soil yield yet another crop. This is where the indebtedness comes in.

Although the Planters live a high lifestyle they usually don't have much cash in hand. Usually, their life of ease is paid for by next year's crop. The obvious problem is that the Planter has not harvested that critical crop. With a crop failure the average Planter is in serious trouble. If he loses two crops in a row they are normally bankrupt. In short, most Planters are supported on a year-to-year basis by banks like the ones we own.

When the North threatens the ownership of slaves one is talking about bankrupting the entire South. Far more money is invested in slaves than in land. Naturally and totally the South resists all efforts to free the slaves. If the slaves were freed the Planter would lose over 70% of their asset base and be left with wore out land that has little value.

The banks would take the property whatever its value and the Planter would be landless and reduced to poverty. Our banks give our clients much more leeway than most banks. After all, we want our borrowers to make money so that we make money. Because of that leeway our banks have a strong regional following.

Sincerely

Your Husband

CHAPTER TWELVE

August 27-59

My Dear Husband

I always read your letters closely because I really do want to understand how the South justifies this market in human flesh. I realize it is hard to run a large business like ours without dealing at times with people we would rather not know. Nevertheless, I know you make a strong effort to do what is right. Unfortunately making an honest living is sometimes difficult.

I want you to know that our children are healthy and happy. They are all making academic progress and are growing up fast. It seems they grow an inch a week. I am grateful to God that our children want to learn, and they want to be prepared for the future. Our local farms are all doing well and are returning a solid profit.

We get good and faithful workers because we pay them a good wage. If the worker is prudent he should be able to make a nest-egg for his future. Our willingness to pay good wages is reflected on our local economy. Our oil producing properties produce vast amounts of money. I check the books very carefully to make sure my bookkeeping is accurate.

The oil profits are nearly clear since we make no direct investment. By taking shares we literally do nothing but put money in the bank. Our names in the area are usually referred to in a positive way.

When I do visit in the South I keep my ears and eyes open. So much of this culture is unspoken. For example, the phrase "those people" means people of the North. I feel I have learned a great deal about the attitudes of the South. I must say the day-to-day manners of the upper classes are without reproach. The ladies make every effort to see the guest is provided with every comfort. Often the hosts will hold social events that are centered around the visitor.

I have been that honored guest on several occasions. One is given an honored position, and the families of the higher social ranking will make every effort to see to your comfort. The manners are so refined it begins to feel like this is a façade to lull the guest from unpleasant aspects of their way of life. It often feels like a formal dance where everyone knows the steps perfectly. It can leave one wondering what is really behind that smiling face.

I have learned there are dark aspects to the Southern Planter's life. I have always tried to gain the confidence of one of my servants when lodging in my host's home. Once that person trusts you then one begins to see under the nearly suffocating social manners.

This subject is so sensitive I must ask you to be extra discreet. I have learned that the master of the plantation often uses his female slaves as sexual objects. The master has access to any Negro female that he may want. The female has no say in the matter at all.

The master can use a female slave for any sexual act that he may want and at any time that the master desires. This is a very common practice, and one sees the results on any plantation. The offspring are called "mulattos." The child is often light colored, and the white blood is obvious to any thoughtful observer.

Even though the master is the father he does not fill the normal role of a father. Since the child has some Negro blood he/she is doomed to be a slave forever. The master often sells his offspring if his slaves are showing too much of his blood.

The amazing thing is that the wife of the Planter typically knows of these relationships and never objects in any manner. It seems to be an accepted social practice. In some cases, the wife is grateful for her husband's dalliances so that she is spared her husband's ardor. It is some type of "men will be men" situation. My confider said that these practices are normal and every young Negro female lives in dread that her turn will come soon.

Quite often the female is a very young child and has not physically matured into a normal sexual partner. Even worse, the master sometimes uses young boys for sexual gratification. This perverse relationship is also quite common. Sometimes this Southern culture feels like Alice in Wonderland. What is real and what is secret?

Love,

Vargia

Chapter Thirteen

September 15-59

Dearest Wife

Yes, I am aware of these sordid facts. These sexual relationships are often not hidden. With my own ears I have overheard Southern congressmen brag about their exploits. Unfortunately, this type of behavior is common. When a master considers his slaves as common property they feel they have the right to use that property as they see fit. In the normal course of life, one's wife ages and these young fresh black bodies are surely attractive.

This activity is heinous because these slaves have no choice in the matter at all. If the slave does not submit they may be whipped or even sold on an auction block. This is one of the reasons so many people want the slaves freed permanently. There really is nothing more that can be discussed about this subject. It is true and it is the reality to the slave.

Let me discuss the political problems between the North and the South. This will help you understand the larger picture. The political problem is more vexing if this is possible. The struggle is related to population. For many reasons, the population of the North is growing much faster than in the South.

Slave states are not attractive to free men. The free man sees much more opportunity for himself and his family in the North. Whatever the reasons, the disparity between the two sections is vast and getting larger by the day.

Under our political system each state bases its number of representatives on population. This is in reference to the House of Representatives. The larger population of the North means that there are more Northern votes than Southern votes. In short, the North can call the legal shots because they have a majority in the House.

Most of the Northern states are anti-slavery meaning they could vote to ban slavery or at least place limits on slavery. The South knows they can never have political clout in the House. The South knows its political strength in the United States is becoming less by the day.

That leaves the Senate. Each state is given two Senators no matter what the population. There is now a fragile political balance between the North and the South. However, that situation could change if more states are formed in the West as seems nearly certain to happen. The huge lands of the West could form any number of states, and it is clear the West wants to enter the Union as free states.

That would mean the North again has the majority and can call the shots. With an anti-slavery majority of both chambers that would spell doom to slavery in America. Presidents have a veto power but once again the North has the population to elect any President because the South cannot match the vast voting numbers of the North. Sooner or later an anti-slavery President will be elected. After looking at these numbers the South sees doom for slavery.

Congress is aware of these problems and many efforts have been made so that the South would remain in the Union. Efforts were made in the National Constitution to allow the slave states to count a slave as 3/5th of a white person for purposes of representation and taxation.

The Constitution also provided a fugitive slave law in 1793 whereas the North had to return all Negro fugitives back to the South. In return for all this it was agreed to stop the importation of slaves in 1808.

This was not benevolence on the part of the Planters. The Planters have enough slaves by natural Negro birth rates. Any importation of slaves would make the slaves they do own to become less in value. In 1821 the slave states expanded their threats, and the North agreed to allow Missouri to be a slave state. In return the North admitted Maine as a free state and slavery was banned from the north 36-30. Time passed and everyone sighed in relief to avoid this difficult subject.

Then a new force came on the political scene: Abolitionists. These people wanted the slaves to be freed at once on moral and religious grounds. These people are not interested in compromise. They are forceful, vocal and tireless. Their literature is extreme, and they press their views upon Congressmen on a nearly daily basis.

As expected, the South rose with great anger and once again Congress appeased them. A "gag rule" was passed that banned these petitions from being discussed. Of course, this violated free speech, but the North passed this odious law in 1831. There the issue remained until 1844.

Now the North is appeasing again. After fierce debate on January 29, 1850 California was admitted as a free state and The Territory of New Mexico was admitted a slave state. In addition, Washington D.C. banned slave trade in D.C. but not slavery itself. The problem is slavery, and it seems this problem will never go away. What was really happening is that Congress kicked the can of slavery down the road in hopes someone else would solve it.

Both sides realize that slavery is something that must be faced sooner or later. This is what is raising tension between the regions. The slavery problem is growing larger and larger, and it is an indigestible mass. Due to the Abolitionists slavery became a moral and religious question. This new dimension blew the lid off the pot.

The entire slavery issue changed overnight when enough people said that slavery is morally wrong and a sin before God. This placed the question of slavery on a completely different level. Through the centuries man has been willing to fight to the death if he believes religiously that God approves the fight.

Up to this point the majority of Northern Americans gave slavery little thought. The North was free and that is where most people lived. Slavery is relatively rare. Slavery was not a day-to-day problem.

Abolitionists changed all of that nearly overnight. Through written material, books, and public speeches more and more people started to look at the slavery issue more closely. Slavery is not an issue that can endure close inspection. Clearly slaves are human. This caused many in the North to view the Southern position as either ignorant or evil before God. Most of the North and the South are very religious in their own way.

The North feels that they are not only responsible for their own salvation, but they are also responsible for allowing evil to being done in front of their eyes. A system that compels people to work under the fear of death or lash is not just.

To have a Negro family split up and sold to different masters is heinous. More and more of the Northern people view slavery as evil. It is difficult for the South to rebut these charges because the charges are true to any reasonable person.

Sincerely

Your Husband

CHAPTER FOURTEEN

Oct 1-59

My Dear Husband

Southern speakers or writers will use the words "pride, honor and culture frequently. I am at a loss to understand how proud one would be of being a slave owner. How would a person take pride in enslaving a human being? How does one take pride in whipping a helpless man?

How can one be proud of taking children from a mother to sell the children to strangers? Especially if some of those children are the result of Planters sexual forays to their own female slaves.

I feel a repulsion toward anyone who claims to be "honorable" who takes part in the enslavement of millions. This same repulsion goes for "honor." How is one "honorable" when slaves live in hovels that are not fit for livestock?

There seems to be a lot of pride in Southern "culture." Their culture is entirely based on the stolen labor of slaves. The hidden vice of sexual bondage is a grievous cancer in the body of Southern slavery. It is a false culture which the entire civilized Western world rejected years ago. I fear that slavery and the so-called Southern culture will eventually end in a savage Civil War. Slavery is the most venial crime known to man. To steal a human life and bind it to one's service is the greatest crime in history.

With Love,

Your Wife

CHAPTER FIFTEEN

Oct. 16-59

Dear Wife

I agree with you totally. Slavery is not moral and those that practice it cannot be honorable. In truth the problem with slavery is financial. The Planters have made this flawed economic system larger and larger. The larger the number of slaves, the more money Planters have invested in them. As part of the 1850 compromise the Northern government agreed to a more aggressive fugitive slave act.

The fugitive Slave Act forced the Northern population to return slaves that had escaped slavery by fleeing North. Most of the North rejected what they felt was morally wrong. This made the law increasingly hard to enforce.

The basic founding clauses of the United States say that every human has basic God given rights: these are life, liberty, and the pursuit of happens." Clearly slaves did not have these rights, and the Abolitionists made sure that the public were aware of it. The Abolitionists spread their message to all walks of life.

Another constant religious sword was the fateful words of the New Testament: "Treat others as you would like to be treated." Naturally, slave owners did not want to be treated as the Planters treat slaves.

The slave owners tried hard to fight abolitionist propaganda. They pointed out the normalcy of slavery in the Biblical Old Testament and the vague approval of slaves in the New Testament. All of this is a fruitless task. Time and again the anti-slave group appeals to "Higher Law." This growing anti-slave movement is gradually but steadily winning the fight for the public mind. It did not help the South when a critic pointed out that slavery has been outlawed by every major power in Europe and beyond. At this point most anti-slave Northern citizens believed that the South was on the wrong side of history.

I must include some thoughts on the reality and the consequences of that reality. The United States is growing explosively. The Northern population has doubled and doubled again. The North has made massive investments in railroads, industry, and telegraph. These are only the top features of the North's ballooning expansion. Extremely large growth in the Northwest is also occurring. Particularly in Chicago which is a boom town writ large. Natural resources must be mentioned.

The Northern states are awash in timber, coal, water, steel ore and undeveloped land where tens of thousands of free Americans see opportunity by riding on the tremendous growth in the Northern economy. The culture of the Northern states is optimistic. They believe in the hope of the future. Nearly every Northern boy is filled with dreams and ambition. The Northern boy with sincere effort has a good chance of bringing his dreams to reality. If a free man is unhappy with his present lot then he can move on for better chances. No slave has that right.

Please keep writing to me. I find the task of writing for your education a useful foil by which I clear up my own thoughts.

Your Husband

Frank

Chapter Sixteen

November 4-1859

Dear Frank

I and the children are doing well. Of our three children Rachel is by far the most interested in the subject of slavery. She has such an intense interest in the subject that it might not be healthy for her. Rachel loathes slavery to a depth that is unusual for anyone of her age. She insists on me reading each letter over and over to her. Of course, I leave out the personal aspects of our letters. When I read to her she seems to ponder every word and every concept. Her response is rage toward the South and its "peculiar institution."

She often asks hard questions. Often I must reply that I do not have an answer. I explain that the Southern mind accepts what most of the world hates. She takes that reasoning but never seems satisfied.

When you get home we should talk about Rachel. There is no doubt of her brilliance but her intensely causes me some worry. She also seems drawn toward interests that one would normally expect of a boy.

She loves to target shoot, hunt and ride horses. In all these areas she is truly expert. Our neighbor Mr. Blake often watches her riding, and he has told me in confidence that she excels nearly anyone in his experience. Since Mr. Blake is considered the best horseman in the county that is high praise indeed.

All our children are doing very well academically although each is quite different from each other. I have no doubt that they will each be ready to face a hard world. Although we are wealthy no-one knows the fickle fate that life can bring us. Our greatest duty is to prepare our children mentally and morally. While having money is a great and comforting thing it cannot solve all problems. And what is money if our children use it foolishly or use it to harm others? Money often makes the load lighter. However, the responsibility of money can also become a heavy load by itself.

The farms continue to do well. The crops are in, and we have had a bumper crop. Several of our hired men seem to be courting local girls. The men are stable hard workers and would doubtless make good husbands and fathers. I often see them in conversation with their sweethearts during the evenings and I know the world will go on no matter what the madness that governments seem to have.

These young people seem to have modest goals and therefore they will meet most of them. To drink too deeply of the glass of ambition often brings unhappiness. The ability to be happy with small things is a blessing given to few.

Many a king at the end of their troubled lives might envy those who reached for lower fruits. One of the great losses of slavery in my mind is the wasted potential of each slave. On their own many of them would become more useful members of general society. Only with freedom does one have the chance to better oneself. Slavery crushes any willingness to advance.

Rachel is constantly upon me to ask for your letters. She wants to know slavery from front to back. I fear we can do nothing but comply.

Love,

Your Wife

Virgia

CHAPTER SEVENTEEN

November 24-1859

Dear Wife

All the news you have given me is good. It sounds like each of us should be proud of our children. In truth there is little that each of us leave behind. Some money, some love, some children and some memories. Beyond that all is lost in time. I am so glad that the farms are doing well. Our oil profits are so large I worry about them. Each of us tends to boast about our achievements but in the end, chance often carries the day.

None of us can coax a drop of rain to fall. None of us controls the intensity of the sun or the timing of the seasons. Who could have dreamed of the income we have received from our oil? Surely it was just luck and God's will. We ourselves have done nothing to receive this bounty.

Perhaps there might be something we can do with these funds so that we might merit this income. We are all small chips of wood that are floating down the great river of life. With our efforts we might push our chip a little to the left or a little to the right, but it is truly the current that sends us to our destination.

Do not be concerned about Rachel. She is a good girl and with our help she should turn out fine. If one is truly interested in something then that is a good sign. I would be worried if our children showed no interest in anything. There are many things much worse than hunting, shooting, and riding.

I hold Mr. Blake's opinion very highly. He has a wonderful eye for horses and those who ride them. I do feel we must discuss Rachel when I arrive on vacation. I too, have noted her interests and her lack of femininity. God makes each of us different and who are we to doubt His choices? It seems Rachel wants me to hold forth on slavery.

Thus:

The South has a different view of the world. The Planters want the present reality of slaves and cotton to stay the same forever. The South cannot see that staying the same is totally impossible. They do not want the world to change, yet the real world is passing them rapidly. The South suffers from the beguiling idea that all work is degrading and should be the task of slaves. With this attitude the South slumbers away as industry and freemen in the North are changing the world for the better.

Ambition is hard to find in the Southern states. Under free enterprise one is the master of his own fate. By this I mean free men can better themselves. In the South black people are held in chains and the Southern boy is bound by the invisible chains of an antiquated culture. There are fewer schools, fewer banks and far less opportunities for Southern boys.

The North has many more educated people than the South. For example, the North has six times more trained engineers than the

South. In nearly any field of advanced study the South is far behind the North and they are falling more behind every day.

It should be noted that the South is not all roses with mint-juleps' for the Planters. Their greatest fear is slave revolt. They know if the slaves revolted in unison it would be a blood bath for the Planters. Every plantation has far more slaves than whites. Should the Negros on any plantation choose to do so they could slaughter the Planter family with little effort.

That is why the Nat Turner case in 1831 put such a chill upon Southern society. Turner was an insane Negro who revolted, and he and his followers murdered over sixty men, women and children. He believed he had a sign from God to revolt.

He and his followers were put down within a few days and I believe he and over 50 black people were hung for these crimes. Nevertheless, the fear of a servile revolution is widespread. Due to Northern agitation the fear of slave revolt is greater than ever.

The South passed many slave laws after the killing spree of Nat Turner. It was believed that Turner was driven to his crimes due to his ability to read and write. In a knee-jerk reaction laws were passed making it illegal to teach a slave how to read and write. It was typical of Southern blindness that the crime was blamed on Negro education without any thought that slavery itself was the underlying problem.

The recent attempt by John Brown to incite a slave revolution has again struck fear in Southern hearts. He paid with his life for his attack on Harpers Ferry and his attempt to lead a Negro revolution throughout the South. Brown appears to be another religious fanatic who was inspired by the abolitionist press. His willingness to die for the freedom of the slaves has made him a national hero.

The North is turning John Brown into a hero and that is driving the Southern newspapers into a blood-red fury. I fear we have not seen the end of Brown's influence. Every great cause demand martyrs and John Brown was a perfect martyr. He defended himself with nobility, asked for no mercy and died with complete courage and devotion. I deeply fear John Brown has taken us much closer to a Civil War.

The South is also absorbing the blistering effects of modern literature. The influence of *Uncle Tom's Cabin* written by Mrs. Stowe is increasing daily. The book has inflamed nearly the entire North and has even influenced world leaders. The book has been sold in the hundreds of thousands. Mrs. Stowe is now a wealthy woman.

The South has raged against the book to no effect. If anything, the rage of the South creates more interest in the book and thus sells even more copies. Mrs. Stowe also makes mock of Southern theory that women are not mentally equal to men. Perhaps someday men will become aware of the potential of women. Without your mind I would probably lose my mind.

Another book that has enraged the South is titled *The Coming Crisis* by a strange man named Helper. He seems to dislike Negros, but his argument is that slavery is wrong because it is not profitable and that morally slavery is destroying worthy Southern men.

This book almost dead-locked Congress because the South said anyone who read the book was not fit to serve as speaker of the house. We had to have over 60 rounds of ballets to finally get someone who the South would accept. Another threat to the South is the growing strength of the abolitionists.

The abolitionist press by people like Garrison is growing daily in readership and power. Educated Negros like Fredrick Douglas are attacking the South effectually and daily. Douglas is showing the world that the intellect of black men is equal to any white. The concept that the Blacks are barbarians with no ability to advance is being disproven every day. I personally believe Negros will eventually be important citizens in our society. However, I must keep that thought to myself. Perhaps I am ahead of my time.

I will now bring up a more sensitive point. It is my firm conviction that the South wants to secede from the Union. They have tried to secede a number of times. However, the North keeps caving in, and the South has not found a good reason to leave the Union. My love, if war befalls us this will be like no other conflict the world has ever seen.

The current weapons of war will kill men faster than any general could ever imagine. I am so afraid war is coming and I am helpless to stop it. This coming war will divide families. Brother against brother. Fathers against their sons.

The power of industry to create monstrous killing machines will be something totally new. The carnage will be horror beyond horror. I predict the deaths will be in the hundreds of thousands.

If this is true then why would the South secede? The South realizes that the North is outstripping them on nearly all fronts. With the passing of each day the North is getting stronger, and the South knows it is becoming weaker. Time is working against the Slave Powers so they want a quick war because they will not become stronger with time.

The South does not want to delay. The South realizes that the quicker a war starts the better chances of victory they will have. Parts of the South have sworn to leave the Union if a "Black Republication" is elected. The elections of 1860 will be decisive. Perhaps a Republican president might form their excuse to leave the Union.

When will war happen? I don't know, but I would bet it is within two years, but the fire could ignite any time. If war broke out in a matter of months I would not be surprised. Congress members are coming to sessions fully armed so that they can protect themselves.

Members of Congress have physically come to blows. Duels have been offered and a few have dueled. I see the clouds of our future becoming darker and darker. Even now at my desk I close my eyes, and I can see flashes of lightning on my mental horizon. In my dreams I see thousands of young men cut down in combat in mere minutes. I am not a seer, but I am afraid.

Love,

Your Husband.

Chapter Eighteen

December 17-1859

Dear Husband

How very frightening this situation is. I had no idea that Congress itself must be armed to feel safe in session. When men are armed it is but a short step to using those arms. When men who are the finest flowers of the Union cannot talk about these problems then we are doomed. When this happens, the issue can be resolved only by arms and blood. The idea of a Civil War is chilling. Is it not time for you to step down and enjoy the company of your own family?

If the storm cannot be stopped perhaps you would do well to come home and take shelter? When I read your letter to Rachel I saw her eyes flash in anger. During these moments, our daughter frightens me. When I tell her that these events might not happen, she is not content with that answer. Once she looked at me steadily in the eyes and said, "The war is coming, and I will be part of it." Her firmness turned my blood cold.

Love

Your Wife

CHAPTER NINETEEN

Jan. 1-1860

Dear Wife

I am retiring from public service. The strain is killing me, and I cannot influence either side of Congress. At times I kid myself that everything will work out. However, I know that is not true. There is going to be a Civil War, and I cannot prevent it. My influence on President Buchannan is fading. I know he is trying his best, but he simply does not have the force of character to steer the ship of state through the coming rapids.

He has chosen to do nothing and that can only encourage more slave states to rebel. As I have mentioned, I have not been able to have constructive dialogue with any party or groups of parties. The very survival of Congress is not certain. The South has warned they will secede from the Union many times, but I feel this time they mean it.

Slavery is so distasteful that it can only exist in the shadows but now the great light of rightness is focused on this issue. Slavery is beyond the pale, and I believe that even the Planters know it is wrong. Slave auctions are seldom attended by Planters. They do not want to see the deploring reality of buying and selling humans. The North cannot live with slavery and the South cannot live without it.

How can one go forward? If neither side yields then only arms will move this nearly immovable rock. I have always tried to avoid violence, and I have always striven to be fair, but the existence of slavery seems to ruin the minds of intelligent men. A strange type of mental blindness seems to possess the minds of even the rational. Please pray for us. I cannot see the path ahead. I can only stumble from darkness to darkness.

Love,

Frank

CHAPTER TWENTY

June 9, 1860

Dear Mary

How do you feel on this great day? I hope you are very well. I am 17 years old this day. I feel so much older. My mother chooses to treat me as a child. My father is so different. He loves me so much. I often catch his eye, and he watches me closely. I wonder what he is thinking. Who knows? On the downside my mother gave me another damn dress for my birthday. I can't stand dresses, but I try to please her.

My father bought me a custom Sharps target rifle. Such a beautiful rifle must have been extremely expensive. That brought tears to my eyes. No-one could ask for a better father. Mama loves me as well, but she is quite different. She believes I will grow up into a fine lady with a high society marriage. At times it seems mother wants to sell me to the highest bidder.

That is not uncommon in the upper classes, and I fear its tightening bonds. In mother's eyes such a marriage can only be with someone in our class who is extremely wealthy. I will gladly take money if my parents wish to give it, but I will never be the lady that she wishes for. I try to remain patient in the belief that someday she will accept me as I am. Oh well, no need to cast shadows over my birthday!

Grandfather gave me a beautiful horse! It is a beautiful bay mare with four short white socks. She is clearly hot blooded and when I ride her I feel I am floating on air. Grandfather said she came from the finest of Kentucky thoroughbred stock. She runs like the wind yet is so well trained she responds to the slightest command. I adore her.

Why do the men in this family understand me so much more than mother? I do wish my grandmother was still living. I loved her so. She did accept me head on. When I did boyish things she would always smile and say,

"Let her live her own life. That's the least that parents and family can do."

She was a tough woman and woe to the man who stood in her way! Even though I have two brothers she seemed to favor me the most. When I reached around the age of fourteen she and father would talk about me in father's office. Every once in a while grandma and father would speak for hours. I confess I once tried to ease drop, but it was hopeless. Father's office is a room within a room and my father would always lock both doors.

My father is a brilliant man, but Grandmother was wise. Perhaps someday I will talk to father about their conversions. As you know my favorite outdoor interests are horseback riding and target rifle shooting. My father says I was born with natural talents in those areas. Of course, I like to hunt as well, and I enjoy that sport greatly. At a young age I insisted on learning how to dress out my own game.

Mama thinks it will be boys soon. That is just never going to happen. I have tried hard to look at the boys and they seem so crude and ugly. In addition, they are poor in their studies. Why go to school if you don't want to learn? The girls in school seem to swoon over them. All I hear is how handsome Michael is or how wonderful Billy is. Which bewilders me since Michael is a pig and Billy is dumb as a stone and can't even read.

When the girls get together they brag about kissing boys. If I did anything that shameful I would never tell a soul. Some hint they have gone further in their sexual lives. This I doubt very much. There is a certain look and a certain maturity that signals a sexual life. These female clowns do not have this poise. If they only knew our intimacy they might lose their childish bravo. Of course, they will never know such things.

What we have is real and far better than many adults. We love each other. Many family unions do not have that inner fire and bodily desire. Love is God's gift, and I cherish this privilege. That means you are God's gift to me, and you are far more precious than gold or diamonds. I certainly can't say that about any boy. I can't stand the thought of having a boy touch me. One of the boys tried to hug me last week and I put my finger in his eye. The big baby ran straight to the teacher and spilled the beans. They pretend to be so tough until you poke them in the eye or kick them hard in the groin. Then they fold.

My teacher had to take a note to my parents. That seems to be the school board rule. She cried to me privately and she knew I was only defending myself from cruel boys. Father later asked me what happened. I told him that bastard tried to hug and kiss me.

The scumbag has not bothered me since. When any boy tries to flirt with me I just tell him to go find a cow. I have not been bothered too much recently. I know the girls talk about me and say I am weird. I suppose I am different. I could care less.

Papa said I did the right thing. He said no human being should be forced upon. He said love is the greatest gift of life and it is such a beautiful flame. Papa is so wonderful. He answers any question under the sun. I began to become seriously interested in sex when I was about twelve. Therefore, we have talked a lot about love and sex. He said that life and sex are part of being a human. Of course, I knew all the mechanics of sex.

He says the desire of the body will let the owner know when sex is wanted and even needed. I have never forgotten his phrase, "the desire of the body will let the owner know what is right for them." We always talk alone in his study. If mother was there she would have run out of the room screaming.

Mother would just look at the ceiling in open terror. At times I wonder about my mother. I tend to think of her as weak yet at rare times I see a real toughness in her character. Perhaps I have not learned that much about mother. Time tells all.

The boys call me names, but they don't come near me. I insist on wearing my hair as short as a boy. I always dress like a boy. I feel right when I am in male clothes. I prefer to dress in work jeans. Papa and Mama have no problem with that. Thank God they are tolerant. Someday soon I will have to tell them about the love and intimacy we share.

Papa says to wear whatever I want; he has talked to several women busybodies in town. He told them plainly my clothing was my business alone. No problems after that. Mama holds firm that I will grow out of it. Papa is so prominent in local government and state government I could probably go naked, and no-one would say anything. As you know my Papa owns nearly all this county and he donates large sums to all the churches and charities.

In this local area people respect him. They not only respect him because he has money, but they also admire him for being a good man. I have seen him help worthy people who are just going through a tough time. Father has said many times there is little risk in helping a good person. Father makes no fanfare about these incidents.

I so wish you had money. It does make life easier. I realize I have a privileged position in our society, and I certainly know how much money is needed. Someday I will have money and on that day you will be with me. I will soon begin doing the books in father's business. I want to know everything about business and money management. I want to stand on my own feet.

I pray for the day when I can help support you. You mean so much to me. One can earn money but to find someone like you is nearly impossible in this perplexed world. You and I are in love. You are a woman, and I am a woman. Women have a right to love women. I swear I will protect you when we can finally live together.

You have given me so much. You have the gift of seeing beauty in this world. Sometimes I must chastise myself, for example, when we look at a hillside I see the rocks, but you see the flowers. You are everything to me. I never knew joyful life until we were in each other's arms. I seriously doubt if I could live without you. I truly love you.

Papa and the whole family went on a picnic, and it was so nice. The sky was translucent blue. The breeze was so fresh and pleasant.

Songbirds were singing for their mates. But it would have been better if you were there. I live for our weekly talks. You were so clever to suggest we write our thoughts and exchange them with each other. I feel it gives you and me a secret world. Even though we can get together once a week I wish it was every day forever. I love you so much.

Love,

Rachel

CHAPTER TWENTY-ONE

June 16, 1860

Dear Rachel

I wish you a happy birthday. Time seems to go slow at times and fast at times. It went slower when we were little and goes so much faster as we age. I am a little older than you, but you are smarter and stronger. I am 17 plus two months. I don't hate dresses like you. I often wish I owned more. But I try to steal my brother's jeans because I am so much happier in them.

Mama does not seem to catch on to my trick. With eight kids in the family, I guess she does not have the time. Let's go fishing next week if we can talk our parents into it. My Pa usually allows it because he claims I have no place in the fields. He literally does not want to see me. In some way I can make him agree if I am humble enough. He says I am just a worthless mouth to feed. I live and pray for my freedom. You are the only human on earth that can save me.

Thank God I have you. Nearly all my education is from the books you lent to me. The last book on Roman history that you lent to me was great. You are fortunate your family is rich. They can buy you things that I could never afford. Pa would not buy me a book even if he could afford one.

The only book in our house is the Bible and that belongs to my mother. Strangely neither of my parents can read a word. My father has not a single virtue from that ancient book. When I read a book I feel like I am in a different world. I feel that all knowledge can eventually be in my hands. You are tutored at home as well as public school. I envy that great privilege. I must go to the free school.

I am aware of the boy thing. I can't stand it when the girls giggle around the boys. I don't understand what they see. The boys are dirty, crude, and stupid. They do not apply themselves to their studies. The boys pick on me and I am not strong like you. I must just endure it. The girls are also catty, and they call me a freak. They talk about being kissed by this boy or that. To them it is a big deal. We have been seriously kissing since we were 13 and it means more to me every day.

My pulse beats faster when I see you. My mouth gets dry thinking of you and when I see you joy leaps in my heart. I feel that desire that your father mentioned. It gets stronger by the day. When we are alone by the creek tucked into the willows on our blanket it is so fine.

We can lie face to face and kiss each other for hours. We touch each other's body, and it seems so good and right. When my hands caress you I feel like I am touching a god. I love you and I know our love will grow with us.

I am growing older, and I can't seem to find my place in the world. My family is so bad I can't find the words to describe it. We live in fifth and degradation. There is absolutely no privacy. My father ruts with my mother and doesn't care how many children are awake. He is raping her. He has not the slightest care as to mother's needs.

I talked to my teacher about my lack of friends, and she was so kind. She said that I am gifted and so much smarter than her other students. She said in truth they should be coming to me for instruction. She wants me to attend a girl's college. I have no money so that is just a dream. She said that sometimes bright students are supported so they can get an education.

You are my only hope and my only star in the sky. She said I was close to the point where she could not teach me anything more. My teacher was modest enough to tell me that I could easily teach all the kids in free school. I tell her that you lend me books and all she could say is "Thank God." That is why your books are so precious.

She said that someday society would give more opportunities for women. She swore me to secrecy on that subject because she might lose her job. Apparently the idea of an intelligent woman is frightening to men. My Pa says nothing is worse than an uppity woman.

My mother told me quietly that being a wife was to be a slave. She regrets the day she was married. Her parents sold her to this beast for twenty acres of poor land. She had to accept this because she had nowhere to go. She had to literally go with this monster or starve to death.

She shared with me that she has never enjoyed lovemaking due to his bestial behavior. She told me that the family could only support three kids at most and we already have eight with no end in sight.

She whispered to me that she prays every night that she will not get in a family way.

She told me that she was wearing out before her time because of too much work, too poor food and too many children. She often has coughs, and she always seems so tired. I worry about her. Thank God I have you. You mean everything to me. I can't wait to hold you.

Love,

Mary

Chapter Twenty-Two

June 23,1860

Dear Mary

The first and most important thing is to tell you how much I love you. Everything else is not worth one hour of my time. This might seem silly writing this way; after all we see each other in Church. After church I may have only a few minutes with you and minutes are not enough. I like the exchange of letters.

It seems more private, and we have a type of hidden world all our own. I agree that we must keep these letters in a safe place. We have often talked about being writers in the future and our letters are good practice.

Somehow I agree with you that our letters may be important to some poor woman struggling to be with her female lover. My parents think I am loaning you a book and they approve of that. My mother says that every child should have books. What they don't know is that we exchange letters hidden in the books.

We have gotten a lot taller this year. Someday I might be as tall as you. I have not been blessed with large, beautiful breasts like you.

Frankly, my breasts are average. I love having an afternoon together with you. When I stroke your breasts I feel I am in heaven.

My father accepts me as I am, and mother does her best to accept me until I am safely married. On such a fragile boat we float toward each other. It is so wonderful to be with you. I dream of your kisses and your hands all over my body.

I relive our intimate hours repeatedly. Your lips convey me to the only heaven I am sure of. The heat of my desire receives your kisses with hunger. I literally burn with passion. When I feel your kisses I just melt with pleasure.

You are my secret world. I have no future without you. I don't have any money now, but I will do everything in my power to see you get out of that hellhole and obtain an education. Our lives belong together. Please do not give up. I promise from the depth of my being that I will get you to safe harbor.

My sisters keep telling me that the day will come when I must marry. I tell them to go to hell. I will never marry a man. My sisters know not to push too hard. I will not be pushed into anything.

I hate boys and I try to avoid them. I want you to know we have our love, our books and our letters. That is more than enough for me. I don't know where our lives take us, but I know we will be together.

Love Always

Rachel

CHAPTER TWENTY-THREE

July 1,1860

Dear Rachel

I always wait anxiously for your letters. I read them over and over. I often memorize them. Without them I will die of loneness and ignorance. To be uneducated is to miss living. I certainly can't do many things but through books I can learn how it is done. Knowledge is freedom. My papa claims books are just rubbish.

I started menstruating when I was twelve. Here are the words he gave me "Stupid bitch. I will sell you as soon as I can. I don't like the look in your eye." Then he usually tries to slap me, and I must run out of the cabin. He keeps telling me he will soon sell me to someone for land or drink. He laughed and laughed as he drank his cheap moonshine.

I fear he will rape me or disfigure me. I carry this butcher knife hidden in my dress lining. I swear to God I will use it. My father is an idiot, a drunk, and a beast. A more dangerous combination I cannot imagine. In a way it is a blessing neither of my parents can read.

Nevertheless, I am very careful with our letters. They are stashed in a dry hidden place. I only read them when I am alone. I can often read your letters in my mind. Somehow I can secretly listen to them, and I don't miss a word. If my father knew of the letters he would literally whip the skin off me.

It is hard to live in the shadow of violence. I am afraid of my father for good reasons. When he hits the bottle there is no one safe in the house. He beats my mother often and I am helpless to protect her. Often he forces himself on her and it is really nothing but rape. He has ripped her clothes off and penetrated her in front of the children. This beastly behavior cannot be love. I loathe him to the depths of my being.

Perhaps someday such violence will be prohibited. I fear we are far from that day. I pray for the day when you and I can be with each other in a state of love and peace. Only with you can I find happiness. I want both of us to keep our letters. I want to be able to look upon these years of love as the heaven that you and I shared. Our love is all that I care about and your life is everything to me.

Somehow I feel our small letters might reach a larger audience. I have always felt that writing was a way to reach a larger world. I have no interest in pride or fame for myself, but I feel our love should be remembered. The Lord knows we are struggling to be together.

Perhaps the letters will help some other women who love each other and just want to live their lives. Hopefully, the world will be a better place. It may help them to know that others have struggled to protect their simple lives and their precious love. I want to share our lives together. I don't know if God exists although I know our preacher keeps his flock together by raw fear.

A God that is violently fierce is not a God to be worshipped. Honestly, I do not know if God really exists. Our joy and intimacy must come from somewhere. I pray every day but shamelessly I only pray for you and me. You are the only one I love. My lover, I am living in hell. I am so afraid. I touch the knife hidden in my dress to be sure I will be able to kill him if I must. I am careful never to talk to Papa when he is carrying on about book learning. Why would one rave over knowledge? He says that no woman alive should be able to read. He claims that is in the "Good Book" although he can't read a line.

I can never forget the hours we spent together. When you are in my arms those are the most precious hours of my existence. The memory of our youthful summers will never fade. May I lose my right arm before I forget those golden days together.

Yes we are young but already we are far wiser than most. We know what a rare pearl we hold in our hands. Should we reject love when true love is hard to find?

I want each of us to savor the gifts that God has given us. When one thinks and lives like an adult then childhood is left behind. I have now sipped from the vessel of pleasure. I have been blessed to know love. I know you will save me. I pray and wait for that hour.

Love,

Mary

CHAPTER TWENTY-FOUR

July 9, 1860

Dear Mary

I have long reached that sexual desire that Papa has told me about and it is growing by the day. Some days my desire for you becomes a fever. The mysteries of the female body and mind are yet to be discovered. I deeply believe in a loving God.

Love, desire, and passion have been given to us. There is no obvious reason why we should take pleasure in these actions. We could simply be wild beasts driven by instinct to thoughtlessly breed for the species to survive.

Pleasure and passion are gifts given to us by a loving God. There is no other logical reason. Papa has several books on sexuality, and I have read all of them. I will lend you one of the books but be very careful to keep it out of the sight of your parents. I am certain that science will tell us much more in the decades ahead.

I told Father that I have never felt anything toward a boy. The idea that a boy would touch me is abhorrent. I told father that at times women in general are attractive to me but that I only have desire for you. The object of desire is the truth of all sexuality. God created us and God has clearly given us objects of desire.

In my case it is a woman for a woman. I am certain we are not alone. There must be thousands of us trying to slip through the chains of intolerance. Father agreed with my thoughts and then he leaned back in his chair and looked carefully at me.

Clearly he was choosing his words with great thought. He told me that some women can only love women. He told me that he had been studying the issue of same gender sex for a long time. He had noticed traits in my personality for many years. He mentioned that he and Grandmother had discussed this question off and on for years.

That certainly was a revelation to me. He is certain I am one of these women. I can't speak of other women. I only know that I love you totally. It does appear that God has made my lesbian love a fact. Father felt that desire was a fact and that the object of desire told which gender was loved.

He told me not to talk to anyone on this subject. To say it is a delicate subject is not enough. In a religious society there is a constant look out for "evil" people. Same sex couples were an abomination to their God. The sadness of this issue was the cruel intolerance and even physical measures that the church placed on the lovers.

Father said that hundreds of women over the centuries have been murdered by the Church for what it considered an abomination. He broadened the injunction by saying never to talk to mother about it.

He said she was a kind woman, and he didn't think she could accept this type of love. I told him that I was not sure about this position. I felt there was strength and love within her which she could call forth. He suggested that time choose its own course. He suggested that I just follow my heart. He said again that it was critical not to discuss this with anyone except himself. He said society would be extremely cruel toward this type of love.

I have the most wonderful papa. He plainly told me that he would always love me no matter what path or pleasures I sought. I was frank with my father and told him openly that I love you with all my heart. He did not fault us in any manner.

He said that he was awed by the power of love, and he would not stand between any couple who felt they loved each other. He said that many adults laugh at young love, but he was not one of them. He said to always follow my heart. Where would I be without him and the books?

Love

Rachel

Chapter Twenty-Five

July 19, 1860

Dear Rachel

You have such courage. I wish I could be more like you. I am not strong like you. Yes my breasts may be larger, but your love is all I am interested in. Your body is so perfect that God Himself must approve. I will still love you as we age. I will still love you totally.

I do not fear age, I fear losing you. I love all of you whether it is on the inside of your body or the outside. I want to live with you here and now. I want us to be together and grow old together. Your body is a sensual banquet, but it is your love I most cherish.

Yes, we have these passions, and I believe God accepts this love. Women loving women must be right for some. After all, God made us. No one in their right mind would accept such a persecuted life. Who would choose a love that has to be hidden from society in fear?

A love you cannot share with your community. A love that in many states is a felony. No, it is not a choice. It is a fact. However, love is love and if we are fortunate enough to receive that blessing we will nurse it and cherish it. Such a gift is given to few.

I also try to avoid boys. Who does not avoid what one dislikes? They are immature and they are animalistic. I cannot beat them in a fight, and I do not want to fight. I want to live in freedom. My papa wants me to fight everyone. Of course, such a constant idea is insane. I love you and that is all that matters. I never lose my temper.

I do not seem to have a temper. Perhaps that is a blessing. I want to create no huge waves for society. Society is not ready for same gender love. This is such a horrible outcome. Someday a woman can simply say, "I love her." What could be more beautiful than love plainly stated?

I do have extreme disdain for petty girls and boastful boys. I try to keep these thoughts to myself. I try to be quiet, and I try to fade in the background. Mostly this method works well. Someday I may be strong enough to try and change some of these twisted thoughts on sexuality. I hope the day will come when I can write on love between women. I am not ready for such a bold life. I hope with prayer, courage, and education I can enter the lists of public discourse.

The older girls are attracted to boys, but I don't understand what they see. Boys are big and dumb. I often help the teacher grade papers after school. I have seen some of the poorest academic work that can be imagined. The poorest performers are boys.

Boys do not attract me at all. They smell of body odor and are hairy. They make my skin crawl. I don't want one to ever touch one for the rest of my life. The ones I see are boastful animals.

Joseph tried to grab my hand yesterday, but I was too fast and got away. You would have knocked his head off but the best I could do was run. A loving partner must have a mind as well as a body. You are my life, my love and my future.

These stupid boys will grow up to be stupid men. Most of them will marry and many of them will lust for other women despite their married status. Married men often commit adultery. When a man commits adultery society often looks the other way, but if a woman commits adultery she is often shunned by the whole community. By the same token when a woman is divorced it is often impossible for her to form another union.

How can society be so cruel? Are women not humans as well? Do they not realize that women also have dreams and goals? Why can't women have lives and careers of their own? Women want the same freedoms of man. Women should have every right to love women. Do men have a monopoly on love? We must be free to choose our own life partners. Until we can own our bodies we will have no hope of political power.

Your father is a wise man. Nature alone tells us which sexual path we will take in life. I believe our type of love is broader than most people think. I am certain we are not alone in this vast society. There are probably thousands of us throughout this country. Our type of love certainly burns with a hotter flame.

How strong our love must be when the world is trying to tear us apart! I know you will find a way for me to escape this hell I am living in. I know you will not forsake me. I have my knife, and I have hardened my heart to use it if papa assaults me. I will not allow myself to be raped or disfigured.

The churches talk of sin but is it sin to love one another? I have read large parts of the Bible and in truth much of it is dreadful. To believe that murdering your son is somehow holy? To stone to death a woman who tried adultery to find some love or pleasure. Many a man in the Bible was guilty of whoring and this fickle God seemed to find these actions acceptable.

Think of the killing of babies by smashing them against a wall? Murdering large swaths of humanity down to the last old woman, babe, and even animals is a crime so unthinkable that no just court could support it. This is not God, this is madness.

Let us be clear: the Bible supports the enslavement of women and men. Never once does the Bible openly renounce slavery. Not once. To accept putting a human being on an auction block is all I need to know about the validity of the Bible. Such a horror could not be the work of a merciful God.

The unthinkable crime of slavery is a blemish that all civilized humans must get rid of at any price. The Bible is a myth written by men to justify their power and desires. Someday the South will pay in blood for these crimes. The Planters in the South are happy to wrap the Bible around them to justify their crime.

Any book that justifies slavery is not written by God. The South is going to pay a horrible price in coin and in blood. They have sown the seeds of slavery, and they will reap the whirlwind. I hope every master who has whipped a black back will die soon.

The world cannot afford such animals. Because of the South this country is going to be torn apart. I fear hundreds of thousands of young men will be slaughtered. Someday black soldiers will be placing the flaming torch under all the buildings and possessions of the slave holder. May I live to see that day.

Please keep lending books. Beyond you they are the most important things in my life. But you are not a thing. Nothing in the world is greater than the love I have for you.

Love

Mary

CHAPTER TWENTY-SIX

June 14,2016

"My God Joyce! What have we stumbled upon?" Ann's eyes were wide with surprise after listening to the readings of the letters.

Joyce took her time answering.

"I really don't know yet, but I know we must keep going. This is a history we must explore. In my heart I feel we have just touched the toe of the beast. We must go on slowly. We can't make haste here. The order of these letters may form the steel backbone of this mystery. Whoever Rachel Summerfield was in these letters. The rest will follow in time.

"These letters have been here for decades we do not need to hurry. On the contrary, I believe that haste can only bring disaster. Later events showed that these matters were not that difficult to understand. The library curators had gone home and would be back in the morning. It was clear that the pair were working hand and hand. Joyce felt confident that the task assigned to them would be done well.

And so, it was. Joyce and Ann cultured modern lesbian women trying to follow the faint tracks of a much younger lesbian couple who were madly in love who lived over 80 years ago. Ann also brought up the excellent point that we should try to find the grave of Rachel Summerfield. At this point no one could have imagined the strange story of these young lovers. A story that would take time before the full depth of the pool could be plumbed.

After a series of calls the harried Robert arrived with our luggage and several pizzas. Robert agreed to be on call 24/7 to try to meet our needs and our needs were not large. The grocery list was short because all the stables had been kept up to date by careful cycling of kitchen necessities. Everything from 1927 to our date has been cycled in the most orderly manner possible. Everything was in its place. Fresh milk, good butter, and fresh bread were all in place. Salt and pepper shakers clean with fresh ingredients up to date.

It was as if the homeowners just walked out the door today and silently went away. Leaving no clear reason why they left. Every normal house's need was on hand. Every staple like flour, rice, and beans were all neatly aligned.

We decided that we would hire a full-time cook to make our meals, keep the kitchen tidy and to provide refreshments. This would allow us to work at leisure and have our meals at regular times. Deciding to do away with fast food and getting more wholesome food should give us the strength to forge ahead with Rachel's letters. This would relieve us of the time-consuming task of cooking. We will ask Mr. Hansel who he might suggest.

Joyce and Ann had time now to look at the living room more slowly. From the bare floor of the ancient farmhouse everything that allowed living was in order. Later they opened the hot cardboard boxes and began the American ritual of eating pizzas on the family sofa. The room was certainly small, about 14x16 feet. The walls were a faint blue, it is cool and inviting.

The ceiling was modestly white. There was no carpet, but the floors were crafted with real planks fitted to perfection. All the wood throughout the house was freshly oiled and waxed. There were several original throw rugs that showed a steady hand and an ideal for beauty. The workmanship was obvious in every stitch.

The room was much smaller than would be acceptable to most modern Americans. Yet there was a coziness that would be hard to find in our current culture. As mentioned the walls were freshly painted. There were no cracks in the ceiling. No water marks on the ceiling or walls. No cobwebs in the corners. There was no dust on the ottoman or on any shelves.

The maintenance was perfect. Not to be forgotten are the shelves and shelves of books. A library any scholar would be proud to own. Mr. Hartman and the cleaning lady knew their job to perfection. Ann and I used silverware that had been unused for decades. No dust at all. All tableware carefully polished and lined up in neat rows.

Unlike so many houses that have been uninhabited for a long time there was no sense of unease. Ann and I felt instantly at home. It was as if Rachel's old house was embracing its new inhabitants and giving them love and shelter. After our meal we went out onto the enclosed porch to watch the day linger with the fading light and we felt the soft cool air of the evening upon our bodies.

It was so peaceful. It was far more peaceful than our city home. We watched the nighthawks go through their rapid swoops and dives.

In the city we never felt we had the time or inclination to watch the day turn into the night. Even in our up-scale neighborhood there was always the slight unease of potential danger.

Without thinking, city residents sought to be behind locked doors before the creatures of the night went prowling. It was so different here. There were neighbors but they were scattered across the flat land. One knew they were there, but no-one had the sense of close encroachment. Of course, we also had our caretaker which gave a comfortable sense of security.

I had thought of asking him concerning home protection and he had looked at me strangely. He said he has his dog and his pheasant shotgun, and he had never needed either one. I took that as a reflection of safety.

It was so pleasant feeling the heat of the day fade into the evening coolness. There seemed to be a sharp drop in humidity after the sun went down and that was a welcome feeling. Ann and I shared an old-fashioned porch swing, and we held hands as had been our custom. It had always been reassuring for our hands to touch. It seemed a quiet way of assuring the other of our love and commitment.

We realized that Rachel Summerfield must have used this swing during the years of her life. Our gentle swing seemed to be a nearly silent call for Rachel to come near us. Our talk naturally drifted to the content of the letters we had read at this point. We marveled at the love and the maturity of the two young lovers.

It was easy to see they were both highly gifted. Their level of writing was high. That their love could span the social classes was a marvel. Normally the rich do not associate with the poor. That is as true today as it was when Rachel and Mary walked the earth. Of course we did not know how long their relationship lasted. Perhaps it ended shortly.

However, we both felt that these romantic lovers showed no sign of a cooling relationship. No drawing back due to the forces that often drive the social classes apart. We had asked Robert to buy some bottles of wine, and he did an excellent job of finding our varieties.

It was a comfortable feeling being with each other sipping cool full-bodied wine. I told Ann that all this inheritance was still beyond belief even though the paperwork was signed and sealed before my eyes. I knew in time the reality would sink into my mind.

When we retired for the night we took a close look at our bedroom. It was small, about 12x14 feet. You had the bed and just enough room to get around it with one set of dressers and a shallow closet. The bed itself was a double and that meant that a couple would have to sleep close to each other. Once again everything was in order. The sheets and blankets were clean and crisp.

I knew I wanted to talk to the house cleaner because I wanted to know how she accomplished this marvel of readiness. We knew we had to contact the housekeeper to arrange cleaning schedules that met our needs. When the bedroom light went out Ann and I held each other close. It was incredibly peaceful. We both fell asleep right away. It seemed like only a moment before we woke up to a new day.

CHAPTER TWENTY-SEVEN

June 15, 2016

At 9:00 a.m. sharp the library workers were on the job. Mr. Hansel called and said he had a cook lined up and she would come out to be interviewed before noon. There was nothing more to be done so Ann and I went to open the next letter in line.

Of course, we still had a lot of ground to cover. Up to this point we did not know what the later letters would tell us. I personally had tasks I needed done. I was able to call my bank in Red Cloud on my cell phone when Ann was not present.

I had something in mind. I told her I had some business at the bank, and would she come with me? Always on the go Ann was in the car before I could find my keys. I felt a youthful spring to my step. I had wanted this action for so many years. We rented a car last week and it was becoming necessary for our tasks. We knew a rental was more convenient.

The short trip once again took us through vast farmlands and the land got more interesting as time passed. There was a strange but good feeling that our feet were finally touching real earth. When one lives in a city the only time one could touch the earth was probably in a city park. Even in a park there was the feeling that man had crafted these small plots. Over the years the citizens of most cities went to parks less and less. There was a steady but noticeable sense of danger. There was none of this feeling here.

Here you could see the sun rise and the sun set. These common sights were becoming less and less visible in the urban giants. Buildings blocked off vistas of the earth that our ancestors took for granted. Here the earth gave off a sense of renewal. The earth breathed and we shared its breathing. The air was new, cool and refreshing. The sky was a deep blue that one sees only occasionally. Again, the towers of man in the cities cut off more and more of our connection with our skies and heavens. This land had been prairie for ages and ages.

There were few trees, and these trees bordered the small creeks that flowed at least part of the year. The trees we saw were mostly Elm and Cottonwood. What the early settlers used for heat in the winter was a mystery. I thought I would talk to Robert about that the next time I saw him. During the daytime, the wind did seem to be in constant movement, but it was not annoying. It rose and fell so smoothly that one could easily think the wind was not blowing at all. In the evenings, the wind often dropped off entirely.

I could see that the winters here must be brutal. There was nothing to stop the Arctic air from plunging across this smooth terrain. How strong the original settlers must have been to survive this fierce environment. Without a doubt many of the first settlers did perish before their time.

The hunger for land must have been overpowering for those who only had a dream and fire in their belly. When the land was settled no one really knew the best times to plant. There was little native wood to put up some semblance of a shelter. There would have been so many challenges to be overcome.

Why did people like Rachel Summerfield come here? The Summerfields' were a wealthy family so why would Rachel leave all those established comforts to battle this soil? What a battle it must have been. The settlers struggled to get the seed in the ground, and then prayed that the right amount of rain came at the right time. They must have fearfully watched their crops grow and hope no giant storm would hammer their crops into the mud.

Perhaps the original settlers had such strong faith because they were nearly powerless in the face of this savage land. She was sure this area would have its own literature. Much of the literature would probably be about the relationship between tough people and a tough land.

To survive on this demanding land must have taken perseverance. She recalled Willa Cather who wrote about this land and the people who settled it. It was interesting that Willa Cather was also a lesbian. As time passed Joyce herself did begin to feel something of the soul in this silent soil.

There is a sense of eternity in this place. One could walk on the land and reach down and grasp the inherent richness of life within it. It seemed to say this is fruitful soil if one was strong enough to pay the price to bring crops to harvest.

Joyce would ponder this growing attachment to the land when she had more time. She felt it was a strange emotion. Owning a townhouse just didn't feel the same. In the cities all was in transit. The buildings, the streets and the people were in constant motion.

There was such a crush of humanity that no one really felt any attachment to the ground. Joyce did not feel that restless motion of man's activity on this flat silent ground.

As we drove down the gravel road we had a light conversation about our observations and Ann mentioned she was also feeling different about this place. The land was mostly flat, but she wondered about its history. What incredible forces of nature made this land so desirable?

How many millions of years had it taken for nature to mold the soil? How many thousands of layers of silt had settled on this land as the waters ebbed and flowed? She marveled how patient the land must have been as it was being formed. Of course, humans came to this land not very long ago.

Ann mentioned the family groups crossing the Bering Strait land bridge about 15,000 years ago with absolutely no idea where they were going or whether they could survive. The only weapon was a simple spear and a human brave enough and strong enough to stab a large beast.

This must have been the same type of courageous and hopeful people to settle and try to farm this land. One could only imagine the primal floods that wiped all life away many times in history. Ann sighed,

Yet this eternal land was slowly sinking into her being and she began to slowly like it. Without conscious thought she was slowly beginning to appreciate these vast lands of eternal mystery. How joyful must the farmers feel when the heat of spring began to force the claws of winter cold to retreat into the distant lands of snow?

How the farmers must have felt when they observed the first blades of grass come up and once again stood in awe watching this new birth of life. To see the newborn calves after they hit the ground during birth and to watch them struggle on shaky legs to reach their mothers tits. Nature here was nearly beyond the reach of time. She knew there was wisdom here if she could only learn it.

Pushing these deep issues away Joyce pulled into the bank parking lot. She asked Ann to remain in the car. She said she would be back in moments. In a few minutes she returned to the driver's seat.

Joyce turned to Ann and said,

"Let me stop at that coffee shop and get something in our stomachs? I'll pick up some donuts as well. We need to pamper ourselves because we have been toiling on Rachel's old correspondence for a long while. If we push too hard we might make errors that would obscure our understanding of Rachel Summerfield."

After we stopped for coffee and donuts I turned to Ann with a smile,

"I remember passing a nice park a while ago. Let's us go there to stretch our legs and eat our donuts."

Ann in return lightly said, "Sure, we have been bearing down too hard. A little while in the early sun would be nice. Spring is coming along so beautifully."

Joyce continued with light conservation for a couple of miles then she turned and entered a large empty park. She looked casually about her. The lawn was freshly mowed. There was a well-maintained running track around most of the park. There was no trash on the ground nor were the trash cans filled to overflow

They left the late modeled car and sat on an old wood picnic bench that was covered with carved hearts and initials. Joyce smiled at these beginning throbs of newly discovered hormones. The young boys and girls with their crude carvings were the innocent signs of children growing up with budding sexuality. Their love was so new that they burned with white heat.

She felt these young loves should be respected as if they were the crown jewels of one's life. They should not be ridiculed as so many people did. These crude hearts and initials were the new emotions surging through their hearts and minds. Their new hearts were still unscarred, and they had yet to suffer the broken dreams and dashed hopes that the world would soon inflict upon many.

She thought: What a loss to all of us that first love often cannot be saved. She sighed and turned to Ann. She thought of Ann's wonderful constancy and her faithfulness over the years. Side by side they had faced life's problems. They had survived the ups and downs of health. They had lost many friends over the years. Most of these were beyond this hard world. Joyce hoped they were resting in peace within the silent earth.

Joyce and Ann had something few couples could have. They had true love for each other. They had their health, and they had peace with each other. Few couples were this lucky. What would these yellowed letters tell us? Up to this point there were several letters between a husband and his wife. Then the letters were between two young female lovers. Where would the letters go next? Joyce knew she would come back to that issue soon. Right now, she had a much more pressing matter.

Ann poured the coffee and opened the box of donuts. She observed,

"It is not at all like the parks on the East Coast. You know how it is, the ground often littered with broken bottles, needles and condoms." Seldom was the fear of violence totally gone. Joyce pondered these issues: The gangs, the drug addicts, and those who lived within the clutches of poverty.

Joyce thoughtfully responded, "Everywhere has its problems but in a town this small the police should be able to control the worst of man's deviancy.

"Anyway Ann, I want to give you a gift. A gift that you deserve, and you should have. It is something I want for you, and I wanted to do this all my life."

She reached in her jacket and handled Ann a small black book.

"This is a savings account in your name at the local bank for five million dollars. I want you to have it."

She handed the thin booklet to a shocked Ann. Ann took the small booklet in total bewilderment. She searched Joyce's face for signs that she was joking. No, the face was calm and loving.

"You can't be serious can you?"

"I am serious, it is real, and it is now yours. I have wanted this all my life. I wanted to give you something like this so badly. At last, I can do it. Please take it with my love. Thank the mysterious Rachel Summerfield for helping both of us.

Ann was numb as she opened the account book. All the particulars of her identity were correctly entered, and the opening sum was 5,000,000. There was also a small note from the bank president fully notarized attesting this transaction was witnessed by him.

Ann rose and tried to compose herself, but the tears were coming. "I don't know what to say. I don't deserve this in any way. I have always loved you completely with or without money."

Joyce stood and placed her hands upon up Ann's shoulders.

"Everything I own goes to you after my death. But I don't want to make you wait for my end. I don't trust the future and that is why I am giving this to you right now. I want your mind at ease as we get older. I want to continue loving you until I die at a very old age.

Please accept it in the spirit it was given. Rachel Summerfield freely gave the money to me, and I am freely giving some of her money to you right now. Later after my passing everything I own will be left to you."

Ann turned toward a large tree and began to cry.

"I don't deserve anything, and I never wanted anything but your love and companionship. I just wanted to love you. That is all I ever wanted."

Joyce turned her toward her face and enveloped her in her arms.

"Hush my love, we have work to do at the farm."

Ann sobbed and sobbed. "Thank you Joyce, you can never know how much I thank you. All I want is for us to stay as we are."

"My dearest love, everything will stay the same. I love you so much."

Never repressed Ann brightly smiled and said, "Could we make love tonight? I certainly would like that!"

"Darling, of course we will. You read my mind. I was going to ask you the same thing. As always after all these years I desire you so often and my love for you has waxed instead of waned. I can barely wait to have you." They fell into each other's arms and wept tears of joy. They wept for a long while and then they turned to go to Rachel's farmhouse.

We drove to the farm with happy hearts. I was so pleased I could do something for Ann here and now. Who can know the future? As I mentioned to Ann I do not trust the future. Tomorrow might never come. It was easy to slip into eternity. Our next step could be our last.

If you have something important to say to anyone do it now. Accidents or diseases have closed the books on many a promising future. I had known people who lost others, and they regretted the conversations they should have had while they lived. It was crystal clear that Rachel Summerfield had made this possible. In my mind I prayed a silent prayer of thanks. "Thank you Rachel. Thank you so very much."

This gift for Ann was the best thing I have done in my entire life. People that say that money is not important have never been poor. It is true money can't buy love, but money can pay the bills. Being able to pay the bills goes a long way toward maintaining a relationship.

I felt that giving money to Ann now would ease her concerns as we each grew older. When we got to the homestead we decided to give our workers the day off with pay. Ann and I wanted to be alone in this house that was growing in our hearts and minds.

We had all kinds of leftovers, and our favorite wines were cold and fresh. We ate in the living room. Afterwards we once again retired to the shaded swing on the porch. Ann and I felt such serenity on this simple swing. We visited the memories of our early days as undergrad students and the emotions that young people often carry.

We laughed at the odd circumstances and events that had occurred in our years together. We mentioned the difficulties that had happened to us and how we overcame them. Each of us had a long life behind them. True, Ann and I were older, but our love was far broader and deeper now since we had gained more maturity. It seemed only a little while before the hot day began to ebb and slip over the horizon.

We visited through the soft evening, and we watched the stars come as the daylight faded. It was so peaceful, and we knew everything was right. We rose and we retired to our bedroom. We faced each other and took the time to kiss each other fully. Then each of us slowly removed the garments of the other. Our eyes never left each other as the garments slipped away.

We slowly brought our passions along. Finally, the bodies could not be denied any longer. Then we slid down gently from that wonderful peak

At last, we were sated and relaxed in each other's arms. Quickly we both drifted into deep entangled sleep.

CHAPTER TWENTY-EIGHT

June 16, 2016

The next day, with Ann in my presence I called my attorney back East to ask her to update my will to reflect my changed financial situation. As always I wanted Ann to inherit all assets upon my death. I asked her to send me two copies so I and Ann could go over them together. I wanted the will to be simple and yet complete.

I wanted the paperwork done in the soonest time possible with copies for myself and Ann. The distant cultured voice said that was no problem and the papers would reach us in a few days. I then hung up and both of us wept freely.

After we composed ourselves I told Ann after we got the paperwork we could both relax.

"It is now time to return to Rachel's Summerfield's letters." Ann nodded and we returned to the task at hand.

Chapter Twenty-Nine

August 3, 1860

Dear Mary

Time will pass and the day will come when we are independent and free. We are still young, and time is on our side. We have our memories of the past and we have the happy passions of the present and we have the dreams of our future. We will burst the chains that presently bind us and perhaps our lives will make the road easier for lesbian women whose lives follow us.

To me the Bible has always been a fallible book written by men. I don't believe for a second that it is truly the words of God. It is nearly all written from the male point of view and normally the woman is assumed to be meek, subservient, and without a mind of her own. I don't fit that pattern, and I never will.

I have a mind of my own and I can make my own decisions. The issue of slavery is a blood red stain upon the South. I have read and listened to all the arguments. Slavery cannot exist in a civilized world.

My father had raised me to hate slavery as an idea and to despise it as a fact. No human being has the right to enslave another. Black is only a color it is not a sign of an inferior human. Beneath our skins our blood is all red.

My father has grimly spoken to me many times on the issue of slavery. He has kept me abreast of the delicate political balance of power that is in our halls of government. For years, the North has tried to avoid addressing the issue of slavery. Many efforts have been made to allow the South to keep their slaves and to legally keep equal political power.

It is to no avail. All the tinkering in the world will never make slavery right. The politicos who are craven supporters of slavery will be added to the list of men with power who did nothing. They support and enable those who want to rule by leg chains and whips. You should live in sack cloth in utter shame. Man has done many wrongs to his fellow man, but none approach the sickness and moral depths of owning and selling humans.

The South realizes that the growing power and population of the North will soon make the South a minority in every meaning of the word. Thus, slavery will not be the will of most American citizens. This is a fact that the South knows very well.

Bloody Kansas is just an example of slavery proponents trying to use violence to intimidate people who do not want slavery. The South's effort to pervert the democratic system is foul. We heard this mantra of States Rights, but it is only a gloss for the right to own slaves.

The South knows their narrow window of opportunity is closing. If they have any chance of winning militarily it must be now while the political power is roughly equal. If the South waits, the imbalance of population will push the South under the waves of democratic majority within a decade or two. So, when they play their song of victimhood they realize it is only a pose to convince others of the justness of slavery. The song of their depravity is the slash of a whip.

Father says a Civil War is nearly upon us and it will be the bloodiest war in world history. The South itself wants war. As I mentioned they realize if they allow time to slip by the power of the North will eliminate slavery.

My dream is to have a world of freedom. A world where any human has the right to seek their own happiness and a world where consenting adults can love each other regardless of social class, gender or color of their skin.

Mary my love, we have the right to love each other, and we should have the right to legally join our lives together. We will always fight to make sure each person has equal freedom and equal rights. I am willing to fight for those freedoms. The history of man has been a sad story of enslaved people.

Women have been under the yoke of de facto slavery from the beginning of time and that must end. Women should have the legal right to be completely equal to a man in every way. A world must come where women stand just as tall as men in the political sense.

We should have the right to vote. We must have the right to an education and the right to enter any profession and any field of commerce. We must have the right to live and to dream. Let us think for a moment of the bumpkin boys that we both know in our schools and in the flow of daily life. These ignorant fools have the right to think for me. I think not. You and I are vastly more intelligent than these sad excuses of humanity.

Papa says he has business interests in Richmond that he must close. He believes the monster of war is nearly upon us. He says he will take me there so that I can see firsthand the fruits and horrors of slavery. Father said it will be within two weeks. Mary I miss you and I yearn to be with you. My heart races when I think of you.

I want to feel your kisses and your caresses. I want to enjoy the passions we give to each other. I believe in God because I believe in love. As you lay upon your bed imagine me with you. I urge you to be strong

All My Love,

Rachel

CHAPTER THIRTY

Sept 1, 1860

Dear Rachel

I also feel the gathering clouds of war. It is on everyone's mind. Everyone has tried to compromise, and they have failed and will continue to fail. One cannot believe in slavery and freedom in the same breath. There is no compromise with the man that wields the whip. My cruel Papa supports slavery, and he professes to hate all "niggers." Black people are not "niggers." They are simply people with dark skins. Is that too hard to understand?

I am sure there are tens of thousands of slaves who have innate intelligence far higher than my crude and stupid father. I sense that everyone must have someone more inferior to dominate. Many people need to have someone to beat. To these moral midgets it matters not whether it is a black slave or a white wife. Who are the animals in this debate? The man who holds the whip or the back upon the man that is whipped.

During our love for each other it is easy to forget the larger questions in the world. I fear the flames that slavery has brought to the world. There are questions that must be faced, and slavery is one of them. Slavery must be fought in the mind of every man or woman. The issue cannot be pushed aside.

Current events will not allow evasion of the issue for much longer. The power of persuasion has failed. Nearly everyone knows this in their heart. God save us but this issue will be settled upon the battlefield. For every drop of blood that has been drawn from a slave's back will be redeemed hundred fold from the citizenry of the South.

The sons of the South will bleed and die on the soil of the South. Their number will be in the tens of thousands. Perhaps the South will lose their sons in the hundreds of thousands. The so-called "value" of slaves will be redeemed by millions of dollars of property lost to the owners of the South. Arms are flowing into Kansas and the natural result will be bloodshed. Unfortunately, the blood of tens of thousands of Northern sons will also soak the ground.

Their blood will be sacred in the courts of heaven. No matter what their errors have been they can declare that they wrapped themselves in the white cloths of freedom. Their deeds will be forgiven. For they have died to set men free.

My beloved Rachel our country is seated on a powder keg. Where the spark comes from is unknown, but it is coming. The explosion will be fearful. Who can say what the verdict of war will be? No-one knows. It is a sad fact that wars are not always won by those who are just.

Moral rights can be lost to the beasts that own the mansions and the cotton fields. If that should happen that means the devastation will just be kicked down the road for another generation.

My love don't forget me during these times of unrest. I live for you. It is you I long for. All that I am is committed to you. I feel your presence when I work, when I think and especially when I dream.

During my moments in the darkest hours my passion burns for you. Make love to me. My strong body yearns for your touch. I know our love is right and our goal of being together will come true. God made lovemaking a joy. I want to give you every sensual delight. Come and join me as we ascend the peak of pleasure that He created.

All my Love

Mary

CHAPTER THIRTY-ONE

September 18, 1860

Dear Mary

I have been gone for several weeks. I accompanied my father to Richmond. His business dealings were settled quickly. His purpose was to sell assets and property. In confidence my father told me that he took some losses on his investments. However, father says when war breaks out his losses would have been total.

It is a strange world down here. The Planters are trying to establish a new aristocracy built on the flesh and blood of slaves. There is an astonishing lack of personal industry. The existence of slavery seems to have blocked all human incentive. Why learn a trade when slaves do the work?

The South thinks they can create a world that rests on pretended manners and with an abhorrence of any actual work. The Planter wants to create and extend aristocracy. He wants to recline at leisure while the enslaved perform the actual work. The Planters want to bask in the profits that other humans have created.

False fools of the past. In the end your repose will be shattered. Your chattel both human and material will soon be gone. Strut upon the stage for just a little longer. Your Armageddon is nearly upon you. Your racism will destroy the world that you thought you owned. So very soon you will be swept from the halls of power. Your sons will be fodder for the ever-hungry cannon. You and your family will be the ashes of a cold dead fire.

Their churches are large and ostentatious. The nerve of these people to pretend they are living a Godly life. The men have affected manners. They bow, nod, and pretend to be cultured men. The women slip along with their affected pose of splendor and delicacy. The Planters like to present themselves as the finest creation of humanity.

Yet when one glances around this vain Planter you see reality very quickly. His carriage door is opened by a black slave. The driver of his conveyance is a black slave. The roads he rides upon were created by black slaves. His fields, his farms, his crops, are nurtured by Negro slaves. Even their children suckled at the breast of a "wet nurse" slave. Their natural mothers are too vain to allow their babies to suckle on their white breasts.

The entire cotton industry was created, maintained, and delivered by black slaves. Every branch of industry, agriculture, and their entire commerce is supported by the life force of enslaved Negros. There is no need to go on. Everything in the South is supported by the work bent on the backs of slaves. All this is true to any person who thinks.

Yet, one must be cautious when one asks questions. The subject of slavery is nearly unspoken. It seems to be a reaction to deep seated fear and shame. The citizens of a slave state have a shame so deep that they use their anger to cover the crime.

Why defend so violently unless they feel deep seated shame? "Me thinks they protest too much". The truth will always defend itself. There is never shame in the truth.

The white citizenry lives in total terror that a slave rebellion will arise. This fear is rational. There are more blacks in South Carolina than whites. They feel the shadow of black vengeance creeping up to their doorstep. Behind every black obeisance there is hate for the master.

Behind every house servant who adjusts the mistress's dress hates her pretensions. Every servant in the "big house" harbors a Negro who has a hate that no amount of faked culture will smother.

Remember this you slaveholders no Negro is going to defend you. They remember Nat Turner very well. They see clearly that their mansions and all their wealth is flammable. They fear the day of retribution. I urge the slaves to rise and strangle the slave owners with their own whips.

I still believe that deep in the hearts of man they realize that slavery is wrong. It seems that Southern society is as much in slavery to the slave system as the slave is to physical bondage. There are many evils that man has done but nothing can match the horror of owning another human being.

As father and I drove through the countryside I saw dozens of slaves working in the cotton fields with mounted overseers with guns. They labor with their backs bent from pre-dawn until dark. This includes everyone from a tottering child to the ancients who are permanently deformed. The fields are baked in scorching heat without a speck of shade. The Negros are prohibited from education because the owners fear that an educated Negro is a dangerous person. I am certain that is true.

Listen up Mr. Planter, the black man will soon aim at your heart. Do you believe you deserve to be spared? Think about these things when you try to slumber after your drunken parties. The torch will soon be at the mansion door. Your cotton in your warehouses will soon feed the dance of flames. Love, Rachel

CHAPTER THIRTY-TWO

Oct 3, 1860

Dear Mary

Thank God I can write to you in the evenings. This place is hot and oppressive. Let me mention the suffering field hands. Despite the slave owner the slaves often sing. It appears that the lyrics of the music are a type of code and that the slaves have a form of secret communication using it. This singing on the surface is often religious. The Planters want the slaves to accept their slavery.

Planters want slaves to believe that their slavery is required by God. Bondage is preached as a natural thing in daily conversations as well as from the pulpit in their churches. This is why I hate Christianity. Christianity endorses slavery. St. Paul endorsed slavery. The slaves are enjoined to be good to their masters.

Strangely Christ Himself supported slavery. Never once does Christianity openly renounce slavery. It had many chances to do so in the New Testament but in truth Christianity endorses slavery. Such contradictions are endemic in Christianity and in Southern society. The women are chastised if they are not submissive to their husbands like little puppies in a box.

There is no law protecting the wife from this abuse. There is no law protecting the woman from de facto rape. After all she must be submissive! It is no secret that the Planters can have any Negro women whenever lust controls their bodies. This practice is extremely common. The arrogant wives know of this behavior but often do not object. Many white wives encourage this behavior so that they do not have to satisfy their husband's lust.

Many men prefer younger women, and the continual supply of young black girl/women is endless. The children born from these couplings are called mulattos. Yet even the child of this inhuman coupling is a slave. Why might one ask? Did not the male Planter sire a child with his own seed?

The reason is based on the premise that any human who has a drop of Negro blood will be doomed to slave toil until the day that poor human dies. This is the universal view of the Planter.

Papa took me to several churches and never have I seen such hypocrisy. The pastor grovels at the feet of the Planters. Such bowing and scraping I never thought I would see on this continent. Without fail every sermon includes the rightness of the slave serving a master. Without fail such behavior will be rewarded in heaven. The lesson is simple: toil until you die and then you go to heaven. Another way to look at it is work for the profit of the master and die as cheaply as possible."

It must be remembered that a slave can be sold at any time or condition. If the slave ages beyond his usefulness the owner can relieve himself of this burden by simply selling the slave. What if the used-up slave has a wife or even children? No problem, the slave has no rights.

He can be sold like an old horse. And like the old horse he will be able to do less profitable work until he has toiled down to the last speck of usefulness. Like all horse traders the name of the game is to never be left with a useless slave. I assume the used up old toiler is just thrown on a bone pile.

The Planters ape their pretentions as so-called gentleman in their tailored clothes and the ladies with their French finery. The landed gentry takes pride in their mincing manners and delicate movements. All this wealth wrung from enslaved Negros who live in structures that people in the North would not give to hogs.

They often speak of "honor." It too is a lie. There is no "honor" in a man that would own slaves. The lowest depravity is to be a slave owner. This is all a sham. There is no "Southern Honor" in a culture that enslaves every Negro man, woman and child. No slave is safe. No matter how hard he may work his children do not belong to him. They are often ripped from their mothers and placed on an auction block to be sold.

Father took me to a slave auction. These are usually held in a poor part of town. The gentry does not want to see humans being bought and sold. They hire agents to do their disgusting business. The local citizens are so used to their evil that they are not even aware of their cruelties.

What under heaven could cause this indifference? How can one human watch another human being whipped and give not a fig? How can a human watch a child sold from her mother's arms and think nothing of it?

I watched as men, women, and children were poked and forced to jump, open their mouths to check teeth to see if they were sound. I saw with my own eyes' children being taken from their mother and sold separately. How can a human watch a child taken from her mother's arms and sold like a hog and think nothing of it?

Typically, the child will never see their mother again. Certain types of cultivation literally kill the slaves, and the owner knows he is working his slave to death. This is particularly true of the sugar cane fields in the deepest South. The slave owner does not care if the slave produces his profit and dies with little cost.

Father then took me to a type of open plaza. Here slaves were often whipped in full public view. This was supposed to be a warning to other slaves as to what could happen to them. With my own eyes I saw slave whipping pillars. Slaves were usually bound to a ring that is inserted into a thick post.

I saw the heavy whips that cut human flesh hanging on a nearby wall. The whipping post clearly showed the repeated trails of blood that had run down the post to the blood-stained ground.

Then I saw several coffin shaped boxes close to the whipping posts. I quietly asked father what they were for. He answered in a low voice, "Come with me and I will show you." Then I saw the inflictor of this evil. Sitting under a shade tree he was spitting his tobacco. He was a huge brute with a malformed scarred face. Father said to him that this was his daughter's first time in Virginia, and he wanted to show his daughter how criminals were justly punished in the South.

My father spoke with a command presence and was clearly a gentleman by all the signs of wealth. The brute just laughed and said, "Goess rite ahead Siree. Busins is sloo taday. Weise hard on themm niggers. Wee ussaly leves them in the box for two or three days. A few days in the box fixes dem niggers rigt up." My father thanked the overseer, and we walked away. I was literally speechless.

Can you imagine the horror of being nailed in a coffin struggling to breathe for three days? They cannot move. There is no water given. The temperature is broiling. The sufferer is lying in the Southern sun possibly screaming to be released. What demented people could do this to another human being?

After we went to a better part of Richmond we found a shady place and my father ordered tea for us and explained more. He spoke about the sexual assaults upon female slaves. These I was aware of but being in a city where this was a common practice is chilling.

If a male slave tried to run away it was common to castrate the slave as a deterrent to other slaves. Some masters castrate all male slaves in the belief that it makes slaves "docile? Father said this only happens if the owner had a Negro "stud" to keep his young negro women pregnant. My Almighty God how long will You step aside against this Evil? I reaffirmed my vow that I would fight slavery to my dying breath.

Then father took me into his confidence. He explained that he had been slowly moving all the gold and silver out of his banks in the South for the past three years. He told me that his banks were only managing existing loans and had lent little money in the past year. He said his banks for all practical purposes were only empty shells.

He was sure the war was coming and had wisely transferred all his real wealth to his Northern banks. He explained he did it so gradually that no-one really noted. I asked him how sure he was of secession happening? He said he has many agents throughout the South, and all agreed that war would be upon us in months.

Mary, I just learned there is a proposed law for Kansas that makes any statement against slavery a felony which is punished by five years in prison? Such a system of government must be devised by demons. The fatal blow will someday come upon the Planters and the entire slave holding empire.

Whether this blow comes from the hand of God or from an enraged North I do not know. But I do believe it is the duty of our nation to eliminate slavery here and now.

Mary my love, let us hope that we live to see the day when slavery is erased from our lands. When Father and I crossed the Virginia border coming home I felt the filth of slavery drop off my body. I literally felt unclean. I asked father to stop right on the Virginia border and I stepped from our carriage and spit on Virginia soil. Father said he was proud of my rage. When father stopped for lodging I sought bathing right away. I did not want the dust of Virginia on my skin.

After I bathed and retired to my bed I wanted you in my arms. I missed you so badly. I wanted your kisses and caresses on every part of my body. I wanted life affirming passion to counter the soul killing filth of slavery. I wanted you so badly. I dreamed you were in my arms. You fill my heart with love. I want you so badly.

Love,

Rachel

CHAPTER THIRTY-THREE

October 7, 1860

Dear Rachel

Thank God you are home. Thank God that we were able to get together so that we had privacy. My body hungers for you. I crave you in every manner. My heart is not complete without you. I fear every day because I am so happy. No human deserves to be this happy. You are the one who has given me such happiness. I was so worried while you were gone.

Your absence showed me more clearly than ever how much I love you and how important you are in my life. Your letter got here before you did. That does not happen often. War is coming and I am truly afraid.

I am a timid soul. I don't know why I am so meek. I just want to live in peace, and I want freedom for the slave. I want the Union because it is the only government that can break this Southern empire. I don't know how I would have reacted to the sights of cruel slavery. At the very least I would have sobbed until I had no tears left.

From the Southern Planter to the least white person in the South they are all guilty. They are all guilty of the most heinous crime that man can lower himself to. For one man to own another man is the ultimate offense against God. To take a precious life and to tear that free life away from a human is beyond any crime I can think of. It is all so wrong. It is all evil.

I know war is coming. The rich and the poor all agree war is coming. On one hand I say, "let it come." On the other hand, I know the cost in blood and treasure will be far beyond anyone's imagination. Tens of thousands of young men will lose their lives in the flower of their manhood.

At the base of this abomination is slavery. Slavery is based on the horrible premise that one human is better than another because of the color of their skin. Everyone that I know can feel the tension. The country is beyond debate. So many efforts have been made to preserve the Union, but slavery cannot be ignored.

No amount of goodwill can bridge the gap between freedom and slavery. Right now, the Northern cry is "Union." I agree totally because only the Union has the power to eliminate this curse from the land. Later in the conflict the North will gradually realize that slavery is the cancer in our social body. In our political chambers men are coming to physical blows. Senator Summers was beaten with a cane until he suffered permanent injury. This was by the hand of South Carolina Congressman Preston Brooks. I believe Preston Brooks should be hanged.

When a republic has sunk so low as to come to blows in our Congress body then words are done, and full-scale fighting will begin soon. Some of our leaders carry guns because they fear for their lives. Many think the war will be short. I sense the war will last a very long time. May justice against the slave system come soon.

I don't have your force of character. Nor do I have your courage. I worry that I am a mouse and not worthy enough to be your lover and life partner. My heart bleeds and bleeds for those being held in bondage. When this war comes I hope I can be of some use. In my dreams I can see the coming carnage. I dream of thousands of broken bodies across vast landscapes.

~ ~ ~

The blood is everywhere. Men torn with frightful wounds asking for help of any manner. They beg for water, and I have none. The battle seems to roll over the dead and dying. I feel I am staggering, lost in the smoke and confusion. I can hear the guns, but I don't know where I am. I cry for the men to stop killing but they do not hear me or perhaps they just ignore me. The killing goes on and on.

Suddenly I feel I am looking upon the battle scene from high above the earth. I see lines of blue and grey soldiers in long undulating formations. The line convulses like a wounded snake. The lines advance and retreat without any logical sense of a pattern. The advancing side surges on but in moments they are retreating.

It depends on fortune to determine who is winning or losing. The musket fire forms lines of smoke, and it takes time before the smoke lifts and drifts. Soldiers are constantly falling.

Unseen cannons are ripping huge gaps in the lines. The noise renders one deaf. Men are screaming in pain, men cursing during the battle, men calling for their loved ones. In certain places the lines become a twisting vortex of hand-to-hand fighting.

I awoke with a start and looked around me. All I see is my family sleeping in any empty space. Some sleeping on my parent's bed, others in makeshift beds, some on the floor, and some are spilling out to the porch. Yet I can't get my breath back quickly. The dream seemed so real that I looked at my hands and clothes to see if I am bloody. I am certain my dreams will be reality in a short time.

At times it seems that hatred rules the world. But I know that is not true. Love is the greatest force on earth. Only love can bind humans together across vast distances and only love can survive long periods of absence. Love gives hope and hatred can only bring misery and death.

Without you my heart is torn in two. The hours that we share passion are wonderful and something that I will never forget. Yes, passion is the temple, but love is the foundation. When you were gone there was not a single hour when I didn't miss you. To say that I crave you is not saying enough. The plain truth is that I cannot live without you.

Love,

Mary

CHAPTER THIRTY-FOUR

October 17, 1860

Dear Mary

I was so glad to get back from Richmond. I thought of you constantly. Mary my love, you are the center of my world. I thank God every day for the gift of your love. I am not truly worthy of your attention.

But I do love you so much and I am so grateful for your love. I swear I will rescue you from your horrible situation. I will come up with a way to get you out of that terrible household.

I am amazed at your poise and your calmness while you are struggling with domestic abuse and sheer madness all around you. I love you so much. I will not abandon you. Soon I will come up with the means to help you escape the slavery of our gender. No woman should be forced to live under the threat of rape or physical abuse. If your father lays a hand on you I will kill him. You must be honest with me. If he attempts to force himself upon you then I swear to the heavens to blow him to hell.

The sights I saw while I was in Richmond were evil, pure and simple. Slavery must be destroyed and each of us who are free has a duty to do our part in the coming conflict. I know that your nightmares are coming true. The blood that must be spilled on this land to cleanse the nation of the stain of slavery will be enormous.

Tens of thousands on both sides will die on the battlefield; Tens of thousands more will die of disease. The grim reaper will stalk our land with a smile and his harvest will be beyond anything the world has ever seen. With each sweep he will take a thousand men.

Our weapons are much more destructive than those of an earlier era. This rebellion will be far more destructive than many of our citizens think. This will not be a short war. This war will not bring glory. There will not be ladies swooning as their men folk die with great pathos with terms of endearment on their lips. No, this horror will be that of a carnage house. Men will be torn to pieces. There will be many corpses that no-one can identify.

My father has told me that the Napoleonic way of war is outmoded even though many of our generals do not know that reality. The insanity of people lining up fifty yards apart and blazing away is chilling to my marrow. This is madness.

The modern musket is deadly accurate to 300 yards and can easily kill at 1000 yards. When one aims at a man at 50 yards with the deadly accurate rifled musket he is going to hit. It is as simple as that. A better system to slaughter masses of men could not be devised.

Napoleon muskets were smoothbores and were seldom accurate beyond 30 yards. Napoleon used massed fire to overcome the accuracy problem. If our soldiers use accurate rifles at 50 yards then survival is highly unlikely. The invention of the Minnie ball has made the rifle far more deadly.

Instead of old-fashioned smoothbore cannons (horribly inaccurate) there are rifled cannons accurate to hundreds of yards. Neither the soldier nor the civilian can imagine the butchery.

The threat of secession is growing by the hour. Father has told me that the coming election will hold the future of the United States in its hand. If Lincoln is elected several southern states have sworn to deflect from our sacred union. Lincoln said that no nation can stand half slave and half free. One or the other must prevail.

Any state that attempts to destroy our Union is guilty of treason. There is no higher crime that a citizen can inflect on a nation than treason. Let us appeal to God that the blight of slavery will be purged from our lands. If one must die trying to destroy slavery then so be it.

There can be no higher cause. To lay one's life down so that others can be free is a privilege that we must aspire to. If war breaks out I will do my part to break the back of the slave holding monster that lives to the south of us.

Love Rachel

CHAPTER THIRTY-FIVE

November 6, 1860

Dear Rachel

Abraham Lincoln has been elected. However, he has not been sworn in yet. That event will happen in March. Nevertheless, the flaming match descended upon the fuse. The flame is creeping toward that powder keg that everyone knew was there. Lincoln has sworn to hold the Union together. He has not threatened the slave states with destruction. He has tried to assuage the fears of the South, but they are not listening.

The South wants war. It is the South that wants to seize this election to provide them with an excuse for treason. The South wants a quick war. She knows she cannot win a long war. The industrial power of the North will crush the South by the sheer numbers of men and weapons that it can bring to the field. No-one knows what the next step will be. One can only wait.

Love

Mary

CHAPTER THIRTY-SIX

December 20, 1860

Dear Mary

South Carolina has seceded from the Union. Now the great contest begins. Woe to South Carolina. In the end she will suffer great desolation. The proud harlot will be thrown down from her high place and stripped of her elegant robes. South Carolina will be exposed to the civilized nations as the soiled slut she is.

Our current pro-slave President Buchanan declared the ordinance illegal but like the coward he is did not do anything to prevent the secession nor did he use any forceful action after South Carolina committed this act of treason. Go to your grave in shame Mr. Buchanan. History called your name, and you were lacking.

My father is a powerful man in political circles. South Carolina is guilty on all counts. She holds the bloody lash and inserts her infamous beliefs that she has the God given right to wield it upon the backs of those who are in bondage. South Carolina Congress man John McQueen stated the case clearly. "The U.S. president elect supports equality and civil rights for African Americans as well as the abolition of slavery and thus South Carolina is compelled to secede." Nothing clearer needs to be said.

The words "all men are created equal" which form the foundation of the US government is somehow null and void to these traitors. It is strangely missing from the thoughts of these racists. As my father pointed out there are more slaves in South Carolina than there are whites. Someday the whites of that state will face armed blacks who will exact revenge for every black child who was ripped from its mother's arms and sold on the auction block. Let the whites tremble in their rich dwellings.

Black Union soldiers will eventually walk into the state of South Carolina.

What will the slave owners say on that coming day? Where will be their boast of white supremacy? As for me, I have no mercy. Raise the black flag and kill them all.

Father pointed out that Church leaders justify slavery because it is justified under the Christian religion. If so, then the Christian religion must go. The Christian religion is not God given. The Christian religion is a harlot used by the South for its sinful pleasures. I wonder how well these fine Christian men would like to feel the lash upon their backs.

How many Christian women would like to have their children ripped from their arms and sold like a pig on the auction block? Your day is coming. Laugh now you scions of wealth. Laugh now while your sons live healthy and strong. Soon your prideful sons will be torn to pieces by the mouths of vengeful cannons.

How will the South feel when so-called ladies have their fine dresses torn from their naked bodies? Soon the day will come when your insolent husbands lie on the battlefield like so many dead chickens. I pray I will live to see these days.

I am proud to be listed with those who reject Christianity. Christ never owned a slave. He never told anyone to own a slave. This teacher never carried a whip. He never asked for wealth and fine mansions. He took no pride in his social position.

However, Jesus did not speak out against slavery. Thus, Jesus is as guilty as the rest of the slaveholders. He did nothing to do denounce the physical bondage of men, women and children. This is a mark of shame that cannot be washed away.

Christianity is false to the core. Those who now own slaves will see their wealth stripped away.

They will live to see their wives and daughters ashamed. They will see their sons torn to bloody pieces upon a hundred fields of battle. I pray I will live to see the South in ruins. To see the South stripped of its wealth and pride. The day will come when armed Black Union soldiers will walk your lands. What shall you say then you false prophets? There are many acts that men do in shame, but none exceeds clasping chains on men that were born free in God's eye.

Is this not nice of the fine Christians of South Carolina to wrap themselves with the pages of the Bible? The Planters have hired men to stand behind pulpits to justify this scandalous crime. Somehow these fine men of God never suggest the truth: The Bible is a fiction from the first day of its fraudulent creation. Would God enslave those of his creation who he created free as the wind?

Mary my love, the weapons of war will soon be used over this land. Let us cling together and pray the Union can prevail.

Sincerely

Rachel

CHAPTER THIRTY-SEVEN

January 17, 1861

Dear Rachel

Our country is holding its breath. Our feeble pro-slavery President Mr. Buchanan by his lack of action is encouraging other southern states to secede. Had strong immediate Union action been coming forth the rest of the south might have thought twice about treason. As history has shown to us many times when the strong refuse to act then the weak will seize power. All eyes are on Virginia.

I cannot foresee the future, and I do not have the experience of our elected officials, but I do see dark and bloody days ahead. I am afraid that all of us will be swept up in this maelstrom. The strong and the weak, the rich and the poor will be thrown together and crushed into this vortex of violence, hate and emotion.

Can no one see that the threat of slavery would doom the new world? Europe with its ancient displays of greed and conquest would like to face a ruined United States. Then by piece meal they could regain the territories that were lost during the American Revolution.

My crude and savage Papa claims that a war would be good for farmers. He is probably right on that point. However, he must remember that one must win a war to keep those bloody profits. No one knows the fate of war. The great statesmen and the lowly citizen are equal in their ignorance. The fortunes of war are unknown when we look through a prism of blood.

Rachel, I only wish for us to be together in a relationship of love and peace. I want you so badly. With the fervor of the young I want you physically as well as emotionally. Doesn't the slave owner see that they stand to lose everything that they currently own?

The great estates of the planters will face the flames or auction blocks in post-war ruin. Can't they see the South will be despoiled? Can't they see their land and estates being bought by the wealthy in the North?

These wealthy northerners will cover the post-war South like starved locusts. Surely the Planters know that eventually slavery will be prohibited just as it is prohibited in nearly every civilized country. The South hopes that England or France will grant them the status of an independent nation. This is unlikely to happen since neither England nor France have or condones slavery.

Currently both the North and the South are amassing huge numbers of men and weapons even though Civil War has yet to be declared. This current lull will not last. Soon all this pent-up energy will be released and then the specter of death will stride unhindered across our fair land. I mourn the coming deaths. The flower of our youth will be left dead upon battlefields.

The old politicians will not be the ones dying. The great democracy of death will litter a hundred battle fields.

Rachel, I know your father has his hand on the national pulse. Please keep me abreast of the political developments. I would rather see the future dimly than fear the opaque future totally.

Love,

Mary

CHAPTER THIRTY-EIGHT

February 1, 1861

Dear Mary

Mississippi, Florida, Alabama, Georgia, Louisiana and Texas have seceded. These states now have joined South Carolina on the road of treason. I fear other states will join this confederacy of infamy. Again, President Buchanan has done nothing but bluster. The nation needs a stronger President.

Hopefully, President elect Lincoln will be the man to save this country. Without a strong leader the Union will fall. This would be fatal for the nation and the new world. President elect Lincoln appears to be an honest man. He is certainly self-educated.

Father says that Lincoln is a thoughtful man, and his enemies would do well not to underestimate him. Father noted that Lincoln did not favor slavery, but he would tolerate it to save the Union with one limitation: He does not favor the expansion of slavery, and he believes privately that slavery will fall of its own weight if limited to the South alone.

It must be accepted that Lincoln does not have the power to abolish slavery by himself. Lincoln knows slavery is a great evil, but he is willing to ignore slavery to save the Union while at the same time limiting its expansion.

Of course, I do not agree with Lincoln on most of his points. Slavery by itself must be cut out of the public body in one surgical cut. A great tumor is not removed one piece at a time. If removed too slowly it will spread far beyond the original infestation and kill the very body one is trying to save. How dare we tell the man that is being brutally lashed that he should wait a little longer! By what leap of logic can such a thought be followed?

Slavery is wrong and it should be removed now. My father knows that only force will kill slavery. The world can no longer endure it. However, I am not patient. This filth must be cleansed once and for all. If we wait for "reasonable men" to abolish slavery this is an agreement to wait forever.

There is never a right time to stop an evil that is total. We do not prohibit murder one piece at a time. The state does not gradually make murder a crime. No, murder is murder, and it is a one-piece crime. One crime and one solution determined by one verdict. The history of slavery shows how depraved a country is to support the enslavement of another human being.

How long will a free nation condone this horror? How many "compromises" has this country endured to keep the peace? One does not compromise with the devil. Think of the mockery of the 1820 Missouri Compromise. Missouri was allowed to be slave, and Maine was allowed no slavery. How silly. Maine for all purposes has no slaves and Missouri is a cesspool of slavery.

Again the 1850 Compromise where California was to be free with all the remainder of the Mexican lands of cession were to be unregulated. This act just kicks the evil cancer down the road where it must be eliminated sooner than later.

Then there was the folly of the Dred Scott Supreme Court decision that found a black man was merely property not a living breathing human being. If there is a heavenly bar of justice than I hope Chief Justice Taney stands before it and goes straight to hell.

Think of Bloody Kansas in 1859 where the slave question was to be settled by ballot. The slave states raced to inflate polling numbers to gain a political advantage.

Lawrence Kansas was ravished by over 1000 southern bandits and murderers. Over one hundred innocent men and boys were gunned down by these murderers who wrap themselves with a Confederate flag. Or the Fugitive Slave act where a citizen was bound to return a runaway slave. What madness! An honest human forced to take part in a heinous crime!

Mary my love, we live in momentous times. Where this violent chaos takes each of us I don't know. I know only that I love you. I worry daily about the threat of your violent father. I pity your battered mother. I want you to be with me so badly. Somehow this impasse with your father will be resolved. I feel that change is coming. I don't know how or when, but I know you will be free soon.

Love,

Rachel

CHAPTER THIRTY-NINE

February 21, 1861

Dear Rachel

There is much I don't understand about these days. The water of reality is often turgid. The hovel that I live in is not blessed with higher conversation. Without you and the books you lend to me I would be as ignorant as any uneducated laborer.

Thankfully, my teacher at the free school allows me to read the newspapers that she gleans from leading citizens. I am often spared the simple lessons that I am far beyond. It is during these so-called "study periods" that I can read the news at leisure.

I often stay after classes and help my teacher grade papers or tutor the truly stupid. I find teaching to be interesting with those rare students who want to better themselves. Reducing the workload of my teacher keeps me in good graces. She is a wonderful person. Her name is Ruth. Ruth hates slavery with a passion but she is not allowed to state such a position if she is to keep her job.

The school has a very limited library. Like you, my teacher encourages me to advance. She lent me her private copy of Harriet Beecher Stowe's book "Uncle Tom's Cabin." The book is deemed too controversial to be available to the class. My teacher has sworn me to secrecy about this book. She says she would lose her job if the school board found out.

I have heard it stated that only the Bible has been more popular in recent times. I have no way of establishing that claim, but I can say that her book does inflame the usually passive citizenry. The book clearly shows how horrible the life of a slave truly is. It gives the face of slavery a name and the average citizen is forced to confront this horror.

That woman Stowe has struck the South a blow that it cannot counter. Let it be noted that the blow was conceived and published by a woman not a man. So much for women not having a mind! Slavery through the eyes of "Uncle Tom" is revealed in all its ugly repulsion.

The book has shown me that the power of the pen is mighty. Nevertheless, the pen alone will never prevail. It takes physical force to end an evil that is hugely profitable to the South.

The Confederate States of American has been formally named by the states that have committed treason. Jefferson Davis has been appointed President of that iniquitous land. History is not a perfect record of the past, but it is a record.

History will record the strange man known as John Brown. John Brown was not an honorable man, but he was at least a man who understood that the time for talking about slavery had to end.

His attack on Harpers Ferry was an attempt to arm the Negro and an attempt to physically attack the Planters and the evil government that the Planters created. He died a brave man on the scaffold, and I believe his crimes will be forgiven in the heavenly court. I hope and pray that Jefferson Davis meets his well-deserved fate upon a similar scaffold.

All the leaders of this "Confederacy" should face the gallows. Unfortunately, before the trap door falls tens of thousands of innocent young men will bleed out on the raw ground of the battlefields. I pray I live to spit upon the graves of the slaveholders.

Rachel, I mourn the simple days when we met with passion in our secluded places. To think that our love is forbidden while slave holders can saunter the land is absurd. All you and I want is the peace to live our lives. We do not seek riches or power. All we want is the right to love each other.

What reasonable person can find that wrong? Surely a woman can love a woman. Why not? Love is a private act that does not threaten the public body politically. Slavery is justified but a woman's love for a woman is not. What madness! I love you and I am willing to stand before the Judge of the universe and state my love. How these gathering clouds of Civil War frighten me.

Love,

Mary

CHAPTER FORTY

March 22,1861

Dear Mary

Abraham Lincoln has been inaugurated as the sixteenth president of the United States. I believe he will respond to the rebellion strongly. My father has told me that Lincoln is a clever man. He believes that Lincoln will force the South to fire the first shot. Thus, the South must take the onus for the beginning of the Civil War.

Lincoln seems to act with careful deliberation, but he does act. It seems the wheels of destiny turn slowly but the wheel grinds exceedingly fine. This huge drama unfolds across a map that covers the United States. The Union will suffer many losses, but I believe that it will and must prevail.

The coming war is not the fantasy time of chivalrous knights joisting to impress handkerchief waving noble women. There will be no glory in this war. War has advanced to become a tremendous machine of slaughter. Men will be fed into this machine, and they will come out merely meat scraps. As the months and years go by the "production" of this machine will increase. Faster and faster this killing machine will whirl.

This machine nearly escapes the control of mankind. As long as one slaveholder is living the killing will go on. Rachel, I feel I can see the future to a degree. I have no method to avoid this war. The fate of slavery must be settled on the battlefield. That men and women should die because of such a cruel thing as slavery seems incredible.

Again, this will not be a short and glorious war. It will demand the death of legions of men and the destruction of capital on a scale that the world has never seen to this day. While I applaud the flag wavers it will take much more than waving a flag to end this rebellion. The flower of our youth will be spent on this holy mission.

The blood of those youths will eventually drown the flames of rebellion. This war will not be easy. It will test the North in ways that can scarcely be imagined. There will be many people who will be war exhausted and want to give in to the forces of slavery, but I believe men and women of stout hearts will continue to wield the sword until the last slave is free.

I share your dreams of our life together. I want only to love you and to live in peace. I am willing to perish fighting slavery. We have no choice in this matter. One either fights or lives with the shame of gaining peace at the loss of our souls. Be strong my love. We must be strong.

Love,

Rachel

CHAPTER FORTY-ONE

April 12, 1861

Dear Rachel

The South fired on Fort Sumter and the fort fell. That brave fort endured 3000 rounds before it surrendered. The enemy flag now flies over that battered hallowed ground. Civil war is now formally upon us. Our president Lincoln has called for 75,000 militia to quell this rebellion.

Nearly immediately after this call to arms our President Lincoln has called for 43,000 volunteers for a three-year enlistment in the regular army. I don't know if this will be enough.

I am afraid no-one knows. All of us in North and South have entered a dark valley. We are all blind and cannot guess the width or the length of that valley. I am so afraid. I have never been strong like you. I know slavery is wrong, but I don't know how to throw my mite upon the scales.

The South is jeering over their victory. Yes, they jeer now but their days of tears are coming. Their youth will soon be thrown into the flames of war that they themselves have kindled. They will sadly learn that the flames of war are ever hungry. More and more of their blood and treasure will be demanded. It is the nature of war to be longer than one thinks, to be more costly than one hopes, and to harden the hearts of normal men. With those hardened hearts the cruelties of war will inspire atrocities. No-one will be proud of the results.

There will be no escape now. The die has been cast and the South has crossed the Rubicon. The sword will be thrust deeply and often blindly. Enraged leaders will throw their troops into battles hoping for the best and often those hopes will not be achieved.

Tens of thousands of troops will die for nothing more than a stupid decision by a stupid General. War has always been thus.

Rachel, I am so afraid. What will happen to us?

Love, Mary

CHAPTER FORTY-TWO

May 25, 1861

Dear Mary

These are uncertain times. Both the North and the South are gathering forces. Father has heard that Union forces have crossed the Potomac River and they have occupied Arlington Heights which formerly belonged to the traitor Robert E. Lee.

So far it is unknown as to whether there was any fighting or loss of men. It takes time to organize an army. Neither the Union nor the South is ready. I think we will continue to see both sides mostly maneuvering and probing each other's forces.

Father feels it will be at least another month before major combat. Typically, the battles must be fought in the summer because the roads are practically impassable during the rainy seasons. There is great pressure on Lincoln to engage the traitors quickly, but his generals are inexperienced in waging a modern war and they argue for delay.

It seems odd that military men who have trained all their careers to fight have so little confidence when the time for real fighting is upon them.

Soon the battles will be so widespread that it will be impossible to name every small skirmish. Both sides are proclaiming that the war will be short. I doubt that very much. It is worth mentioning that President Lincoln has never spoken of a short war. It will probably take time for Lincoln to find the correct General to defeat the South.

The South claims that one Southerner can whip five Union troops. That remains to be seen. The South must win a short war. If the war should be longer than the chances of a Southern victory diminish rapidly. The South is aware of this reality, and they will make every effort to fight a decisive battle to end the war.

Thankfully, you and I have had two recent occasions to be together privately. These meetings were passionate and wonderful. The war has had the favorable effect of giving the public something to focus on. That plays into our hands. If we continue to be careful the reality of our love will not be noticed. I pray this will continue to be true. I am convinced that God has provided these passions so that love can survive difficult times.

God has given his creation many gifts but the greatest of all gifts is love. This war prevents love from flourishing. Yet I love you so much. I think of you constantly. When I am within your arms the rest of the world is blocked out. Our reality of love completely overcomes the horrors of this war. Bear with me Mary.

I want you to be safe and I want a future for us. This war against the Union places a firm roadblock to our future happiness. I know difficult decisions must be made and I pray God can give us the strength to do our duty.

With Love Always,

Rachel

CHAPTER FORTY-THREE

June 22,1861

Dear Rachel

I heard through rumor that a battle had been fought at Big Bethel. Although the information is thin it appears that the Confederates won a narrow victory. Apparently around 5000 troops were engaged in the battle. The number of dead was low considering the number of troops. The Union lost around 20 troops, and the South lost less than 10.

The northwestern part of Virginia broke away from the rest of the rebel state of Virginia. Beyond these things I really know nothing.

Love,

Mary

CHAPTER FORTY-FOUR

June 24,1861

Dear Mary

My father found out that a small battle was fought at Philippi in the western part of Virginia. Apparently the battle of Philippi was a victory for the North. The result of this battle has increased pressure to launch a major drive to Richmond. Father says this would be a big mistake because the Union Army is just not ready.

I must ask you directly has your father abused you since my last letter. This is the one crime that would be his last. If he raises a hand against you I will certainly kill him. My father is engrossed in the news about war, but my mother has descended into depression.

She mopes around and has no interest in anything. She has ceased to talk about my grandiose future wedding. She had spoken about matching me with some grandee. Now she only sinks into a world of silence. My father has tried to raise her spirits but so far he has met with no success.

My mother can only thrive in a peaceful place and the current world is anything but peaceful. My father on the other hand is a rock during the storm. He seeks the best possible information and reports on it with an unbiased mind set. As a prominent figure he is in the highest circles of the state.

Of course, emotions are running high, and the president is receiving pressure from many sides. It appears there are many armchair generals that are enflamed with their viewpoint. I fear my father is right and that any major campaign with this untrained army will come to failure.

Please remember me when you are alone at night. I would give you anything to share your bed. The pleasures we have are intoxicating. I want us to share our lives together. It is only right that our love for each other is to be cultivated. In a world that is swirling in madness we must keep our eye on ourselves and the future.

Love should be our touchstone. If each person focuses on love then one does not get lost in this disintegrating world. Soon I will take you out of your world of violence and hate. I live for that day.

Love,

Rachel

CHAPTER FORTY-FIVE

July 25, 1861

Dear Rachel

News has reached me about the first major battle of the Civil War. It was called the Battle of Bull Run. I despair to say that for the Union it was a total defeat. Apparently Union General McDowell was defeating the Rebels to his front until General Johnston struck the flank. This folded the green Union Army upon itself which was then driven in terror back to Washington D.C.

A new Rebel officer has made a name for himself. I fear we will hear more of this "Stonewall Jackson." The sack of our Washington D.C. capital was a near thing. Thank God the Rebels are as new to this war business as we are. I am now told that a series of fortifications is being built to defend our capital. I assume this is a good thing, but I fear we will hover around the capital and fail to take the battle to the Rebels in the field.

Love,

Mary

CHAPTER FORTY-SIX

August 30, 1861

Dear Mary

The last few months have had few serious battles between the North and the South. Both sides realize this will not be a short war. A long war tips the scales toward the North. Yet we all know that a true debacle could give the war to the South. The theme now seems to be both sides building a larger and better trained army.

The North is also growing in sea strength to blockade the seaports of the South. Efforts are also being made to regain the inland river waterways. These waterways are important supply routes that the South depends on. The Mississippi River is the most important, but the Tennessee River and the Cumberland are also keys to Union victory. Over time I am sure many smaller rivers will play their part in this huge human drama.

I have reached a serious personal decision, and I must talk to you first and frankly. I am going to volunteer for the Union Army. I am slight and with care I can easily pass as a boy. I have successfully passed as a boy at many major shooting matches. I have all the necessary qualifications.

I am in excellent physical condition; I am an excellent rifle shot and I am a good horseman. I have my own high-quality long-range rifle. I have researched the situation carefully and the need for the military is so pressing the recruiting offices are not looking too close at any issue. I will not leave until I am certain that your needs are taken care of. That means in simple terms getting you out of your dangerous home situation.

For this I must talk to my father. He is a wealthy man, and my hopes are high if he can be convinced of our situation. I know this is a life-or-death situation, but I could not live with a clear conscience during our country's hour of need. I cannot live in a slave state or a destroyed Union.

The South wants to expand their evil system all over the United States. I have cut this letter short because we have both listened to all the arguments. Once again I will not leave until I am convinced you are safe. You are the most important person in my life. My family and country are distant seconds. Mary, I feel I must do this. I will await your response.

Love,

Rachel

CHAPTER FORTY-SEVEN

September 20, 1861

Dearest Rachel

I have long known this situation was coming. I have known of your rage against the South. If you decide to join the Union Army what can I say? I know how much we both hate the slave system. We know the slavery system and we have been strongly against it. I know the South wants to destroy the Union and only their defeat will save the Union.

I know all these things, but I also know how much I love you. If I lose you I will surely die. My selfish desire is to flee with you to any place where we would be beyond the horror of this war. But where could we go? Our conscience would always haunt us. All of this is in the hands of you, your father, and God Almighty. I can only wait for a decision to be made.

Love,

Mary

CHAPTER FORTY-EIGHT

October 19,1861

Dear Mary

These are grave times. I spoke to Father and in turn my father spoke to my mother. Then I spoke to them as a couple. It was a difficult situation. I spoke to Papa for over two hours.

He pointed out that as a girl I did not have to be concerned about the war at all. He was aware that there were other girls serving secretly as men. In some cases, they joined with their husbands. In other cases, the women served alone. The higher command of the Army was suspected of knowing these things but due to the needs of the Army they were not looking closely.

Papa did agree that having my proven marksman talents might get me off the direct firing line. It was possible I could obtain duty as a sharpshooter. He had heard that good sharpshooters are in high demand. Father also said that a draft was probably coming. He felt I stood a better chance of getting a sharpshooter slot as a volunteer.

He had heard from good sources that substitutes would be allowed for those that had the means to pay the price. He indicated that such evasion was not attractive to him on principle. I in turn said that such a substitute system would not appeal to me at all. It was simply an evasion of duty.

The discussion moved on to the subject of your situation. I repeated what I had said many times that I was in love with you and wanted to be with you for the rest of my life. I carefully explained the dangerous situation that you live in. I openly said that our relationship had been intimate for a long time. To that information Father only nodded. I asked if money was the issue. He said he was awash in money from the high prices of crops and especially the extremely large sums that he was getting from the oil that had been discovered on many of his properties around Titusville.

He is receiving a royalty for every barrel of oil that is extracted from his property and oil engineers have assured him that the reserves were vast. They were sure oil would be the energy source of the future. I again stressed that your safety and financial security was extremely important to me. I told Papa that my death would impact you financially and emotionally.

I had to be sure you would be safe from your father and somehow be secure financially. Papa leaned back and stared at the ceiling for long moments. He turned to me and said he might have a solution, but he would need to talk to mother before this discussion could go forward.

The next morning father and mother were in his office for over three hours. At times I could hear my mother crying. This situation was hard on me and very emotional. At last, I was called into the office. My mother had gained control over her emotions and only dabbed at her red eyes occasionally. My father came right to the point. He and mother were in reluctant agreement that I could serve.

He said he had political influence and would try to use it to place me in a sharpshooter slot where my talents could best serve the Union. I say I had no objection to influence, and I wanted to serve if possible as a sharpshooter. In any event I wanted to serve.

Then we moved on to the most important issue: your welfare. To my amazement, mother in this case did most of the talking. She had been greatly moved at your need to escape the current hell you are living in. I was surprised how much she knew about you personally as well as your intellectual potential. She informed me that she had been in close conference with your free schoolteacher for quite some time.

The teacher had assured her that you were gifted and with opportunity you would excel. Once again this showed me that mother was no fool nor was she as soft as many people believed. The facts are that mother knew a great deal about you and was very interested in helping you escape that horrible situation.

Mother said she did not understand our sexuality but at times like this with our nation on the line such issues were small and private. I was astonished at her practicality. Mother said she knew the family was doing extremely well financially. We had been wealthy for a long time.

Now we were far better off than mere wealth. She said this gave the family more means to help. The offer that mother and father were willing to make for you drove me to my knees in tears. Mother comforted me and said, "Stop my darling, you know soldiers can't cry."

They offered to get your father to sign a release that granted you all the rights of adulthood including the right to leave his residence, and he was to surrender all parental rights and authority forever. Father said he would offer a sum of money to gain your father's agreement. Secondly, my parents are willing to legally adopt you as their legal daughter with all the rights of a natural child. They said this was the best buttress they could offer.

I wept and wept for a long while. Father said this would take some time. He thought about a month or so should wrap it up. He told me that there would be plenty of time for me to take part in the coming battles. In his opinion the war was not going to be settled this summer. My father, my mother and I prayed for strength, and we prayed that I would do my duty and return home alive. I have never prayed more sincerely in my life.

Love,

Rachel

CHAPTER FORTY-NINE

November 11,1861

To Rachel

I am free!! Totally and completely free!! Your father sent his attorney to see pa and offered him 100.00 for the release. Papa signed it in a heartbeat and told me good riddance. I had only rags as clothes except for my Sunday dress and shoes. I am currently at the residence of a friend of your mother's. Here I met your mother, and we hugged and cried for a long time. All I could say was thank you repeatedly. All she could say was "poor child" over and over. She bucked me up with a smile and said it was time for some serious shopping.

The next thing I know is we are on the train to Pittsburgh. Your mother burned my Sunday dress and shoes. She had clothed me with Titusville best and that was the dress I wore to Pittsburgh. Under your mother's wing we went from one fabulous dress store to another. She viewed many dresses and picked out the best. Each dress was then tailored to make me look my best.

Your mother exclaimed a hundred times "What a beautiful girl! What a lovely young woman." I now own several dozen beautiful dresses, shoes and accessories. I don't know how to accept this dream. I will be arriving at your home in two days. I can't wait to see you and the rest of your family. Your family has saved me from death or disfigurement. I have gone from hell to heaven in one swoop.

Love,

Mary

Chapter Fifty

December 11, 1862

Dear Mary

You are now at your new home with your new family. We have decided to keep writing to each other, so we have a record of our love. I can see my two siblings love you and will wear you out with all their activities.

The fact that you wear jeans and ride horses was enough to gain their affection. You claim that you are not brave, but my brothers say you take your horse over the highest fences and think nothing of it.

I will teach you how to shoot with both revolvers and rifles. I am sure you will soon become proficient. We live in a dangerous world, and I want you to be able to protect yourself. Father has had many conversations with you and told me privately that he is well satisfied with your intellect. You have leaped into my mother's heart. You are much more feminine than I am in some ways yet masculine in some areas. To my mother this seems to mean adventurous and independent.

You have mentioned that you are astonished that our home has eight bedrooms. You commented that just one of our several living rooms would easily hold the old shack that you were raised in. Our separate bedrooms are upstairs. These bedrooms used to serve as a nursery. As a planned nursery the area was designed for family quiet. The baby would be in one room and the nurse in the other.

We have a connecting door between the rooms, so it is easy to have privacy and yet not offend sensitivity. Of course we are discreet. I have discovered that no-one discusses the issue, and it has become a non-topic. Since we did not flout our affection for each other the rest of the family has ignored our relationship. It is like the heterosexual relationship between father and mother. Of course, there is sex, but no-one gives it a second thought.

I am glad that both father and Mother have taken a strong interest in your education. We have several tutors, and mother insists on French as one of your subjects. To my surprise, Father insisted on mathematics and science. These subjects are augmented by history and writing. I know you will throw yourself into these disciplines with the fervor of a religious convert.

Mother is already astonished at your linguist skill. French is coming rapidly to you and father is quietly satisfied with your progress in mathematics and science. Both mother and father sought my audience and confided with me that you and your welfare is most satisfying to them. They are very happy with you, and you fit in with our family perfectly.

I was amazed at mother's friendship with you. The truth is my mother has fallen in love with you. You are a daughter in her heart in every way. She dotes on you. I am so happy and greatly relieved.

Father has preceded the adoption papers for you. So many men have gone to the war the backlog of legal cases is light. All formalities were settled in less than two weeks. In this instance the influence of father's power and money is impressive. The Judge and father often hunt and fish together. The Judge and his wife have dined here many times.

Last year father had been able to help the Judges son acquire a good farm as the son had no interest in the law. Normally I do not like the idea that money and position can influence the law but in this case I am overjoyed.

You recall we had a large family party to celebrate your entry into our family. I couldn't restrain myself and wept for a long time. Your horror is behind you. It was mother who welcomed you into your new home. I was finally able to stem the tears. The family and all our servants were encouraged to join the festivities.

Mother and Father waltzed again and again. They were so brilliant. They once again seemed like a couple in their teens. I pray I will remember this blessed day when I am a tottering ancient.

Now there was no more time for delays. My Mary is safe. It was time for me to go to war. I gathered my few things and carefully wrapped my rifle, shells, and tools. I led the dark bay that my grandfather had given me and called my family together. It was a somber time. Of course, there was a good chance I would not survive the war. God knows thousands of good soldiers who would never again answer the bugles call.

I hugged each of my dear brothers and they did their best to hold back the tears. I shook my grandfather's hand and looked him steadily in the eye. He nodded to me and told me to shoot straight. "I will Grandpa. I surely will." My father was next, and he looked so sad.

"Don't worry Father I will do my best to return." He replied with emotion that he was proud of me and wished me Gods speed."

My mother could only hug me and pled that I must come back over and over. You were last of all. We each put our hands on each other's shoulders and looked deeply into each other's eyes. "I love you Mary. No matter what the world may say I love as deeply as any human can. Pray for me. I will write as often as I can."

You could only nod through your tears.

"I will be here to meet you when this horrible war is over."

We hugged each other and kissed each other gently on the lips. I quickly swung into the saddle and rode away. I forced myself not to look back.

Love,

Rachel

CHAPTER FIFTY-ONE

June 17, 2016

Joyce and Ann decided to make it a day. The story in the letters was compelling but they knew they had to work slowly. Our newest employee was a new cook named Stacey Jones. She is a short stout woman with sharp sparkling green eyes. She is in her early seventies. She has cooked all her life for families, large work crews, and high-end restaurants.

We were surprised that Ms. Jones had learned her trade in Chicago and later with crews building the railroad. After the railroad she cooked for large crews that were building state highways in North Dakota. Her cooking ability was beyond any doubt. We merely told her the cuisine we desired, and she produced excellent food. I doubt that few cooks in the East could match her repertoire.

Once again I was surprised as to the talents that exist in this flat farmland. Her food was so delicious that we had to constantly watch our weight. She was pleasant to be around, but she left no doubt that the kitchen was her domain. She holds her talent in high esteem. She had cooked at several high-end restaurants in Chicago, and she was unflappable.

She had left the big city to share a life with an up-and-coming farmer. Her husband had built up a large and successful farm but unfortunately he suffered an early death with cancer. Others now work the farm, and she is able to live off her share. But it seemed that work was the only thing that is helping her with her grief.

We also employed a helper for Ms. Jones. Her name was Barbara, and she was responsible for helping Ms. Jones, food preparation and washing the dishes. As time went by we noticed how freely Ms. Jones passes on her knowledge to Barbara. It was refreshing after the common guarding of secrets that we so often saw in the over competitiveness of the east coast.

As was our custom, Ann and I would spend the cool of the evening on the porch swing. Naturally, part of our discussion turned to our findings. Neither Ann nor I had spent a serious amount of time on Civil War history. It had always seemed a dark and ugly part of United State history.

And the letters exchanged between Rachel and Mary made it all too clear how grim that time really was. However, they both agreed that they needed to get a more solid foundation on the subject. We had taken a brief look at the body of writing on the Civil War and we found there was an enormous body of available literature. It should not have been surprising that the library in this home carried dozens of volumes on the Civil War.

We pondered how interesting it must have been for Rachel to be reading on a conflict that she had been a participant in. As a citizen I should have been more aware of this history, but the huge size of the Civil War was overpowering. Even during the main battles that hugely shaped the war there were literally dozens of smaller military actions going on at the same time. "Small" being an operative word.

Even small battles consisted of thousands of soldiers fighting for their lives. Even more complex was the factor that there was a vast Union effort to control the high seas. The history of stopping the blockade runners was a huge subject.

Actions on the sea very much affected the battles on the land. The opposite was also true. Land actions shaped what the navy did on the sea. Another vast subject was the diplomatic efforts that were being made on all sides to gain favor and oversea support.

Keeping England or France out of the Civil War was critical to understanding what was going on. For the South huge battles like Antietam and Gettysburg were specifically aimed at trying to woo France or England to acknowledge them as a real nation.

The complexity was the incredibly issues of slavery, racism and control of a democratic government. Counting votes in Congress being critical to the survival of the United States. Just keeping control of all these interwoven interests made the war complicated beyond all reason.

As a woman fighting illegally as a soldier in the Union Army Rachel showed how desperate the North was looking for ground pounders. After all it could not have been too complex to check the gender of any would-be soldier. The Union Army knew perfectly well there were a surprising number of women serving as combat soldiers.

They also knew the ranks contained many child soldiers under twelve years of age. They knew but made no effort to eject these people who had no legality in a national war.

During this same era women were beginning to escape their subjugation. The long and slow fight for women's rights and civil liberties really began at the time of the Civil War. The war showed clearly that no modern nation could cast aside the productive potential that women had. The simple but critical need for female nurses and eventually female doctors grew out of the Civil War experience. The war was a clear dividing line between a nation that was primarily rural to a nation of industry.

The booming population made it clear there were only so many farms that could be profitable. The critical need to employ the surplus population was just beginning to be understood. For good or evil the United States was becoming a world power. As a world power the need for a large and professional army was necessary.

All these issues were silently fighting for women's rights. The non-stop drive for women equality began there and has not been completed as of the present day.

Joyce and Ann fully realized that women of the modern era often take for granted the sacrifices that women of former days made for their ultimate benefit. Rachel's entry into the Civil War showed clearly that many women were just as interested in political issues as men.

The war had the additional effect of freeing the blacks from stereotypes that were not at all true. By the end of the War fully ten percent of the Northern Army were blacks. When the blacks were properly trained they performed superb ably on the battlefields. Men that had faced enemy bullets were not likely to revert to servile treatment.

So, Ann and I rolled these issues around on the comfort of the porch swing. We both found this quiet time to be so relaxing and we began to understand how these simple comforts made the endless toil on the farms more endurable. It was so pleasant to be on the swing in the cool of the night.

The screening prevented the entry of mosquitoes although we could hear their eager buzzing just beyond the wire. We found ourselves lapsing into long periods of silence. In the busy city true silence is nearly impossible to find.

The deep silence here was most welcome. It gave each of us a chance to think objectively. Although each of us had regrets we decided we had led reasonable lives. Granted our status has much changed since we had heard of the name Rachel Summerville. Even without this huge event we felt we had done some good. We had our love for each other and love makes life worth living. I found myself watching the stars as the darkness intensified. I seemed so small on the galactic scale.

Here I sat worth over fifty million dollars and it still does not answer the basic questions of existence. Why am I here? Is there a conscious life after death? Is there a God? What is our purpose and how does one live?

I could not escape the feeling that being on this gentle swing felt good and right. We were forced to relax and let time pass. We wondered how often Rachel Summerfield had sat on the same swing. Was she able to find peace after the turbulent life she had endured? Did her relationship with Mary last? How did Rachel end up here in Nebraska? In time nearly all questions of Rachel Summerfield were answered.

After a solid breakfast we went back to the letters.

CHAPTER FIFTY-TWO

April 18,1862

Dear Mary

I am aware of a terrific battle at a place called Shiloh. This was the first major battle in Tennessee. It appears to have been a narrow union victory. Albert Johnston of the Confederacy was killed. He was considered one of the best generals of his generation.

Thank God he is gone. A new Union general has come to national attention: Ulysses S. Grant. Little is known about Grant. He has been called a drunk in some quarters. I say give the man more liquor if he gains us victories.

Grant has been known before. On February 16 he forced the surrender of Fort Donelson in Tennessee. This left the Union in command of the Cumberland River which was an important victory for the North. Here he gained his nickname "Unconditional Surrender." May God give him more victories. It is important to understand that the Union Army is divided into a western sector and then the eastern sector.

Love, Rachel

CHAPTER FIFTY-THREE

April 28, 1862

Dear Mary

Supplied with ample funds I preceded the long journey to Washington. The fields of Pennsylvania are green and bursting with life. The grass is growing high, and the farm animals have already glossed up from the rich food.

Thanks to my father I can stay overnight with his friends as I travel. I can bathe and eat good food. The homes I have stayed in have been gracious. My horse gets proper care, and I am spared some of the hardships of sleeping on the land.

I had to camp outside several times. In truth I must be careful where I camp. There are many men footloose and running from the law. I carry my sidearm openly and I made sure that all passerby's see I am armed. I always camp far from the road and make a cold camp without a fire. One is defenseless when one is asleep. I sleep lightly because of the danger.

I had one face-off on the road when a rough man stopped and asked me for money. He was a huge man tall and burley. He must have weighed over 220 lbs. lean pounds. He wore a reddish beard that had not been trimmed for months. He said he was hungry and had no further resources. He seemed aggressive and tried to walk closer to take my reins. Before he got close I drew my revolver, cocked it and held it pointed at his head.

He then said, "You are only a little guy and would not use it."

"Take one more step and I will kill you."

That seemed to convince him not to come closer.

"Maybe you ain't as little as you look."

I rode by until I was 50 or 60 yards away and placed a small amount of money on the road.

I shouted back, "Here is some money to eat with."

He shouted in return, "Thank you. Would you have killed me?"

I shouted back. "Yes Sir. I would have killed you instantly."

From there the rest of the day was peaceful. On the eighth day I reached Washington D.C.

The frantic scene of the capital is difficult to convey. It was like a large dirty incomplete building being erected in a swamp. The streets were open sewers and stench filled the air. Hundreds of horses and mules kept the streets mired in mud. At one intersection a team of horses was up to their knees in the morass. The fool driver was lashing the poor beasts.

A few of the buildings had boardwalks but most streets did not have this luxury. Knots of drunks gathered on many corners. I paused at a fist fight that was surrounded by idle men placing bets on the outcome. One sees war material and men going every which way. Open corruption was everywhere. I saw enlisted men selling army blankets to well-dressed civilians. The blankets were handed over from a government wagon

The chaos had to be seen to fully understand. I held up my horse and looked for a long while at the incomplete Capital building. I vowed to myself that I would help win this war of rebellion and against slavery even if I died. Naturally, I also hoped I would live to see the capitol dome finished and complete.

The streets were rutted and in some places water lay in small lakes. The stench was everywhere. There was a sense of rawness in the air as well as a general sense of fearful danger. Every other man looked like a professional criminal. It was not hard to see the presence of the Army. Officers and enlisted men in blue were in every establishment. There seemed to be a sea of blue uniforms. I thought to myself if one could gather these idle troops it would be possible to conquer the world.

There seemed to be little order or discipline. It mattered not whether the establishment was of class or of the pits. Most officers walked the streets as if the war was not of the slightest interest to them. Many of them were indeed interested in women. It mattered not to these malingers whether the woman was of high station or a woman selling herself. Every soldier attempted to gain the favor of either class. I wondered to myself why these heroes were not on the field facing the rebellious enemy?

The prostitutes were indeed legion. The variety of clothing was beyond my meager imagination. Red seemed to be part of every garb. The whores were hawking their bodies with a wide range of prices and services. I felt nothing but pity for these poor wrenches.

Life had been harsh to them, and they were simply trying to survive through the most degraded means. They had no place to seek constructive employment. Hopefully in the decades ahead women would have the same employment opportunities as men.

If only a women could be as freely employed as a man this would relieve much of this travesty. I realized again that there were only a few places or occupations that a woman could be employed. At most small businesses, the wife of the owner would leave her husband if he had the baseness to hire a woman employee. Why was it that the bulk of men wished to exploit the weak? Sometimes it seemed that the world was formed for the sole purpose of enslaving women.

I asked a well-dressed bystander where was a good stable? That man was so engrossed in his own thoughts he did not appear to hear me and walked on. The next person I asked was clearly a laborer and he gave me directions. It is impossible to know what is in a man's heart. Some have a good heart, but many do not.

There has been many a good man in poor clothes. I found the stable and it was a good one. I carefully took the tack off and found a brush to give my horse good care. I found a stable boy who would guard my horse and my tack for a fair sum of money.

I braved the streets of the capital until I arrived at the Willard Hotel. The Willard is known to be the best hotel in the city. The Willard was an inland of comfort in a sea of depravity. The floors were constantly being scrubbed in a futile effort to stay ahead of the foul mud. The lobby was large by any measure. At least 200 people could stand in it easily. The lobby counters were made of an exotic wood I was not able to identify. Many surfaces were clad in the finest marble.

Hanging from the lobby ceiling was a huge chandelier of the finest crystal. The chandelier spanned over twenty feet. Surely it weighed two tons. The workmanship in the building was of the highest level. Holding the dome and chandelier high were six pillars of beautiful white marble. When I paid for my room I noted that the bill was quite high.

I tipped a bell boy heavily for his help with my meager luggage. Before he left my room I asked him many questions. It seems that bell boys hear a great deal about the military and political situation by merely being in the presence of powerful men.

Strangely, important people do not notice the lowly hotel personnel, and openly talk around them. Having seen the multitudes of well-dressed men and ladies in the lobby it was not hard to imagine enemy ears soaking up valuable information.

The bell boy told me that the war up to this point was not good for the North. There was a great fear that the Union Army did not have a good general in charge.

There were strong feelings for the need for a Union victory. Some traitors were talking about making peace with the South. Of course, such an action would doom the entire continent to slavery.

The boy told me that nearly everyone in the hotel was either Union Officers, important political people or men with large business interests. I learned one of the best lessons in life. Often the lowly employee knows a great deal about the larger sphere of war and peace.

I was to meet a Captain Miller the next day in the hotel. It was agreed that I should meet him in the lobby next to a red leather sofa. The captain was prompt and did not want to brook any delay to get away. He gave the impression of a busy officer who did not approve of these civilian errands.

He was to take me to a powerful member of the General Staff by the name of Colonel Henry J. Hunt. Colonel Hunt was a staff member of Major Gen. George B. McClellan headquarters. At the present time the Army of the Potomac was located about 25 miles southwest of Washington D.C.

Colonel Hunt was the soldier that organized the artillery branch of the Army of the Potomac. He had risen on his merits. Many modern cannon tactics had been invented by this enterprising officer. Colonel Hunt had gained fame during the First Battle of Bull Run by providing a rear guard during the panicked retreat.

As bad as that battle was for the Union it could have been much worse. He and a few cannons stemmed the Rebel drive. His actions had not evaded notice, and he was properly promoted to his given rank. Had the South been able to overcome their lack of experience they could have ridden into the capital city and seized the national government. That would have been that.

Captain Miller was a rigid professional officer that asked no questions and gave no information away. He was tall, probably over six feet. He was very slender and had a small scar on his left cheek. His eyes were striking. They were gray and piercing. His hair was cut short, and it was a light brown. He said few words from the time he met me. He seemed focused on distant vistas. He did not express any interest in me or my mission.

He was an excellent horseman, and his mount was a high-quality animal. I learned later that the horse was his personal property. It was not hard to imagine this man leading a charge into hell. I was certainly impressed.

He was armed with a Colt side arm, and he had the standard Sharps in a scabbard. My Sharps rifle was also well protected in a scabbard and I gave it the utmost of care.

The captain did notice the special rifle and I thought he might ask some questions. However, he remained silent. Clearly here was a man who could keep a secret. He rode at a stiff pace, and he seemed surprised that I kept pace with him easily. I fear if he had known I was a woman he would have dropped dead of a heart attack.

I and my mount were in excellent condition, and I had not found any man who could outride me. In a couple of hours his mount was lathered, and my sturdy steed had not broken into a sweat.

Several times I caught him looking at me surprised at my ability to keep up. I was tempted to ride him into the ground but wisely I thought better of it. In any event I did not know where I was going.

We camped for the night about 20 miles southwest of Washington in a loose Army camp. We joined eight men around a campfire, and they were a lively bunch. One soldier had a harmonica and was good with it. The singing was off key and overall atrocious.

Referring to their strength these men had a cursing vocabulary that was most impressive. I had never heard such emotive words. I got the impression that the sheer depth and velocity of these vulgar words would peel the hide off a Union mule.

My rigid Captain did not join in on the festivities. I watched a beautiful sunset, and I thought about the horrible mission that I and these soldiers were facing. The captain provided a long Army coat, and it was clear that I was expected to sleep under it. As expected the ground was hard and uneven.

That was the first night I lived under Army conditions. Perhaps in the months to come I would consider that first night a luxury. For food I was given several pieces of hardtack. At first it seemed inedible but perhaps in the months ahead I would learn to appreciate its merits. I am sure that hardtack would stop a bullet.

I awoke at the sound of a bugle, and it was a new day. The bustle of human activity was overwhelming. I had never seen so many men in my life. Even more remarkable was the impression that each soldier seemed to know what he was supposed to be doing. The sky was a crystal blue and there was a soft breeze that moved the spring flowers.

The spring air still had a cool bite and it was totally refreshing. I wondered why men killed each other on such beautiful days over such an issue of Union and slavery. My poetic thought ended when a coarse soldier crushed the most beautiful flower with a careless indifferent step. I wondered whether that crushed flower was a warning of coming days.

There was also the stench of dozens of latrines. Many soldiers did not bother to use latrines. I had not been exposed to men who were raised in primitive conditions. I wondered if disease might kill more soldiers than bullets. Perhaps I would adjust my attitude toward these rough men.

We arrived at the general camp for the Army of the Potomac at about two in the afternoon. There were several picket lines that had to be crossed before admittance into the general camp was allowed.

It was easy to see these were untried men. Their clothes were new and clean. They were still uncertain as to the protocol. I think they thought they were playing soldier. I am so brazen, and I think I know all about fighting. I hope to learn from my errors.

Later it may be difficult to greet these new replacements with their new rifles. One knew many of them would not survive the first battle. I could not imagine how to write a letter telling his mother that he had died in the fighting.

It would be hard to express the vast horde of soldiers that met the unlearned eye. They appeared to be a rolling blue carpet as they went about their business. It took time to be able to grasp the thousands of men involved in this morbid trade. The tents, wagons, and artillery seemingly stretched for miles.

The Army had thousands and thousands of weapons, wagons, and lines of tents to the distant horizon. Some of the men loitered and but vastly more were drilling to perfect the complications of battlefield maneuver. I will soon join those hundreds of soldiers learning the basic duties of soldering.

The captain escorted me to a large walled tent. In front of the tent was a tall strong guard. Captain Miller asked for an audience with Colonel Hunt. Upon my entrance the captain saluted and then walked away as if he was depositing a bag of flour.

I had come a long way to meet this man, and I carefully took his measure. He was a fine-looking tall man with broad strong shoulders. He walked with professional grace, and he took my hand firmly. Deep blue eyes examined me.

There were worry lines on his forehead, but he had a strong black beard that was shaped like a flat sand shovel. He was large, at least 230 pounds with no fat. He looked like he could whip the Rebels by himself. As I looked him in the eye he said, "So you are the son of Mr. Summerfield of Pennsylvania fame?"

"Yes Sir, he is my father, and I am instructed to give you this letter from my father."

The Colonel took the letter and retired to a small folding desk to peruse the message. He appeared to carefully read the contents several times.

"Son, have you read the letter yourself?"

"No Sir I was just told to give it to you."

"Frankly, this is a most unusual request. Typically, important people are trying to get their sons out of service. In this case it is quite the other way. You want to serve. Well, men like you are needed. How old are you?

'I am seventeen Sir.

"Well, you look young, and you are a small man, but our country is in peril. Physical size means little on the battlefield. It is your mental strength and courage that count. The Union has lost several major battles, and we are at low tide.

We need strong men who are willing to do their duty and serve willingly to save the union. Your request would commit you to a three-year enlistment. This is the Army and life in the Army is not easy for a person of any rank. That includes me. You understand a man with the wealth and influence of your father could easily send a substitute to replace you from the service?

"Yes Sir but I am a citizen who wants to serve his country. I have no interest in evading my duty."

The colonel seemed to take that information, and he rolled it around carefully.

"Your father suggests you have a special skill that might be of benefit to your country. It appears you are a sharpshooter of some repute. It further states you have brought your own target rifle to serve in that capacity. Are these points true?"

"Sir, it is true, and I have won many rifle competitions. I believe I can contribute to the restoring the Union."

"Son, would you mind showing me this weapon."

"Not at all, it will take only a moment to remove it from my scabbard." I quickly retrieved the rifle and brought it in for his inspection.

Colonel Hunt looked at it carefully. "It is a beautiful rifle. A Sharps if I am correct."

"Yes, it is a Sharps, and it shoots extremely well."

"What is the sight mounted on the barrel?"

"It is a Malcolm 6 power rifle scope. It magnifies the image six times for finer shooting."

"What is its effective range?"

"Sir it is absolutely deadly to 700 yards in still wind and a serious threat at 1000 yards."

"I have read your father's letter, and I am impressed with your patriotism. However, I am an officer in the Army of the Potomac. I am expected to think clearly and not be influenced by civilians. What do you have personally that would uniquely impress me?'"

I reached in my battered travel bag and took out a target I had recently shot at a Titusville Long Range Shoot. It showed my winning group of ten shots in a six-inch circle at 700 yards.

"Sir, all I have is this target."

He studied it carefully. "This is an unusual argument, but I am favorably impressed."

Let me explain the situation and allow you to decide. You would need to sign up for three years. That is an absolute commitment regardless of who your father is. You would go through the accelerated course in field maneuvers and Army discipline. This would require three weeks.

Our summer campaigns are looming large, and we need every man we can scratch up. If you fulfill these requirements I will take you as an aide de camp. You would always serve me when we are not in combat and certainly between campaigns.

You would be personally responsible for my welfare and an aid in my workload. This would put you directly under my command. Your official unit would be staff artillery, and you would travel with the artillery section.

You would be permitted your horse and the use thereof. On the battlefield you would be assigned to an experienced sharpshooter. He will teach you the ropes and I will use his judgment as to your suitability.

Then I will make my final decision, and you will have to live with it. If your performance as a sharpshooter is unacceptable you will probably be assigned as a common soldier on the main battle line. This is not a game. Do you understand your choices, and do you have any questions? Before you answer, realize that when you are in the Army obedience is everything.

The Army will own you and they will spend your life if necessary. Indeed, the Army may cause your death with no military gain. If you need to gather your thoughts you may leave for fifteen minutes to reach your decision."

"Sir, that is not necessary. I am here to serve."

"So be it. Camp with my tent guards and be prepared to be sworn in promptly after sunrise."

Thus, it was. The next day I was Private Summerfield and in a training company preparing to fight.

Love,

Rachel

CHAPTER FIFTY-FOUR

May 14, 1862

Dear Mary

The military life of a private is hard. One is up before dawn and is expected to have eaten breakfast before the morning light. Most of the remaining day is drill. Drill is easy to understand.

Drill is simply marching. We drill hours upon hours. One drills regardless of the weather. Drill during the hottest hours and drill in the rain. Endless drilling until you think your head will fall off.

The soldier must know when and how to get to battle and how to get into the correct formation to best defeat the enemy. Typically, you march distances like a long snake in ranks, but fighting is normally in linear lines. Ideally the fighting line is two rows deep.

In practice, a single line of battle is more common. It sounds easy but is quite difficult. Large bodies of troops can mill in chaos which on the battlefield can lead to general slaughter.

Typically, drill is taught by sergeants of the regular army. Most of the young officers are also new and have yet to learn their jobs.

The hardcore professional sergeants are the ones that really know their job. The vast majority of the day is spent drilling and most soldiers (myself included) hate this constant redundant exercise.

Nevertheless, any clear-minded soldier can see that this discipline is critical for fighting and surviving battles. Having an illiterate sergeant screaming in your face is tiring. The temptation to come to blows is strong. However, military discipline is harsh. The easiest way to get through this training is to learn as quickly as possible, keep silent and simply do what one is told.

In the Army, every function from cleaning your rifle to maintaining one's clothes has a fixed method. It is true that there is a normal way and then the Army way. It is offensive that one is considered an idiot but having a uniform standard has its critical function. In just a few more days I will be done with this process and assigned to my permanent unit. Please read these letters to the family. Naturally omit the personal parts.

I love you and I miss you so much. Please remember me in your prayers.

Love

Rachel

CHAPTER FIFTY-FIVE

May 21

1862

Dear Mary

The Army is moving. This huge killing machine projects unremitting force. The Army moves on like an unstoppable law of nature. I am assigned to an artillery unit but stay close to Colonel Hunt. As an aide de camp I am assigned to Colonel Hunt, and I am not helping with the cannons. I am deployed during combat as a sharpshooter. Between battles I see to the needs of Colonel Hunt alone. Colonel Hunt in turn serves under whoever the General is that is in overall command.

Thus, Generals may come and go but Colonel Hunt is on the general staff permanent. That is why the letters you write are my name but addressed to the General staff.. As a rule, soldiers are discouraged from listing the unit one is attached to. The Army wants nothing that might give the enemy an advantage.

Thank God I am permitted to ride my horse. All the other troops must walk endless miles in the dust and heat. Many soldiers drop out from exhaustion and heat stroke. Some recover and can make up for lost time and rejoin their unit. Colonel Hunt speaks quite frankly to me.

"We are marching toward Richmond. Somewhere in front of us the rebel army is waiting."

The joking common among troops is gone. Everyone is alone in their thoughts. Many of us will not survive. I hope I am one of the lucky ones.

Artillery plays a vast role in modern warfare. Properly trained a cannon crew can kill dozens of enemy soldiers in one shot. A battery of cannon hub to hub is a fierce some sight. Each cannon crew consists of eight men with an addition four men to hold the horses.

An Army on the march is awesome. Screening by the cavalry on all sides prevents us from walking into a trap. There are often single shots at any time. These are usually pot shots just testing our line and to keep new troops on edge.

However, some of these single shots are from Confederate sharpshooters. Usually, they shoot straight, and a soldier is dead. Most of the Confederates are rural born and have been raised hunting squirrels and deer.

They know the value of patience and making that one shot count. It is discouraging to the troops because the deaths seem so random and somehow unfair. I know that soon I will be tested under fire.

Colonel Hunt gives me constant lessons of what to do and what to watch for. He says when the shooting at the front becomes more constant that is when the army is engaging the enemy skirmishers. These skirmishers are usually around two to three hundred yards in front of the enemy's main battle line. Depending on the ground the cannons are at least two hundred yards behind the line,

The cannon has its own section of line and normally does not shoot over the infantry. Cannon can be used against soldiers or against the cannon of the enemy. Quite often the cannon is hundreds of yards from the main battle line. The eight-man crew must get the cannon in place and ready to fire in under two minutes.

Riding twenty yards away from me is a soldier called "Old Joe." Joe is much older than the average soldier. I would place him at 30 to 32 years of age. He is a small wiry man with quite dark skin. He has deep sunk eyes that appear to be without emotion. He has several scars on his arms and a long one on his face. I am told that knife fighting is common in the Deep South.

I heard his mother is Negro. His father is a Frenchman. He was raised near New Orleans. I have not noticed much expression from him. Seemingly he is quiet and withdrawn. I learned he had never held any rank above private. Apparently he is outstanding in combat but cannot endure Army discipline. Hence, the Army appreciates him but does not reward him. In many ways he is a solitary man that does his job without fanfare.

He is aware of his duty to me, but he has yet to say a word to me. He rides in a slouch on a grey mule, and he chews tobacco. At times he swallows his tobacco juice. A repulsive habit. His uniform is dirty with mud stains

Like me he carries a Sharps rifle in his scabbard and a spyglass in a pouch. When the army is engaged I am to join him and learn what I can in a life and death situation. Apparently there is no training that can prepare one for sharpshooting.

Old Joe will be my instructor in this violent trade. The army thinks in large numbers and has not had the time to become a truly trained unit. I am only a tiny gear in this huge killing machine.

An army moves slowly. We camped here overnight, and this is when I am writing this letter. Tomorrow the battle will begin. The enemy is rumored to be less than five miles away.

Love,

Rachel

CHAPTER FIFTY-SIX

June 8, 1862

My Dear Mary

Thank the Almighty God I survived my first battle! I will do my best to give my impressions but believe me the conditions were one mass of killing, noise and chaos. I will try to keep my account as clear as I am able. A huge problem was that there was no time to just look around. One was trying to do their duty and stay alive. The name of the battle was Seven Pines, and it took place May 31 to June 2. It was all so frightening it is possible I got some things wrong.

It started like Colonel Hunt said it would. Rifle shots were pot shots, and I still did not feel any real fear. In fact, my emotions were anticipation and excitement. The shooting quickly got more rapid but one could still hear individual shots. During this time, we are still going toward Richmond.

I think we were within 20 miles of Richmond. I remember thinking this war was going to end in a couple of hours and Richmond would fall. I sure missed that prediction.

Unfortunately, the rifle shots melted into a solid and constant roar. I could not pick out a single shot. Colonel Hunt ordered me to go with Old Joe. We had handed our horses off to a private and I could barely keep up with Joe. For a man I had thought couldn't move he could run like a deer.

Joe and I were about five hundred yards from the main battle lines and our cannons were spread to the left of us. Bullets were literally flying everywhere it sounded like you were next to an aroused beehive. These bullets were raising dust impacts all around Joe and me. I wanted to drop down to try and take shelter which I hoped might keep me alive for a little bit longer. But Joe kept on running and I was right behind him. I don't think I have ever run so fast.

Joe finally hit the dirt, and I landed right beside him. We were laying down next to some trees that were about 8 inches in diameter. I lay prone behind a tree and got into position to shoot the enemy. Joe told me to catch my breath for a couple of minutes. Thanks to youth and fitness I recovered my wind fast. Then Joe pointed out several enemy officers through his spy glass.

I could easily get my crosshairs on any one of them. The officers were controlling their line by riding their horse up and down the line that they controlled. The enemy officers thereby urged steady fire and brave hearts. The officer is the brains of the battle line and the riflemen on the line are his body.

I tried to keep my sights on one, but they seemed to be constant movement. Joe said to be patient. He said the officer would pause when he reached the end of his sector, and he would then turn around to ride to the other end. Joe asked me what I thought was the range and I answered five hundred and fifty yards. He thought that was about right. He told me to set my sights on the center officer.

Joe said he would time the pause in movement and tell me when to shoot. I was nervous but I felt under control. Joe said to be patient. Again, he said the officer would pause when he reached the end of his sector, and he would then turn around to ride to the other end. That pause before or after turning was the time to shoot.

Joe said, "He is about ready to stop. I will tell you when to shoot."

I said, "I am ready." I saw the horse pause and it turned around.

Joe said, "Shoot"

I shot and watched the officer slump over and drop. Joe tugged at my sleeve, "Time to move fast."

I got only ten yards or so when a bullet hit exactly where I was before. If I was still there I would have been killed. I learned the enemy often has counter shooters. These are sharpshooters with a specific job. Their job is to look for rifle smoke from single shots on the edges of the battle. They know that single shot probably means an enemy sharpshooter. Without Joe I would have been killed in the first hour.

When Joe ran I ran. He dropped behind a large rock, and I dropped next to him. I couldn't catch my breath. I thought my heart would beat through my chest. I still was in control, but things happen so fast there is not enough time to be afraid. When battles started you were too busy to think too much.

We were on the back slope and could not be reached by rifle fire. Only air bursts from cannon could explode over our heads and kill us. There is nothing a lone shooter could do so one ignores it. In front of my astonished eyes Joe casually took out his pipe and slowly packed it. He lit it and took a couple of draws.

He saw my bewilderment he said, "Take it easy son. Those Rebels will be there all day. Let me smoke a pipe and then you should be ready."

That is exactly what we did. Finally, Joe knocked out his pipe and said, "Let's go."

We went back to the slight rise, and he set up in a small clump of bushes. He carefully checked where we were going to run after the shot.

He took out his spy glass and picked out a large bright suited officer with a white hat with a feather.

Joe asked, "What do you think is the range?"

I thought about 550 again. Joe said, "I think he is a tad further but let's take the shot."

I had a slightly longer time to check out the officer. He was a large man, and he carried a bright sword. He was shouting mightily but I am not sure anyone could hear him in the din.

Joe said, "He's about ready. I will say shoot."

My crosshairs were as steady as a rock on the center of the man's chest.

"Shoot."

I did and the bullet hit below his belly button. He slid off like a wet sack of flour.

"Run son,"

I ran. Joe had been right about the range. The officer had been about 575 hundred yards. I was off about 25 yards therefore the bullet hit low, but Joe called him dead.

When Joe ran I ran, and it seemed I was running all day.

One must be careful that one is not too close to the cannons. Their blast when they fire feels like it will take off your head. Ideally one is above and beside the artillery. Often the artillery batteries are dueling with the enemy artillery. Everyone serving cannon is cross-trained so that any one of the crew knows how to do all the steps necessary to keep firing.

This is important as one artillery piece can kill a lot of men very fast. If the enemy cannon is within rifle range it is essential to kill crew members. Joe told me that artillery crews are seldom within rifle range. The Sharps has a maximum range of 1000 yards. Hitting an enemy at that range is not likely.

The wind is the greatest problem. The bullet is going slow and during its flight it drifts. One must think carefully whether to shoot or not. Every time you shoot you may lose your life. The smoke gives one away instantly.

Joe taught me that one had to learn judgment. Joe taught me the most important rule for a sharpshooter: Never shoot from the same spot twice. Many sharpshooters die for this reason. The only exception is when your position blends in with constant fire all around one.

Then one's shots are lost in the storm. That is rare. If one is in a stationary position like a siege never use the same spot as you used the day before. The same rules apply. Never take more than one shot from a given position.

We were setting up again when I glanced to the left and saw an entire Union artillery crew killed. They just went to pieces of bloody flesh. Joe had to shake the sense back into me I was so frozen in horror. Of course, the battle went on without pause. That is the most frightening thing. Hundreds, thousands of men dying before one's eyes and the battle goes on as if nothing happened.

It is so impersonal. One is breathing heated air. The arid taste of gun powder irritates one's throat. The smoke makes one's eyes water. Your ears are throbbing.

I killed four rebels that day. I killed three officers, and one artillery man. The artillery man was by far the most difficult. We noted one enemy cannon crew working smoothly like a clock. I judged the leader as being 885 yards away. Joe had me shoot at a rock near the artillery man.

Joe explained the first shot was to get the wind correction and the drop correction. This is a deadly tactic. One rarely hits a man at that extreme distance but sometimes it works.

I will try to enter more details because I did see more as I learned. The basic fighting formation is both armies facing each other at about 50 to 100 yards and blazing away. This is an insane way to fight. This is the old Napoleon tactic. In those days, the battle rifle was a very inaccurate smoothbore rifle. One would be lucky to kill a man at 50 yards. Thus, the officers pushed their troops forward.

The modern military rifle has rifling and is quite deadly to 300 yards. At fifty yards the first man to shoot will win because the modern rifle is dead accurate at that range. Therefore, for a modern officer to push his men forward is not a clear-headed tactic. Ones losses will be catastrophic. The same can be said of the modern rifled cannon. They were far more accurate than the old smoothbores.

Men like my superior Colonel Hunt are working hard to modernize cannon tactics. As odd as it sounds Colonel Hunt had to convince higher officers to change the way they fought war. I learned a wise statement in this war: Old officers use old methods. Tens and tens of thousands of good soldiers died because their commanders could not get their head out of the past.

The Union and Rebel line was like a writhing snake. It twisted and turned depending on the steadiness of one's line. At times one side would charge forward and the opposing line moved back. In a matter of seconds, it can be right back to where it started. Occasionally the lines would move like a vortex.

This twisting tangled pattern means hand to hand fighting. There is much I still do not know. About 35,000 men on each side fought. Each side lost about 3,000 men killed and wounded. The outcome was a draw. The end of the war is not one inch closer.

Then the rain came up heavily and the exhausted armies drew away from each other. There was no more action for Joe and me. I was exhausted and dropped to the ground when I returned to Colonel Hunt. He said the battle was called Seven Pines. You may show this letter to father. Let him be the judge as to whether to show mother and my brothers.

I would give anything to be in your arms. I am haunted with memories of our former passions. When I think of you at night I become aroused. I am driven to take my hand to myself to sate these passions. I imagine my passionate hours with you and that brings me to the peak of passion quickly. I hope that you can understand. Someday I will be home with you. I pray for that day.

I learned from Colonel Hunt that about 35,000 soldiers from each side were engaged in the battle. General Johnston led for the South and General McClellan for the North. The battle was considered a draw. Neither army was forced from the field.

Both sides fell back exhausted. Each side took over 3000 casualties and it had no effect on ending the rebellion. They probably lost at least as many soldiers as we did. I must live with the fact we are not an inch closer to final victory. We must win this war.

With All My Love,

Rachel

CHAPTER FIFTY-SEVEN

June 15, 1862

Dear Rachel

I pray for your safety every waking hour. We get some news on battles. Probably more information than you do. Around May 25 Stonewall Jackson drove Union forces out of Winchester Virginia. General Jackson is a fearsome opponent of the Union.

Around June 6 The Union Navy took Memphis giving the Union control of the Mississippi except Vicksburg. Your mother and father have drawn faces nearly all the time. I know they worry about you constantly. Your Grandfather reads all the newspapers religiously trying to glean knowledge of your whereabouts and the state of the war.

Oh Rachel! Why do so many men on both sides have to die over the evil issue of slavery? Surely no serious humane human can condone owning another human being. Yet we are fighting the most horrible war in United States history over this issue.

I often feel the same burning passion for you. We are young and in love. Our sexual needs are high. I too must sate myself at times. Without that release I think I would go mad. I pray for the day we can get together. It seems to be a wild dream. Why are people so reticent about passion? In the present world where men in their madness are killing without restraint why is passion something to be ashamed of?

Passion is God's gift to mankind. Making love is not a sin. It is a joy. If two women find love with each other who is anyone to criticize? To love one another is truly the greatest commandment. God even gives passion to our enemies. I would shout my passion from the rooftops if that would return you to me.

Love

Mary

CHAPTER FIFTY-EIGHT

June 17, 1862

To My Beloved Son

It is with great fear and great love that I write to you. This is no time for hints and half thoughts. It is time to speak honestly and completely. Let me directly say that I love you totally and I respect your decision to fight totally. I want you to be fully aware that slavery is the cancer of this Union. Do not be fooled by any political sophistry of the slave states.

Slavery has always been the desire of the South, and the South wants to spread this immoral heinous crime to the entire United States. The South has done everything to kill the Union.

I have battled slavery and all the forces that have tried to destroy the Union for decades. This contest is literally between freedom and slavery. Never be deceived by the words from the South or their mouth pieces.

The South has done everything they can to keep and expand slavery. They have used dishonest practices, promoted violence in Kansas and used any method that would allow them to keep and expand human bondage.

Do not be deceived with their cries of "States Rights." Do not be deceived with their vague gloss of "property rights." These bland phrases are simply words to cover their crime of human enslavement. The South has even tried to steal Cuba to spread their noxious poison. The South has lied, bribed, cheated and used violence to promote slavery. There is no base practice that the South will not use to continue to keep and expand slavery.

The truth is that you may lose your life defending the Union and freedom for all men. If you should die for the cause of Union and freedom I would want you to know how proud I am of you. I have pride that you realize that the enslavement of men by others is evil and must be resisted to our last drop of blood.

Your death would crush me and your mother. However, to lose your life in the name of freedom is to die for the highest cause known to man. I would mourn for you to my dying day. Yet my pride in you would support me and your mother until our own deaths.

It is our deepest prayer that you will survive this dreadful war. If God should take your young life then your family hopes to be with you eventually in the heaven beyond.

Love,

Your Father

CHAPTER FIFTY-NINE

July 9, 1862

Dear Mary

We have just finished the most horrible series of battles that I can imagine. The last week of June was one continuous slaughter. The ground is covered with thousands of the dead, pieces of the dead and the wounded for hundreds of yards. The wounds are horrible and practically beyond description.

I have seen many bodies literally torn into several pieces. Often one seems only a piece of meat with no clue as to where the rest of the body is. Arms and heads are often asunder. The military musket makes a big hole. Often there are dozens of dead that are in a large pool of blood.

One can often see entire artillery crews hanging dead limply on their cannon. One often sees smashed cannons with no crew in sight. One could easily walk 100 yards on dead bodies and never touch the ground. The cries of the wounded tear my heart apart. Understandably they call for their wife, their family or loved ones.

Some are appealing to God to take them or relieve their pain. I pray a merciful God will receive them.

In the heat of the battle there is no time to help a fellow soldier. Sometimes the wounded can be propped up or given some water. Hundreds and thousands of soldiers die of wounds they would have survived if they had received the minimum of medical help. Typically, the non-injured soldier cannot pause one second because he is fighting to stay alive.

It is a vision of hell to see hundreds of men desperately bayoneting each other or clubbing each other to death. Sometimes a soldier is grappling against the enemy when another enemy soldier stabs or shoots him in the back. Luck or the lack of it often decides who lives or dies. I don't think I could survive on the main battle line. I do not have the strength to match an enemy. Their greater strength and longer reach would do me in.

The non wounded fighting soldiers are so encompassed in confusion, anger, or hate that nothing is done except loading and firing at the enemy. It truly is a killing frenzy. I have absolutely no doubt that men on the same side have killed each other in the melee.

Quite often during the midst of the battle the wounded are walked upon by soldiers or horses. This can be fatal for the wounded especially if the ground is muddy. They get pushed under the mud and drown. It is just the way it is in this type of war.

As I mentioned, the Army does not have nearly the doctors or ambulances to care for the wounded. If the service multiplied the medical help by a factor of 10 it would not be enough. Look at our horrible losses in the thousands and there is no help. Many is the man who dies alone that should have lived.

Our lines are often several miles long. This is just the part I can see. To be able to see the total battlefield must be mind numbing. This conflict was called The Seven Days Battle.

Once again our Army got close to Richmond. General Lee, who replaced Johnston attacked us fiercely. General McClellan does not resist he only retreats. The men are fighting the war by themselves. Our field officers do their best to hold us together but without overall leadership we have been constantly driven back. We have been driven down the Virginia Peninsula.

We have clearly lost these battles. The men are fighting like lions, but our leaders are letting us down. If I see our artillery withdrawing I must retreat as well. Sharpshooters must not be overrun by the main lines. We must shoot from a distance. Here we can do our best work. The rank and file doubt the quality of General McClellan. He never seems to attack.

I have fought every day for seven days. I am exhausted. I can barely stand. My clothes are rags and mud. Colonel Hunt is tired and looks to have aged at least ten years. On the brighter side Joe and I make a deadly team. I killed 8 of the enemy over the entire battle. I was constantly shooting and moving. I was so flooded with emotions, but I know how many I killed. It is a number that is hard to forget. I wish I never had to do this killing. It is a soul-destroying task. However, what can I do?

The overriding principle for a sharpshooter is one must stay calm no matter how dire the situation. Every action of the sharpshooter must be thought out. Acting without thinking gets one killed quickly. Joe has taught me so much. He looks like the stupidest man you ever saw but he knows every nuance of sharpshooting.

He can see and correct any error that I may make. Despite my experience with long-range shooting, he outclasses me by miles. He knows where the bullet will be at any range or with any wind. He often corrects my range estimation to the target before I shoot and never once has he been wrong.

He has taught me so much about shooting in unfavorable conditions. He sees immediately something I would not see in a week. He is death itself on the battlefield. He also has an uncanny feel for which side is winning or losing. I am certain he knows the pulse of the battle line better than the line officers themselves.

I would have been dead a long time ago without him. Thank God I have Joe. I pray we can both survive the war. I would like you to meet this unsung genius. Without a mentor like Joe, I would have been dead in one hour.

Most Northern troops have no experience with shooting. Most of our raw soldiers have never fired one shot at a target. Apparently our leadership considers that a waste of ammunition. What kind of insanity is that?

You throw a man into this hell and expect him to instantly turn into a cool marksman? This is simply murder of the common soldier and the fault is with our leaders. It is true that many innocent soldiers must die so our bumbling officers can learn to lead.

Yet we must defeat the South. We have now fallen back to a good position. It is called Melvern Hill. I am fearful of the lives that must be lost to obtain this goal. Around 55,000 troops from each side were engaged in this battle. We lost around 3000 men. The Rebels probably lost twice that. Rebel infantry repeatedly tried to take

Melvern Hill in the face of Colonel Hunt cannons. The Confederates were slaughtered.

Colonel Hunt bravely walked back and forth behind the artillery. If he sees a frightened crew that is about to run he talks to them calmly and that usually gets them back on the line firing. During this slow walk the Colonel is under serious fire.

During this battle of Melvern Hill very few of the enemy got close to our main line. Our artillery cut them to ribbons at a distance. Colonel Hunt's efforts are critical, but it must be horrible mowing down hundreds of farm boys with his cannons. This battle was called the Seven Day Battles. I am so tired I must get some rest.

Deepest Love,

Ray

CHAPTER SIXTY

July 23,1862

From Mary

To Ray

Dearest Beloved Ray

I am horrified by these terrible battles. It is hard to understand the scale of these tragedies It terrifies me that there is so much random death even between battles. Apparently men can just be walking along in his company of soldiers and be killed by a sharpshooter.

The victim is not even in a battle. We read in the newspapers (which your father gets all of them) of the massive deaths from disease. Naturally, the articles in the papers are censored. However, when one reads different accounts from different papers it is possible to form a clearer picture.

How dreadful to live through battles and die a victim of some raging disease. Our father has access to Southern papers. He finds these to be invaluable. He says we must be aware of our enemies' thoughts. Everything good or bad begins with a thought. He feels in the long run we must not only conquer their armies but also win their minds. The latter he feels will take decades. But such thoughts are idle. We must win or all else is moot.

The Union must win this hideous war. It is through soldiers like you that we may achieve our just cause of freedom for all mankind. Imagine being a black slave breathing his first breath of sweet freedom! I pray every day that you will come home and be ready to forget these bitter experiences.

I am afraid that I will lose you. I pray multiple times a day that you will survive. I will encompass you with love. Please hold the memories of our passions.

We will once again drink from the cup of ardor. My passion burns with the strongest desire. I burn with the need to have you in my arms. You own my whole body. I in turn seek yours. The killing is necessary to stop this madness of enslaving human beings. By what right does the South commit these crimes?

They take the entire God given life of a human being and deprive him of his chance to pursue a trade and to seek his happiness. This horror must end. If we do not stop slavery in the South then the entire new world will fall to these deprived people. God save us from their warped set of values.

Your family has been so good to me. It has been such a blessing. I am surrounded by gentle kind people who truly care for me. Your brothers are always so kind and courteous to me. Your mother insists on being addressed as mother.

She often addresses me with endearments like "blessed daughter" "my love" and "precious child." I am so humbled. Your father also wishes to be addressed as father. He says I have been a source of joy to the entire family.

Father (note how easy the word is to say!) is thinking of some way he can help during this war. He often sits in his study, and I wonder what he is thinking. I know that father will do something. But I have told him that you are in the direct fight. What more can a family give? I cannot even visualize so many people in one place. I am just a local girl, and it is thanks to you I have such a hallowed life. You and your family have not only saved my life but have also given me a new life. I often tremble with gratitude.

Please thank Joe for me. I am so glad you have a mentor to help you. I will pray for both of you daily. May God allow both of you to survive this indescribable war. Please tell Joe that I thank him from the bottom of my heart. Why the South has brought this war upon all of us is difficult to understand. May God have mercy on all of us and allow the Union to win shortly.

I have such love and passion for you. I know these are simple words, but I mean them to my grave. I would die for you. Please write to me and the family.

Love

Mary

CHAPTER SIXTY-ONE

August 2,1862

Dear Ray

I know how horrible the war is going. You may be killed at any time and the Union is not winning. What can a mother say when her child is fighting in this horrid war. To say that I love you is surely not enough. I borne you and you are still such a part of me. You are flesh of my flesh.

I try to keep up with war events but in truth I can hardly bear it. The endless lists of the dead, wounded, and dying just take my breath away. I am drawn between knowing the horrible truths of the day and a total personal withdrawal into blessed ignorance.

I will try to say what I would want you to know as if I could never speak to you again. I love you. I would do anything to spare you this agony. If I lose you I will mourn every hour until I die. I would also say that my child gave his life to save our Union and to destroy slavery. No mother could be prouder than I am to have nourished such an unselfish and brave child.

Each of us lives and we all die. Few have died for such a noble cause. I cannot fully understand the horror you are going through.

Be strong my child and bravely face those who would destroy the Union and enslave human beings forever. I pray nearly every waking hour for your safety. I pray to a God of mercy who would not want his human creations to be chattel for the gain of evil people.

I can't understand the desire to enslave others, but I know to the last fiber in my body that it is completely wrong in both the holy and human sense. Remember on your days of battle that your family is with you. In the chaos, blood, and death we will be at your side.

We pray for your strength and your bravery. If it is God's will that you shall die then we are at your side as you pass over the river of death to the shade of trees of heaven. We prepare to meet you on that blessed shore when we cross the river to rejoin you.

With all possible love,

Your Mother.

CHAPTER SIXTY-TWO

August 20, 1862

My Adored Mary

The Army is refitting, and another battle is coming up. I am no longer a private. Based on my performance Colonel Hunt promoted me. I am now a corporal. The Colonel said he spoke to Old Joe and my teacher praised my work to high heaven.

He apparently told the Colonel I was a natural. The Colonel asked me how many kills I had made. I told him that to the best of my memory it is 24, most of them being officers. The Colonel said that my performance had been excellent and that my probation was over.

I was now a full-fledged sharpshooter. Colonel Hunt added that the decimation of Southern officers has a strong effect on the battlefield. The main factor is the loss of leadership during battle. This is exactly the time troops need their leader. To kill that officer often means the troops may fall back in their confusion or even drive them to desert the field entirely. Rattled troops make poor soldiers.

I asked if I could continue teaming up with Joe. He was receptive to that. In closing this conversation, the Colonel said my father should be proud. That was that. Tell my father that I would be nothing without him and mother. Their support and guidance formed me from the ground up. Tell them that my heart breaks thinking of them.

As I said, we are preparing for another battle. My position as aid ad camp of Colonel Hunt gives me a wonderful way to get a feel for our leaders and their plans. I am just a mouse in a corner. However, I am an attentive mouse. I learned that our leaders have no clear plan for winning the war. Nor do they have any established plan to win the next battle. Typically, there is no agreement as to what the Army is to do next.

There are arguments and discord. It is frightful to watch this small group of leaders. They have the lives of thousands of troops in their hands. The egos and vanity of many officers are clearly in play. Some of the officers are unmistakably "yes men" who are seeking promotion. Failing to realize that there will be no promotions if we lose this war.

The biggest mystery to me is General McClellan Here is a brilliant man who has had a brilliant career. Yet his greatest days are obviously behind him. He has a "Messiah" complex. He feels responsible for everything in the present, yet he is truly chained to the past. He wants to rest on his past reputation, and I have concluded that he does not really want to fight. All he is worried about is losing his prestige. McClellan will not take any risks, but wars are won by risk takers.

We have rebel deserters who tell us that the enemy had no more than 50,000 men and McClellan claims he is vastly outnumbered while our Army had 120,000 men. Even with that margin he refuses to fight. To his credit, he is wonderful at building and training troops. That should be his role in this war. He will not fight.

Colonel Hunt is often a critic of McClellan. He is not afraid to express his opinions right in the face of McClellan. He told McClellan that he would lose the next battle without taking the battle to the Rebels. He added that if he (McClellan) continued this path we would lose the entire war. Colonel Hunt does not receive McClellan's praise. I fear the next battle.

Total Love

Rachel

Chapter Sixty-Two

August 27, 1862

Dear Beloved Ray

Please come back to me alive. I am so afraid. I fear losing you. It would mean my life as well. I know I can't live without you. I want so much for us to live in peace and be together. It matters not whether we are rich or poor. I only want you. I would happily work at the lowest stations in life if I only had you. I want to grow old together. I miss you so badly.

I am appalled at the dissention between our military leaders. The very existence of the Union depends on them. Our cause is so much larger than personal egos and ambitions. Your father is very interested in your observations near the leaders. Father tells me that there is a thin line between war and politics.

On these issues I do not know enough. I do know that the Union is swamped with traitors. The Democrats want Lincoln's head, and they are willing to destroy the nation to get it. These traitors have the right to criticize the very nation that allows critics to live! The entire life of a Negro slave serves his masters profits only.

Don't these military leaders realize that the fate of our civilization hangs in the balance? This is no time for puffing and preening. The overall tide of the war has been against us, and we can't survive if this flood keeps overwhelming us.

Many politicians say they only want the Union. We will have no Union without the freeing of the slaves. Why did the South leave the Union? It was solely for the right to keep slaves. The constant theme of 'States Rights" is just a gloss to keep slavery alive. How hollow their statements are. The Planter's right to own slaves is their idea of a perfect life.

What does the slave have to say? What of his rights? Nothing. The slave can say absolutely nothing. He has no right to think because the slave owners don't believe black people can think.

How absurd! Let us test their premises. Free the slaves and see how long they would work for nothing. How long will the free Negro allow himself to be whipped and subjugated? How long would a Negro man endure seeing his wife and children being sold?

I know in my heart that the day will come when Negro soldiers march into the heartland of the South. When the Negro man raises that rifle and aims at the Planter does the Planter still believe the Negro man can't think? He will indeed think, and he will blow the Planter to Hell.

Woe to the South I pray for the day when their pride and boasts are utter ashes. Their famed mansions will burn with all the dross of their false civilization. Utter doom will be their reward for the chains that they clamped on free human beings. I pray for the day when Southern belles are stripped of their finery. Let them walk their ruined plantations naked without the clothes that they have gleaned from the toil of slaves. Let the tears run down their faces like the tears of a thousand Black mothers. Black mothers who have shed them when their very children are ripped from their breasts and sold for mammon. Their day is coming, and I pray for that day.

How brutal we have all become. I am a simple farm girl who wants to see people blown to hell. God forgive the hardness in my heart. Yet slaves must become free even if every Southern must die. How can any human believe that taking humans for slaves has forfeited their right to live. I will stand on that belief until the day I die.

Love

Mary

Chapter Sixty-Three

September 10,1862

Dear Mary

On August 30-31 the Union lost the Second Battle of Bull Run. Once again our Union Army took flight toward Washington. My shame runs a mile deep. When will we get proper leaders? Thousands of our men lay dead on hallowed ground because of the errors of our commanders.

The troops are fighting at a fierce level, but our leaders do not direct this awesome body of soldiers. Our leaders do not deserve one drop of blood from these fallen giants. I am so angry I can barely contain myself.

I killed six Southern officers in two days. Three Rebels each day. This is a poor harvest. Sharpshooters must not let the main lines fall back too far. We must have distance behind our main battle line.

I was constantly falling back, and this does not allow me to pick the right ground from which I can shoot the enemy. At times, our Union lines were falling back so fast that I barely survived.

Actually "falling back" is not the correct phrase. Most of our troops were running toward Washington as fast as humans could run. Joe was my infallible rock. During the storm, he knows where to go. If I stumble he quickly drags me on my feet again. I trust him without thought. If I live through this war it will be because of Joe.

Joe is a master of surviving. He does not look like much. His dress is beyond bad. However, at this trade of war he is vastly superior to our Generals. He is cool under pressure, and he can see the value of terrain. He has saved my life many times.

When I was so exhausted by flight he kept me moving. He told me to think of my sweetheart and run another hundred yards. Think of my mother and run another hundred yards. Think of your home and run a hundred yards. I ran and ran because Joe did not leave me.

Finally, Joe stopped, and I collapsed on the ground: We had reached safety. Only then did Joe give me sips of water until I cooled off. It took me about two hours to gain control of my body. God only knows how many miles we ran.

My morale is at a low level. The morale of our main troops is beyond bad. It approaches utter despair. Our Generals at the highest levels are quarreling between themselves as to who was to blame for this shameful battle. From my viewpoint there is little doubt on this point. General Pope on the front line waited for McClellan and his reinforcement of troops.

McClellan moved as always: at a snail's pace. Finally, he quit moving at all. This left his generals hanging on the main battle lines and this directly led to the Union defeat. The words of my partner Joe are not fit for print. I share his opinion but not his words.

General Lee of the Southern forces did not dilly dally. He struck immediately and the Union Army folded. Our Union Army was completely out general-ed. Clearly General Lee easily maneuvered our forces and inflicted this terrible defeat. This defeat will give ammunition to Lincoln's enemies.

It is true that General Lee is a brilliant commander, but he is not God. He has made mistakes, and he will again. Lee has yet to face a General to match his steel. Our Army in the West is doing well. I hope Washington takes note of that brighter light.

By being the mouse in the corner, I have been able to get some numbers of this battle, and these are probably correct. The Union troops numbered about 70,000 and the Southern army had about 55,000. The Union losses are around 14,000. It is believed that the Confederacy lost about 8,000. This clearly is a massive Union defeat.

If the country can hang on we will surely have victory in the longer run. I have heard how troops must have courage to win. There is some truth to this but what does one say of the soldier who stands and fights when the position is lost?

Many of our troops did exactly that and they lay dead on ground they did not retreat from. Most troops are brave enough. It is their combined force that must be directly by our generals. This is the critical point.

The rumors are flying that Lee will refit and attempt to invade the North. If Lee does this and can have a big victory then the cause of the Union might be lost. Many Union Generals are defeatists, and they are of no asset to our cause of Union/slavery. Heads will roll after this defeat, and I feel McClellan should be first in line.

He refused to put his troops into the battle claiming he had to defend Washington. This is a total lie. Washington is well defended and cannot be overcome. At the very least McClellan should be removed. He has caused the deaths of thousands of Union troops, and I would be hard pressed to see where McClelland has done any good for the North at all.

Pray for me and pray for our troops. Our Army is at low tide. I hope this victory causes Lee to get a big head. I hope and believe that Lee's Waterloo is coming. Mary do not forget my love for you. I fight only because I believe I must. I am aware that good causes sometimes lose.

I believe the Union will prevail, but I have no understanding of why I feel that way. Despite this terrible defeat Colonel Hunt believes we will be re-fitted to face another battle shortly.

Love,

Ray

CHAPTER SIXTY-FOUR

September 20, 1862

Dearest Ray

This setback has struck me to the core. We must hang on. We have no choice. If the Union Army fails then the Union will fail. If the Union falls then slavery will cover the new hemisphere. As long as possible we must girt ourselves and go forward. You are my brave soldier. All I know how to do is to support you, love you totally, and desperately wish you were in my arms.

Where do all the men come from to die in these numbers? These terrible losses of men and yet armies can fight on. Surely both countries will run out of men. I ask myself: why does this war have to go on? This is madness. Slavery is madness. Does the greed of the South need slavery to make their profits? The South is guilty. The Planter's profits come from the body, blood and souls of enslaved human beings. May the South burn for eternity!

Ray, I have had a dream lately and it has occurred three times. I see a massive Union Army burning a path of destruction through the heartland of the Confederacy. I see plantations destroyed, mansions converted to ashes, and huge cities burning. I see this Army ravishing the land in a huge swath. Anything eatable is being taken to feed this Army. Civilians are driven to utter despair.

I see thousands of slaves coming from the South to seek the protection of this Army. I see citizens of the South starving. It is a fearful sight. This dream has a clarity I have never had before. I don't know the future and I don't believe in the truth of dreams. How I would love this dream to become reality! I hope the Union takes the war to the heart of the South and burns everything in its path.

Father is certain that the South will invade the North. All the Southern papers are encouraging such a move. Father says we cannot lose another major battle, or the Union will be lost. Father believes a major point of this war is near. He feels it will be within two weeks.

The South believes that Lee cannot be beaten, and Father says pride goes before the fall. How deeply I hope he is right. Father says he is close to a project that would allow him to make a difference to this war. He is certain the war has at least two more years. I am sure he will step forward with some plan.

Love,

Mary

CHAPTER SIXTY-FIVE

September 25-1862

Dear Mary

Father was quite correct about Lee's Army attempting to invade the North. The battle of Antietam was on September 17, 1862, in Maryland. Today was a banner day for my sharpshooting. It had been a busy day. I had killed four officers and at the end of the day as the light was fading Joe spotted a small group of officers about 750 yards. They were nearly on the crest of a hill. It seemed to be a group of 6 or 7. The shadows were lying long on the hillside and the only rider I could see clearly was on the right hand of the group in a narrow ray of sunshine.

I asked Joe whether I should shoot. He said they were officers and to take the shot at the rider we could see. I made my adjustments and put the crosshairs in the center of his head. This gave me some margin. If the range was longer than we judged I would still hit his chest.

The wind had no current as is quite common in early evening. I did not need to worry about the wind drifting my bullet. When Joe said to take him, I squeezed off the shot. The officer was hit right where I aimed, and his head exploded. His body instantly slid from his saddle as dead as a stone. Joe and I moved to our second spot immediately.

All the remaining officers fled at high speed except one. He had dismounted and was raising the victim's body. I would have shot again but the shadow had drifted, and I could not see well enough to shoot. This kill was my final officer of the day. Joe and I went back to our camps in the early darkness. I had barely reached my rack before a private told me that the Colonel wanted to see me right away. This was unusual and I wondered what I had done wrong. I will try to recall what was said.

"Corporal how many men did you kill today."

"I answered that I had killed five officers that day."

"Did you kill an officer late in the day?"

"Yes Sir, I killed an officer that was part of a group of officers on a hillside during early evening. The officer I shot was the only one in clear light."

"Joe was with you when you made the shot?"

"Yes, Joe was with me, and we worked as a team as is normal. I took the shot, and it was a perfect head shot. Of course, the man was dead when he hit the ground. Sir, have I done anything wrong? We knew he was an officer of the enemy, and I shot him." By this time, I was getting nervous.

"No, you have done nothing wrong. You killed one of the most valuable officers in the Confederate Army. You killed General Branch who came from a highly esteemed family in the South. He had been a three-time Congressman and one of the most educated of their officers in the entire army. The loss of this officer was extremely demoralizing to the South.

The news of his death filtered from Confederate skirmishers to our skirmishers nearly immediately. Listen to me carefully. I will be with you but be aware that General McClellan wants to see you at our evening staff meeting.

I am sure you are receiving a battlefield promotion. Ideally you should only say "Yes Sir or No Sir" and take what he gives you. Then bow out immediately. Do you understand?"

"Yes Sir"

"Report to me in exactly one hour. You are dismissed."

I left immediately. My present circumstances were dire. My head was spinning. I was to meet the top General in the entire army, and I am a girl. If someone sensed my gender then I would be busted of all rank and thrown out of the army. When the press got a hold of the story, the army would make a laughingstock of the nation.

I did not have a clean uniform to wear. My uniform was dirty from the day's work, but I could only go on.

I met the Colonel at the appointed hour.

The Colonel was sharp with me.

"Is that the best uniform you have?"

"Yes Sir."

"Well, in this case it might work." He replied.

The Colonel took me into the staff tent and saluted General McClelland.

"Sir, this is Corporal Summerfield the sharpshooter who killed General Branch."

General McClelland turned to me, and I sharply saluted him.

"Sir, Corporal Summerfield reporting Sir"

McClellan turned to me and looked me over. I was determined to look him in the eye. If I was to be booted out I wanted to face it head on.

"So, you were the sharpshooter that killed General Branch."

"Yes Sir, I am."

"Your uniform looks pretty rough, but I like to see soldiers that are here to do their job and not afraid to get dirty."

I said nothing.

"How far was the general and where did you hit him?"

"Sir he was 750 yards, and I hit him in the head."

"That was one hell of a shot Corporal. How many soldiers have you killed in this war?"

"Sir, I have killed 14 officers and four enlisted men Sir."

"Corporal, I wish we had more of you. I am promoting you with a battlefield commission to second lieutenant. You have surely earned it. Colonel Hunt will do the details. You are dismissed."

"I saluted and said, "Thank you Sir."

I turned immediately and went to the distant dark side of the large tent. That was that. My secret was still safe. As always I was the attentive mouse in the dark corner. After the meeting I rejoined Colonel Hunt. On the way back he said:

"Well, lieutenant you conducted yourself well and I congratulate you on your rapid advancement. I will tell one of the guards to set up a separate tent for you. From here on out you will be living alone. If you need a service feel free to address any of my guards to assist you. If any of the enlisted men present any difficulty to you let me know immediately."

"Thank you Sir."

That was that. I will add the details of the battles as I understand them.

It was rumored that Lee had political goals which he hoped to exploit by a battlefield victory. He hoped by a victory to achieve international recognition from England or France. In addition, Lee had hopes of possibly sacking Washington and thus bringing the war to an end. Third, Lee wanted to take the war to the North rather than fight on the tired land of Virginia. He also had hopes that Maryland (a slave state) would join him in arms and secede from the Union. On all these points thank God he gained not a one.

At Antietam, Maryland the two armies clashed. General McClellan claims a massive victory, but the rub is that he did not commit all his troops. He had several chances to destroy Lee's Army, and he let Lee's Army slip away intact. It is true in a limited sense that it was a Union battlefield victory. Lee was forced to retire from the battlefield. Yet it was a hollow victory. Not only did McClellan fail to destroy Lee, he did not follow up and he would probably have won the war.

For a brief time, Lee had less than 12,000 soldiers facing the Union Army with 120,000 men McClellan was so slow he allowed Lee to gather his split command which allowed him to put up a real fight. McClellan's generals did a respectable job of gaining their objectives in the view of battlefield surprises.

This event takes into consideration reverses brought on by new Rebel armies being fed into the battle. However, the Union Army takes its cues from McClellan. He sent his troops into the battle in pieces thus allowing Lee to defeat them in pieces. Had McClellan committed his forces properly the Rebel Army would have been destroyed.

Therefore, Lee's Army lived to fight another day because of McClellan's lack of courage to attack. This so-called victory came at a huge loss of Union soldiers. The Union lost around 12,000 and Lee lost around 10,000. This was a battle of failed opportunities.

I fear many thousands of Union lives with be lost on future battlefields because McClellan did not have the courage to attack with all his troops. As always McClellan claimed he was facing an army of 120,000 when in fact Lee had around 50,000.

This is a constant and deadly trait of McClellan. He sees phantom enemy armies despite all evidence. The evidence was very plentiful. The Union Army was given deserters by the hands full, our own scouts, and direct field observations of his own line officers. McClellan even was given Lee's entire battle plans by chance.

Even with Lee's battle plans McClellan moved so slowly it was fatal to our success. Lee gathered his widespread forces before McClellan even moved. We lost thousands of good soldiers because they were led by a bad soldier.

The terrain was good for my work. I was able to get a good standoff range of around 600 yards. This is a solid distance that combines distance (which is safety) with the shooter above and behind the battle line. The word "safely" must be taken with salt. There are counter-shots from the ranks of the Rebels. Many of these shooters are excellent shots.

Death is never far on a battlefield. Rebel cannons are a huge risk. The cannon can make a midair explosion that throws storms of hot iron that kills by the dozen. As sharpshooters we cannot avoid that risk. With Joe as my spotter, we were able to engage targets quickly. Using our standard shoot and move tactic we had good success. I killed four officers that day. In a couple of cases I shot leaders that took command after I killed their true officers.

Although I tell of four kills this is not without deep moral pain in my heart. These are humans I am killing. They are someone's son, someone's brother or someone's husband. We must never become so cold that we do not regret this war and regret the deaths of those who are our enemies. I kill because I must.

I must do my best to save the Union and obtain freedom for the Negros. This is a skill that I must use. One can see immediately the behavior of the troops when they lose their officer. Typically, the rate of fire goes down because they are looking for guidance.

The troops often fall back on the line as if there is more safety further behind the old firing line. In rare cases part of the line simply runs away. However, the forces of the South seldom run. They fight like tigers. It is strange because the average Rebel does not own any slaves and never will. The deserters tell us they are fighting because we are in "their country."

They seldom have been far from home. Most have never been more than 20 miles from home. Washington is like another planet for these unlettered simpletons. They never have had a sense of the

United States as a whole. What they really mean is that they are fighting "invaders".

The common soldier seems to take pride because he is not at the bottom of the social levels. The Negro slave is the absolute bottom. It must be clearly understood that the lower-class whites in the South are even more racist than the Planter class.

The greatest thing about this battle is that Lincoln announced the Emancipation Proclamation. On January 1, 1863, this frees all slaves in the Rebel states. Our greatest goal of freeing the slave is now clearly on the table. Lincoln's enemies are in a red fury. However, the fateful word "emancipation" has been uttered and nothing will put it back in the bottle. Now we must win the war, or this proclamation will be moot. Nevertheless, I have lived to see a great thing. At last, there is a legal basis for Negro freedom. I hope I live to see you again.

Love

Ray

CHAPTER SIXTY-SIX

Oct 6, 1862

Dear Ray

The battle of Antietam will be known as the greatest loss of life in one day of combat in Civil War history thus far. The figures now available are 12,000 killed and wounded on the Union side and 10,000 for the Confederate side. It seems that the Union Army numbered right at 87,000 and the Confederate side numbered around 45,000. Again, our generals refused to throw the weight of the entire army on the battlefield at once.

The death of General Branch by a sharpshooter was in all the papers. Thank God your name was not mentioned. Your father was very proud of your promotion to the officer class. However, father seemed somewhat depressed at the death of General Branch. Perhaps he will communicate with you later.

We outnumbered the rebels nearly two to one. We must pray that Lincoln can find the proper General to fight winning battles and destroy Lee's Army. Again, Lee's army was able to slip away. Most of the Union newspapers are playing down the Emancipation Proclamation and playing up the stopping of Lee's troops in his invasion of the North. Of course, both successes are of tremendous value.

Father told me that the Southern papers are no longer claiming that one Rebel can defeat five Yankees. The fantasy of the superiority of the Southern troops has been proven wrong on many battlefields. The Northern troops have proven to be more than a match for the South. Even Northern Cavalry has developed to such a degree that the Southern Cavalry is not making its boasts of domination as in former times. The North is learning its skills, and all the Union lacks is the right general to direct this force to crush Lee's army.

Father does not expect much more fighting this warm season. Our current Generals choose any reason not to fight and every reason to retreat into winter quarters. Father believes the year 1863 will be a year of great battles and desperate times for both the North and the South. He is convinced that the war will last until 1865 at the very least.

War weariness has settled into the bones of the Northern people. The South is facing the same challenges with her population deploring the price of this war. Simple endurance may be the key to which side wins the war. Both sides are stumbling like drunk boxers.

I pray the North can see that the future of the New World depends on who wins this Civil War. We must believe in the verdict of God on this issue. The curse of slavery will either have explosive growth or slavery will end forever. These are the only two viable options. The North must hang on so that its former losses will not be in vain.

We of the North must honor our dead by winning this war and freeing the slaves. The Northern population must consider the lives that have fallen on many battlefields. Their blood demands that we must stay the course. I believe in my heart that the North will prevail in this horrible conflict.

I want to share with you father's plan for helping the simple Union soldiers in this horrific conflict. He purchased the large Miller holdings from Widow Miller. This property abuts a part of father's holdings. Upon the property are several very large buildings. He is converting these buildings to take at least 250 wounded soldiers for rest and treatment. Father has hired four experienced doctors/surgeons from Canada. These doctors have already signed contracts.

He chose married doctors who will then have their families. They will be open for business on January 1, 1863. He has made all the necessary contacts in Washington D.C. to obtain the proper certification and paperwork to function as an approved government medical facility.

Also, the hospital needed Government approval for a national cemetery on hospital grounds. Unfortunately, many of the patients will not survive their wounds. All these costs are being paid by father. He feels this is the best way he can help the cause of the Union. He is grim daily but this decision to build these hospitals has raised his morale greatly.

The White House has expressed profound gratitude for this facility and has promised full government cooperation. President Lincoln himself sent a small, signed note with his signature. The note was also signed by Secretary of War Stanton. Both the President Lincoln and the Secretary of War noted that your son Ray is serving in the Army as a sharpshooter and again thanked father for his support of the aims of this war and they again expressed their thanks.

The hired doctors will have the latest medical equipment and supplies that money can buy. He houses the doctors in the former Miller home which has always been noted for its luxuries and comfort. The doctors will be furnished with a full-working household staff to cater to their every need. All the aides and caregivers will be hired from the surrounding population.

Father says this facility will be second to none in the North. The construction crews are already refitting the buildings for their future work. He has thrown his full energies into making this faculty a true diamond of modern health care. How blessed we are to have a father willing to give this service.

Mother approves of this venture with all her heart. She believes that being of service will help her daily worries and fears for your life. Many of the soldiers that come to this hospital will be saved because they will receive the best care available at this facility. Father has indicated that if the facility needs more doctors he will find them and entice them to come here.

Ray, please come home to me. I am so afraid of losing you. I could not go on without you. Keep writing to me. There is no need to color a rosy picture. Tell me what is truly in your heart. I need you to in my arms. I would work at your feet for the rest of my life if that were what it would take to get you home alive. My fear is growing with every battle. I am lost. I don't know the future. Rachel, I am so alone without you.

I have never been strong like you but no-one on earth could love you more than I do. You are everything to me. Please come home when this horrible ordeal is over.

All my Love

Mary

CHAPTER SIXTY-SEVEN

October 15-1862

Dear Mary

Thank you for your uplifting letters. There is nothing that is treasured more than mail. A letter is a breath of paradise to the soldier. This is true regardless of the soldier's rank. I often overhear officers telling another officer that they just received a letter from home and were in tears to receive them. Without letters for the soldiers, I believe they would go insane. That is certainly true in my case.

My parents should take great pride in forming this new hospital. I have not heard of any private person who has performed such a service. The wounded soldier has a good chance if he can get medical care. I am sure many lives will be saved and my parents should take great pride in their effort. I am so proud of my parents I could burst. I hope beyond hope that I can return home alive and in good health.

I would like to tell you a little about my life between battles. As the aid de camp I do not live as badly as the main line soldiers. I do not socialize in any way with anyone. I am regarded as a stone-cold assassin. I encourage that thought. As such I am an outsider.

Sharpshooters are generally not liked by the rank-and-file soldiers. It is felt I am not taking the same risks as battle line soldiers. Sharpshooters take very high risks but not in the same manner as the line soldier. The line soldier has the sense of seeing the man who might kill him. It is felt both adversities stand on equal footing. To be killed by a sharpshooter is to never see the man who killed them. They resent this type of killing and they dislike sharpshooters.

This attitude is extremely helpful to me. I never talk to my mates unless directly addressed. Even then the answer is extremely short. On rare occasions that I am approached in a friendly manner I just coldly brush them off. I let it be known that I do not want friends.

Since I have been promoted to officer rank there is much less chance of interaction with the troops. I never talk about my personal life or my background. I tell the friendly person I don't like idle talk and to stay away from me.

Basically, I am rude. Often I act like I didn't hear the question or comment. I often play deaf mute. Sharpshooters by nature are silent. After the first week or two I am just ignored. The Colonel knows of this attitude, but he says nothing.

I do my job and that is all that matters to him. Officers know this attitude very well. It is exactly the relationship between an officer and an enlisted man. They have basically no personal interaction at all. Thank God for my promotion.

Some may wonder how it was possible for me to hide my gender. I will put some thoughts down in no special order. The truth of the matter is that it is not easy. Calls of nature can be trained to late hours when one is apt to be alone. Being small is the key to long term suppression as to being a woman.

When a person is seen as small then further attention does not seem warranted. For some reason when a person sees a small soldier they dismiss them from their thought. Maybe it is because a small person is not seen as a threat to the larger person.

Wearing a uniform that is mildly too large is helpful. The main factor is living quietly. Do not mix with the other troops. Maintain a demeanor of aloneness. Most soldiers talk because they do not want to be alone. When the talker is speaking to someone who does not cultivate this relationship they simply tire and move on.

I have small breasts that I can bind with wound bandages. Hiding gender would be much more difficult for a woman with a large bust or a large bottom. Another factor is the manpower shortage. Officers do not see what they do not want to see. This is why mere children were able to serve. I learned that the roundness of hip and bottom is my greatest problem. The only approach to that problem is the oversized uniform.

In addition, Army food is such that one did not gain weight. The norm is a slimmer body. After a while, a persona is made of a person who does not stand out, does not socialize, and does not seek company. Ones every habit is to stay as low key as possible. Another factor was the turnover of personnel.

The costs of battle make it easier not to get involved with anyone because so many are getting killed or wounded. Another point should be made. As noted, I gained rank very rapidly. This means I outranked all enlisted soldiers. It was well understood that higher ranks were not associated with lower ranks. That made it easier to pull off the "aloneness."

My relationship with Colonel Hunt is strictly business. I do not ask off topic questions and I do what he wants done. I speak only when I am spoken to. I do not speak at all beyond that point. I don't ask for favors of any kind. I don't chat and I don't gossip. I don't complain about anything. I have learned that when a higher officer finds a person good enough to do this job and is not a chatter box he wants to hang on to him.

Between campaigns Colonel Hunt engages me as a personal secretary for him. The paperwork of an officer on the general staff is mountainous. A large percentage of the paperwork is not critical. The Colonel answers such things as changes of personnel letters, letters to quartermasters, letters to concerned family members, letters of promotion, and so on.

The direst duty is writing a family that their son/husband/lover was killed in action. This is a form letter although if time can be taken I try to add a personal sentence. After about two weeks I was writing all such letters, and the Colonel just proofreads a few of them. The most important aptitude is not gossiping. Soldiers are the worst gossipers in the entire world.

That is particularly true of soldiers in winter camps. The personal flaw of gossiping is by no means an activity of the enlisted soldiers alone. Gossiping between officers is endemic. Naturally not all gossip is neutral. Officers commonly back stab other officers for influence or promotion. Officers, like any human, are fond of complements.

The activity called "buttering up" is surprisingly effective with officers of high egos. I learned that one never gives flattery. Good officers' distain being "buttered up." It is the bad officers that reward flattery.

When an officer has a good secretary good things can happen. Since I don't ask for anything Colonel Hunt will often give me small things. Officers are observant, they know their soldiers and how they get along. It is easy for an officer to make life easier in myriad ways. For example, the officer might give guard duty to a favored soldier at a better time. Small things can be done in a thousand ways. It is ironic that by asking for nothing one often gets some things.

By being silent it is common for other officers to confide in me occasionally. The officer, like anyone, is often lonely and they like to ease their burdens by commenting to a trusted aid de camp or a secretary. This type of relationship is worth gold to the officer.

Like any other aid de camp I still polish boots. I often lay out uniforms applicable to the occasion. I commonly polish his saber. I serve him his meals. None of this is onerous.

Winter camps are horribly boring. To keep the troops from killing each other they must be kept busy. Typically, that means drilling all day. The soldier learns the skills he will need during the fighting season during the boring times in the winter. The last thing I want is drill.

As far as current military actions are concerned, I know nothing. As far as actions next year it is the consensus of the officers that 1863 is going to be brutal. By this time, the armies have a solid core of seasoned soldiers. Likewise, the officers overall have gained much experience in handling large numbers of men. This means the battles will probably be bloodier and the overall cost of battles will be grim.

The refitting of troops, supplies, and mount replacement is going on at great speed. The trade of sharpshooting will be more and more dangerous. The remaining sharpshooters have been proven in battle. They will not make beginner mistakes. The poor sharpshooters by now are dead or wounded.

Sharpshooters also take large losses. Part of the reason is that sharpshooters are often close to artillery. The artillery in battle is commonly dueling with enemy artillery. This means a lot of air bursts near the artillery batteries. Sharpshooters are commonly killed by this random shooting because they are in the general area of artillery.

There is little a sharpshooter can do to defend himself from air bursts. Joe and I have talked about these issues at great length. We mutually agree to try to place ourselves as far from artillery batteries as we reasonably can.

The downside of this tactic is that it means enemy sharpshooters will see those isolated shots and realize instantly they are from sharpshooters. Thus, we are going to make a strong effort to shoot between small cracks in the rocks to give us more direct safety. In war I have learned that it is easy to get killed.

Luck has saved more soldiers than talent. The truth is that every soldier does the best he can and whatever happens will happen. The fatalism of soldiers is universal.

Mary my love, I miss you so much. It seems I have been away from you for ages. I still remember every inch of your body and I wish I could be home to enjoy you. The hours of our passions are burned into my memory. I want to smother you with kisses. I am dizzy with desire. The sooner this horrible war is over the sooner I can come home.

Please don't forget me Mary. You are my entire world. I know I must be here doing my best to help save the Union and defeat slavery. This is my duty, and I must fill it. Yet I am so lonely, and I want you so bad.

Love

Ray

CHAPTER SIXTY-EIGHT

December 20, 1862

Dear Mary

On December 13, 1862, our Union Army suffered a horrible loss to the Rebels at Fredericksburg Virginia. This battle is painful to write about. General Burnside led the Union Army, and the South was led by Robert Lee. This was a classic case of young men dying because stupid men led them. Burnside attempted to take a strongly held position using the same old frontal assaults that have never failed to be complete losses. There was no element of surprise, and our troops had to assault a long upward hill.

On the crest of the hill the Confederate Army waited behind a stone wall to butcher them. Of course, it was butchery. To compound the error of the first assault Burnside made several others. All total losses. Burnside ordered thousands of brave young men to charge an impossible position, and they were destroyed. Rumor came across from the Rebel side that General Lee could not believe any General would be stupid enough to try to take that hill.

Nevertheless, the Union Army did have someone that stupid and his name was General Burnside. As seems to be standard with the

Union Army when Burnside was licked he ran back toward Washington to reform. Would the Union Army ever find a General that understood basic tactics? At the general staff meeting it was the same debate as who was responsible for this debacle.

Thankfully, the debate was short because everyone agreed that Burnside was totally responsible. The raw numbers are grim. The Union Army had about 120,000 and the South had 80,000. The Union suffered 12,000 losses to 5000 for the South. It is the most lopsided battle to date. The Northern papers savaged Lincoln and Burnside. Lincoln is trying to find some general that can fight and win in the East. I certainly pray for that day.

Love

Ray

CHAPTER SIXTY-NINE

January 7, 1863

Dear Ray

This is a proud moment for the United States. President Lincoln's Emancipation Proclamation went into effect on January one. All slaves in Rebel states are now and forever free. Of course, this decree can only become effective if the North wins the war. The Southern papers are in an outrage over this action.

Jefferson Davis is calling it the most dam able document in the history of mankind. Abolitionists like Garrison and Douglas are overjoyed. Most of the people of the North took this event in calm stride.

It is unfortunately true that most people of the North are still not interested in freeing the slaves. The overriding interest is to bring this horrible war to an end.

As always the Democrats are beside themselves in a terrible rage. They are hoping they will return to power in the fall when the national elections will be held.

The Democratic traitors are wearing the broad yellow strip of cowards. They are the social rot that is feeding upon the bottom tier of our Union. They bring dishonor to the cause of universal freedom for every human color in the world.

Our father is deeply concerned about the direction of the war. He feels we need some big victories this year to keep the Northern hopes alive. Both the South and the North are reeling with war sickness. The Southern papers are now carrying articles that criticize Jefferson Davis.

Separate states are talking about rejoining the North. These states claim that each state can do this under the authority of "States Rights." It appears that a confederacy is fine if they are winning but not so good when they might lose.

The Northern blockage is stopping the flood of cotton to England. This means in simple terms the South is going broke. The Southern currency has no practical value. Northern greenbacks and gold are secretly becoming the de facto currency of the South. There are now mountains of cotton sitting upon the docks with no legal market.

The blockage is killing the South financially. The real business money in the South knows they cannot exist without trading with the North. New Orleans is legally selling some cotton to the North with dubious authority of the United States. The North is not thinking clearly. Any United States currency will enrich the South and allow them to buy war materials to fight us. How illogical can one be?

Love Always,

Mary

CHAPTER SEVENTY

June 24, 2016

I and Ann spent many hours upon the swing on Rachel's porch. The gentle beguiling movement seemed to encourage deeper thought and surprising contentment. We were both engrossed in this story of passion, love, gender and war. We wondered how many times in history lovers have been separated by the fearful demands of war. How many times did women conceal their gender to serve their country? These personal journals gave amazing insight into the times and pressures of people who lived in the confusing disturbing times of the 1860s'.

The curse of slavery seemed to run like a rapid infection through the social body. To Ann and me it was still amazing that logical human beings could justify the most dreadful condition of man: namely slavery.

That the South would hold on to this inhuman system for as long as it did was truly amazing and sobering. Even at the cost of 620,000 men who died in this conflict the South would have maintained the war if they had the physical means. It was not until Lee was completely decimated did he sought to end the conflict.

They agreed the shadow of racism and sexism still exists today. There is still a corrupt thread twisting and winding through social classes. America now has gated communities, and they certainly do not contain blacks. Indeed, there is more separation of the races now than there was in the 1960s. Red lining to housing is still a secret reality. Private clubs still have unspoken but real racism. The unwritten assumptions of behavior based on age, gender and skin color alone still exist in real time.

For example, young black males are assumed to be dangerous without any actions or signs of aggression. Stereotypes still held sway over race and gender issues. If any member of the Planter class was to talk to the average American of today the conversation would be easily understandable.

The educated cultured voice of the Planter would be clear and mannered. It was as if the South had blinkers on their eyes which caused them to not see the inhumanity of slavery. It was astonishing to see their collective blindness.

To us the utter fury of the South leading up to the Civil War was difficult to understand in this modern era. This rage had to come from deep-seated doubts as to the rightness of their beliefs about slavery. In many ways the entrenched racism of the past and present is not very different from the taboos against same gender love. The battle against lesbianism is still going on. Sometimes the social climate is liberal and permissive.

At other times, the social attitude is regressive and cruel. But always the social climate is unpredictable and unclear. Lesbians must swim in changing water. Naturally, social attitudes are not always going in a progressive manner. The world is not going constantly upward.

This is not an example of people becoming freer and more tolerant. It is quite possible for a liberal era to lose freedom when the society is swayed by a regressive group. Rights can be easily reversed or even lost.

Much of this has to do with the Christian religion. When modern pressures seem too much to bear then the return to rigid simplistic religion is attractive. Fundamentalism is alluring to those who face a world that is changing and becoming increasingly complex.

These troubled people need to find simple and understandable rules of life because modern life is so overwhelming.

During Civil War times persecution toward lesbian love was rigid. Conformity was nearly total. The luxury to go one's own way did not exist. The assumption of gender station was nearly total. The women stayed home and raised families.

Decisions and authority rested with the husband alone. Divorce was rare and the women seldom used the courts for relief. There was no reasonable way for women to be financially independent. The few employers who might hire them were often predatory. The overwhelming belief was that women had to dependent on men alone.

The greatest crime of all was the insidious belief that women were not as intelligent as men. This fallacy had not been exposed during Rachel's and Mary's time.

In their time total submission was desired if not demanded. Sexism with its deep and ancient history of discrimination kept women under a man's heel. The primeval curse of all women was uncontrolled pregnancy. If women could not control their own bodies' freedom for women was impossible. Naturally, Christianity was involved in this social structure. Its mythology believed that God only approved male headed families.

All this drove same gender sex/love underground. The entire madness of Christianity was based on sexism, racism, and slavery in its open or overt manifestations. Open same sex love can exist only in a world of tolerance.

Without open tolerance, same gender love was nearly impossible. Lesbian love was deeply driven underground. In most states it was a punishable felony. That was the world Rachel and Mary lived in.

In Rachel's case even her desire to serve her nation had to be approached in a clandestine manner. Since only men had rights Rachel had no choice except to cloak herself as a man. Ann pointed out that female freedom only began to grow when birth control was possible. Men could enjoy sex, but the woman constantly existed in fear that she would become pregnant. The condition of pregnant meant total dependency to a man.

Naturally, the fear of pregnancy reduced the enjoyment of sexual activity for women. Joyce pointed out that freedom for females only began to grow when the woman had escaped pregnancy and had options to earn a living without a man's oversight. The interest in this journal remained high. It was interesting to read an account of how a lesbian couple had to function to live through an oppressed time.

CHAPTER SEVENTY-ONE

January 14, 1863

Dear Mary

Between December 31 to January 3 a large battle called Stones River was fought in Tennessee. The North won but at great cost. The margin of "winning" was so narrow the battle is objectively a draw. Apparently the loss on each side was the highest percentage of troop fighting so far in this terrible war.

The Union army had about 43,000 and the Confederacy fielded around 35,000. The Union had about 9000 killed and wounded. The South on this scale also had 9000 killed or wounded. The battle was too close to call. However, it raised the spirits of the North after the horrible Union debacle of Fredericksburg.

Many Southern losses occurred charging a fortified hill. Thereby the South made the same mistake that the Union made at Fredericksburg. In this war, assaulting fortified positions is always a disaster. One would think our stupid officers would learn that simple lesson. Even the vaulted Robert E. Lee is making that mistake, and I hope it will be fatal to the South sooner or later.

However, I am sure fatal charges upon secure positions will happen again on both sides. However, this battle cost Rebel control of middle Tennessee. So, the terrible losses did serve some purposes. Apparently the battle cost the confederate general Bragg his job.

There has been a great debate over a military draft. With the huge Union losses there are not enough volunteers to fill the ranks. The war has lost most of the glory and adventure of the first months of fighting. The bravest soldiers are already dead. The war now is close grinding combat.

This is the slow war of stark attrition. Each army trades bodies for bodies until one side runs out of bodies. Is this not a horrible thought? There are no pretty girls giving away flowers to the brave departing young men. Certainly, there are no marching bands encouraging young men to arms. The war is far beyond such simple mindless actions.

The war now is young men dying in the mud of trenches or charging stone walls with great losses. Ironically, many men who dug those trenches now lay dead in them. Trenches are handy for mass graves. To fill our emptying ranks, we need more men.

Those men are going to be compelled to do their duty. The big trick is not just getting the men but the deadly fact of training them to be good soldiers. Putting green troops in battles is simply murder.

The Confederacy started drafting one year ago. The Rebels had little choice because they cannot match the North's population numbers. There is much to be said about a citizen army, but others point out the sincere need for professional soldiers. This is one of the interesting contradictions of wars. On the one hand, one is looking for sturdy citizens who have a stake in their future but on the other hand one needs professionals to win battles and thus win wars. The divide between each premise is vast.

Love

Ray

Chapter Seventy-Two

April 16-1863

Dear Mary

The fighting season is upon us. The spring rain has moderated, and the roads are drying. As always the general officers are talking about occupying Richmond Va. Against Robert E. Lee this goal has been difficult. The Union has not seriously threatened Richmond yet. I have heard that the Army will try to go north then flank the enemy and destroy the enemy army on the spot.

Like all seasoned soldiers I am very doubtful such a plan will work. So much depends on whether our general gets all his troops in action at one time. The battles have shown that armies fed in by pieces are destroyed by pieces. It really does not matter if one outnumbers the enemy if all your assets are not in the battle at the same time.

The draft started March 3, 1863. The draft is not popular, and I have heard rumors of rioting in New York. The Union has little choice in this matter. The losses the Army has taken must be replaced by new soldiers. The grimness of this war has crushed all talk of glory.

The mathematics of war is depressing. If one assumes a 20% loss per battle then at the very best a soldier can only expect to survive five battles. Of course, some soldiers are lucky and survive at any odds. I hope to be among the lucky survivors.

It is also true that the bravest soldiers are killed first. These brave soldiers do not run, and they are killed at a higher rate. Thus, these fine men usually die first. Officers do not escape these risks. Typically, officer losses are about two times the rate of the enlisted soldier. The officer is the most exposed and they are constantly rallying soldiers in the most dangerous spots. As a practical matter, officers on horseback are above most of the ground smoke and therefore are a target for soldiers looking for someone to shoot.

My own work as a sharpshooter exploits this weakness. As noted earlier killing an officer during a battle causes confusion and confusion can often be exploited by our Army. General officers get killed at a fast pace because the common United States soldiers have a reputation of "shooting at the braid." The eyes of the nation should also be watching the western fronts.

General Grant is attempting to win against Vicksburg. If Grant can take Vicksburg then Union will control all the Mississippi River. This would be a horrible blow to the South. General Grant's star seems to be rising. It would be funny if the Civil War is ended by Grant. So many charges have been made against Grant because of an alleged drinking problem. As noted earlier, the Union should make sure that Grant has more of his famous booze. He fights and he does win.

I cannot keep my mind off you. I would love to be home so I could make love to you. Please don't forget me. Remember the times when we rested upon a soft blanket hidden deep in the willows during the dog days of summer? I am so lucky to have you.

Many soldiers suffer the loss of girlfriends or even wives while they are serving their country. It is hard to love a man who has been away from his sweetheart or wife for months. The girls are usually young, and nature encourages them to wander to an available man. Please hold firm. I love you so much and the only reason I try to survive is because of you.

The battles we fight are so depressing. I do my duty, and I pull my weight. It is work that I am gifted at performing but it is hard. At times, my duties are very hard. All I seek is the restoration of the Union and the end of slavery. At this point most soldiers do not feel they are fighting for slavery.

There is racism everywhere. Sooner or later there will be black men in uniform and I am certain they will fight well. Once people see that they can do as well as us the barriers to equality will begin to go down. From a practical standpoint when a colored man kills a Rebel that is one less man the Northern white soldier must deal with.

There is an also a great secret in this Army. Suicide is quite common among the troops. The horror of war just overcomes some men. The wounds of war can be both physical and mental. This causes them to seek final relief through suicide.

Others choose this death when they learn that their sweethearts have traded them for another man who is available. Take away a soldier's hope and he is often a dead man.

War is such a horrible place no-one has the right to judge another. The reality is that when a soldier loses a girl or wife the soldier often loses his life as well. With no hope and facing dashed dreams he often seeks his own death. On a battlefield it is easy to die and if the soldier seeks death he will find it without any trouble. Father and mother should be able to get plenty of patients before long. I fear the cost of these coming battles is going to be high.

Love,

Ray

Chapter Seventy-Three

April 29,1863

Dear Ray

I will never leave you nor will I betray you. Mother and I look at your picture daily so that we will never lose our memory of your features. It is I who will probably be a disappointment to you when you return. In the short time you have been gone I fear I have aged several years from the strain and the worry.

We have been informed by Washington that battles are coming soon and to prepare to receive patients. We are as ready as we can be. The doctors are present, and we have young women ready to step into this service. We have a vast storeroom of dressings and medical supplies of all kinds.

Mother and Father have been clear that I must continue my studies full time. I am allowed only a few hours a week to work in our hospital. Both parents held the wish that I was not to work in the hospital at all.

I did my best to ask for a few hours of war service and with their misgiving they agreed to a limited role for me in the hospital. My duties will consist in writing letters to loved ones from soldiers too injured to write for themselves.

Of course, I am aware that many of our soldiers cannot read or write. I would read letters from home to them and conversely I would write their thoughts to their loved ones. I feel I would be performing a service to these young men by helping them to reach out to their sweethearts, friends, and families.

I accept this duty because I know I could only endure the vision of horrible war wounds for a short time. I fear I would be so traumatized that I would not be a worthy person for you. I am not strong like you. Mother and Father insist that this reading and writing service would fill a huge emotional need for the men.

I have thought about our parents' loving demands and I will respect their judgment. I love our entire family so much. They have accepted me totally and I would do nearly anything to help any member. They all accept my total love for you, and they tactfully respect our intimate sexual actions.

Mother told me that with mature thought she realized she had no right to condemn love between two people regardless of gender or age. She said love is too precious to criticize. I hugged her for a long while. All I could say was" thank you and thank you."

Your mother said "My dear daughter let us not worry about small things. All these private issues are between the lovers and God."

What did I do to be blessed by such parents? I would never do anything to hurt or disappoint them. I love you with all my heart and mind. I pray for your safety nearly every hour of the day. One day your mother saw me in the apple grove, and I was weeping. She came and placed her arm around my shoulders.

"Dear child God knows your heart. Be patient and trust in God. Neither of us knows what is to be Ray's fate. However, we know it is all in God's hands. We must give each other strength so that we can survive over the long road."

"Mother, you are so good and forgiving. I don't deserve you or Rachel. I am so frightened at times."

"My precious child I am so happy you are part of our family. Everything will work out. I don't know what that means but I know we must be patient."

Then she took me into the house for lemonade and fresh cookies. I am ashamed to say how good they tasted.

Please come home to me Ray

All my Love Forever

Mary

CHAPTER SEVENTY-FOUR

May 15, 1863

Dear Mary

A huge five-day battle has just ended. Colonel Hunt said it would be called the Battle of Chancellorsville. In anguish I must admit a massive Union loss. This loss will have a negative impact on the political and military opinion of our wounded nation. General Hooker was in command. Hooker was an aggressive leader, and the country had high hopes that he would use the huge Union Army.

The Army was trying to get past the "never move" McClellan. It appears that Lee split his limited army to attack the flanking army. This he did successfully. After Lee beat that part of the Army he rejoined his troops to attack the main body of the Union Army. It appears that Hooker lost his nerve and then lost the battle. It was a shameful defeat.

Colonel Hunt was extremely angry because Hooker forced him to break up his cannon batteries. This meant the power of the artillery was diluted to the point that it was of limited help during the battle.

I don't believe I have ever seen the colonel so angry. I did my best to be of service to him and I tipped toed around him.

Joe and I remained with the main body of the Union Army. Since our Artillery was spread out there was less cannon fire on our position than normal. Joe and I were able to do good work over the four days we were in contact with the enemy.

I killed three officers the first day, one officers the second day, two officers the third day and two officers on the fourth day. The complete list showed seventeen officer kills. It was a good result for Joe and me.

As always after a Union defeat we shamefully retreated toward Washington. It took about three days to get some order in the demoralized troops. I have no official word, but I doubt if Hooker will get another chance at this level of command.

It appears that Hooker had a strong advantage for a short while but was too fearful to take his chance. The basic battle numbers are as follows: 130,000 Union troops and 60,000 for the Rebels. Union losses were about 17,000 and 12,000 for the Rebels. Once again the Union had the numbers we just did not have a leader to put this complete force into action.

Splitting our Army and then feeding it against the enemy in small pieces means Lee defeated us in series. Again, we lacked a leader who would use the full force of our numbers to attack Lee at the same time. Lee is not God. He cannot make new troops out of the sky. He does not have unlimited troops. What he does have is a strong instinct to attack.

That he was willing to split his small army into two pieces goes against normal military wisdom. Lee saw that as his only chance, and he took it all the way to victory. I feel in my heart that Lee will soon blind himself with his successes. He is not above mistakes, and I feel in time he will make a major mistake.

There was one bit of good news. The famed Stonewall Jackson is dead. He was killed by friendly fire as he scouted the land in front of his nervous troops. His troops put the fatal bullets in him. Thank God that Jackson met his end. Many people in the South had the impression that Stonewall Jackson was some type of demigod. "Stonewall" was killed by bullets like any other soldier. He made a mistake, and it cost his life. I feel Lee will make his mistake in the future and that mistake may be fatal to the South.

Five days after the battle Colonel Hunt questioned me directly. He asked how well I did in this confusing battle. I told him I have made 8 officer kills in this battle. He was surprised and told me that I had been the only soldier in weeks that was truly encouraging. I openly said Joe was also a large part of the system. The colonel took that in and said:

"I am well pleased with you. If we had such talent in overall command the war would have been over by now."

"Surely not Sir"

"I hear you are a solitary man and have nothing to do with other soldiers."

"With respect Sir I have no time for idle chatter from the troops. Their attitude toward this war is different from mine."

"It has been said you don't drink, smoke, or gamble with the soldiers in the guard tent. Is that true?

"Again, with respect Sir I consider these vices to be wasted time. I prefer not to socialize. I like to be left alone to do my job. I want to help win the war. I must focus on doing my job. It takes great concentration to perform at a high level.

I always study each kill to determine what I did right and what I did wrong. I must also maintain my rifle to keep it at its highest functioning level. I need to be left alone. My job is to kill the enemy. Nothing more or less."

"How many kills have you made? How many misses during this last battle? How would you feel about a promotion to a higher rank?"

"Sir: I have killed 42 men, nearly all officers. During the last battle I missed two shots.

Sir, promotion would be an honor, but I would prefer reaching a kill number of 75 to feel comfortable about a promotion."

"You will take a promotion when I say so. When your kill list hits 60 you are ordered to report to me immediately. You are dismissed."

With that I retired to my quarters. I am a tiny cog during this war. Thank God I do not carry the large responsibilities of the higher officer ranks. It must be crushing.

You are everything to me. Without you I could not go on living. I think about you day and night. I wish for Union victory and to be in your arms again. I am not in this Army for fame or for excitement.

I never had such thoughts. I want to do my duty to bring victory to the Union. Then by far the most important thing would be to return home to your kisses and to be in your arms. I don't need promotions, medals, fame or any of that silly stuff.

I only want to be with you for the rest of my life. I am not ashamed about our passions. I thank God that He has given us such joy. Whatever the state, the church, or society says is nothing to me. God provided us with these pleasures to help us in our daily toil and our constant worries. We are not animals that come in heat blindly and recreate without conscious knowledge.

God has given us minds and bodies so that we can enjoy them to the fullest. I have nothing but pity for any person who feels lovemaking is shameful, something to be hidden, and something to never talk about. What are these fools thinking? God made us and made sex possible. Unlike animals we can fully appreciate these joys and thank God to the highest heavens for this gift.

Someday I will be home, and these questions will be academic.

Pray for me my Love,

Ray

CHAPTER SEVENTY-FIVE

May 27,1863

Dear Ray

The news of the debacle of the Chancellorsville is all over the newspapers. The cry for Lincolns head has risen to a roar. Very few people have had the fiber to defend our President. Surely no man in the country has a greater load on his shoulders. It appears the masses of people have a shallow view of this horrible war. When we win a battle the former foes praise Lincoln.

When we have a reversal they join the cry to draw and quarter our elected leader. Lincoln has never said that this war would be easy or short. The evidence clearly supports those who have constantly warned the people that the path to victory will be blocked by bitter rocks. There will be many stumbles on our way to the crest of ultimate victory. However, you and I know our cause is just and with God's help victory will be ours.

After Chancellorsville, the government has been sending patients to our hospital in steady numbers. We were forced to turn back patients once our numbers reached 300. The highest number our small hospital was designed to hold is 250. Father and mother try to shield me from the horrid reality of the direct costs of war. However, the sights, smells and sounds of the wounded are overpowering. One cannot shut one's mind and ears to this mountain of anguish. This torment has brought sickness to my soul.

Father has already appealed to Washington for permission to build a facility which would hold 250 patients who are past danger but need a good environment to finish healing. Within a week, father had the government permission to expand his mission. This need was important because those beyond danger still filled a bed that a critical case needed so badly.

The soldier in less danger could move to another area to recover. We are overflowing with the wounded and frankly the dying. We have received a letter from the hand of Lincoln himself thanking us for our service and his pledge to support us. What a blessing from a man who must be dying of sorrow.

Sadly, the burial crew has never stopped digging graves. Despite every effort, many cannot be saved. Their bodies are interned here with solemnity. I am assigned to the patients with the greatest need as far as my letter writing or reading.

It appears to be a great relief to the soldier in need. This duty also has its problems. Does one write the letter in exactly the manner that the soldier speaks or does one write with more correction and clarity? I always add a note that the letter was dictated to me and hopefully that will help the recipient.

Often I must write a letter that the dying soldier wants so badly to send. I have not broken down in tears in front of a patient yet, but I have had to leave the hospital for a few minutes to collect myself. Outside I often cover my garment with my tears.

What a horror this all is. I gather strength knowing that I am performing a vital service to the soldier. In some cases, it will be the last words that his family will receive before the patient succumbs to death. Of course, I often must-read letters from his home to a dying soldier.

This is extremely taxing upon my heart. Again, I say, I am not as strong as you are. I am doing my best, but our parents were wise to limit my exposure to this tragedy. If I had to do this duty full time I confess I would perish. It is so important that I work within my limits because I am afraid I will break down emotionally and be of little use to you when you return. Please forgive my weakness. Why dearest God must this horrible war go on?

I do have some war news that you may not have received yet. Grant has begun a siege upon Vicksburg. This is of the greatest importance. If Vicksburg falls then the Union will have complete control of the Mississippi as well as split the Confederacy into two pieces. Once again Grant has placed his name among the greatest of generals.

On June 9,1863, a huge cavalry battle between Northern and Southern troops at Brandy Station occurred. It appears to have been a draw but clearly Northern Cavalry is equal to the Confederate cavalry. It seems the Union had 11,000 troops and the South had about 10,000 involved.

J.E.B. Stuart boasts of Southern supremacy have been answered with Northern might. It is crystal clear that Stuart did not win the day. It is the belief of many that the high-water tide for Southern cavalry is past. From here on it will be the Union Cavalry that holds the high cards.

I could care less what anyone or anybody thinks of me and my love for you. With you at my side I am not afraid of the world.

With Deepest Love

Mary

CHAPTER SEVENTY-SIX

June 17, 1863

Dear Mary

Please be kind to yourself. Everyone in this sordid war has their limits. Just accept these limits as personal facts. None of this suggests you are strong or weak. The truth is that you are giving as much as you can and beyond that no human has the right to ask of you. Your service to the wounded and dying is beyond praise.

What if we lacked people such as you? The wounds and horrors of war would mean nothing, and we would have no human limit to the horrors we inflict.

People of deeper moral feelings such as you are the natural criers of human limits. People like you say this is too much. We must strive to never cross this line from human to beast. I love you so much. We all want this war to end but it is so necessary that the Union prevails.

I don't have much information but apparently a battle was fought in the Shenandoah Valley. It sounds like the Union troops under Milroy were pushed completely out of the valley. This is another sorry Union defeat. This means the Valley is still controlled by Rebel power. The Shenandoah Valley is the food basket of the Confederacy. In time we must take this Valley if we are going to win this war.

There is strong evidence that Lee is pushing Confederate forces north in another effort to bring on the final battle of the war on Northern soil. I have dreams that Lee is pushing north to win once and for all. I fear this may be true. I have had the darkest dreams lately. I look across a great plain of a mile or more and men are marching toward the ridge. During this time, the cannons roar so hard that it is difficult to think.

The rifle fire is only one constant throbbing eviscerating sound. Hundreds and then thousands of soldiers are falling. It is a monster of a battle. It is if Death is striding the land and gathering humans by the division. I don't know who is winning and who is losing. All I see is death in every direction. Pray for me my love. I am so tired and so afraid. I fear I will break down and somehow fail to do my best.

Many people say they are not afraid of death. I am afraid. I am afraid I will be ripped from you in the prime of my life. I worry I won't be there when we age and need each other more in our infirmity. I am afraid that I will not be able to enjoy a lifetime of lovemaking. I fear I will lose my humanity upon these fields of blood. I am afraid. I am afraid. I am not ashamed of my fears. I must not let these fears take control of my present.

The Union needs me in some tiny sense. Every time I kill a Rebel I feel everyone is that much closer to the end of this war. I certainly must function. I love you so much. Without your letters and love I can't see how I could survive. At times, each soldier feels they are at the limit of human sanity. I have felt that emotion several times. I must fight the thought that I am going insane. If the question is in my mind then I know I am sane and functioning.

Deepest of Love

Ray

CHAPTER SEVENTY-SEVEN

June 28,1863

Dear Ray

The entire country is in fear. It seems clear that Lee is marching north, but I have no sure information. We have heard that Confederate forces are going through York. Rumor has it that Union Militia has burned the bridge over the Susquehanna River and that has slowed the Rebel advance. We have heard of a small skirmish near Harrisburg but that is only a vague rumor.

This appears to be heading toward a huge clash. The land is open in that area and of course that provides a huge area by which armies can maneuver. I fear that gives the advantage to Lee who has proven to be a master of maneuver.

Our hospital is still filled. It is nearly like a machine with soldiers arriving with different levels of injury. The doctors assign each patient as to the degree of severity. However, some soldiers are clearly dying. These poor souls are given the best care possible but cannot receive the supplies that could still be used by a soldier that has a chance.

What a horrible duty that selection process must be. If the soldier becomes stable he is moved to our recovery section to be nursed back to health. The soldier often takes months to recover. At some point the doctors evaluate whether the soldier returns to active duty or is sent home on furlough or medical discharge.

My duties are light, but they weigh heavily on my heart. Mother wants me to share with you that my education is going very well. I am already quite fluent in French and am making solid progress in mathematics and science.

Father says I am quite gifted in math, and he wants to advance me as I master different levels. My work in science is theoretical but it teaches me the method of scientific investigation and keeps me abreast of the state of the field. Many people are skeptical of science, but I can attest that science for good or evil will change the world.

Ray, I am so frightened of this stage of the war. Clearly huge battles are coming, and the fate of our nation hangs by a thread. I fear you will be in the heart of the upcoming battle. I tremble in agony as I fear your death. I can't go on without you. Your mother and father are stoic about the dangers, but I tremble like a little leaf in a storm. How can I hang on?

I pray, but not to a Christian God. I will not accept any religion that supports slavery directly or indirectly. I pray to a God that is far vaster than our small human imaginations. I ask him to bring you back to me alive and well. I so want to cover you with kisses. I feel I could rest in your arms for months.

Forever Loving You,

Mary

CHAPTER SEVENTY-EIGHT

July 10, 1863

Dear Mary

You have probably heard rumor of a great battle at Gettysburg in Pennsylvania. The battle raged from July 1 through July 3. This vast storm of violence and death lasted for three days. Each day the fate of our nation hung by a spider thread. Thank the God of all gods the Union has won the most important battle in American history.

I believe that had we lost this battle we would have lost the nation. The Union General in command was General Meade. For three days the battle was too close to call. I have long said that Lee was beatable and that his victories might go to his head. That is exactly what happened.

I cannot give you a blow-by-blow account. As I said before, a single soldier can only see a small part of the battlefield. Yet, I saw the most important action, which was Pickett's charge that cost General Lee the battle. Lee very foolishly attacked uphill against an entrenched enemy.

The war has clearly shown this to be a fatal losing tactic. Colonel Hunt's cannons were parked hub to hub facing the open field. As I earlier said Generals are only human and too much victory may be worse than close losses.

General Lee made the old mistake of believing his men could not be defeated under any circumstances. When a General drinks such a fatal draft he is blinded to reality. Lee ordered the fatal charge to General Pickett. A full division marched up a clear slope for nearly a mile.

They marched into batteries of cannon that were wheel to wheel. Colonel Hunt fired his cannon non -stop during the entire approach. Huge holes were torn in the enemy ranks as they stoically marched uphill towards us. Then at 300 yards he told his batteries to load with grape and cease fire.

He allowed the Rebels to reach 200 yards and then he ordered the entire long line of cannon fired at once and that infernal volley wiped those enemy soldiers from the face of the earth. That volley from hell was the last sound hundreds of Rebels heard in their final moment. Pickett's division was killed almost to the man. The Union kept a steady fire with musket fire starting 400 yards from the natural stone ridge of Cemetery Ridge.

It was a slaughter. Very few Rebels got to our wall. Those who did were quickly killed or taken capture in just a few minutes. When the Rebels finally broke their attack and filtered away the entire Union line called "Fredericksburg" repeatedly. This taunted the Rebels for the killing they gave the Union on that long upward hill toward a fortified position at Fredericksburg.

Again, the Union Army allowed the remains of Lee's army to get away. I am not sure the Union could have destroyed Lee after such an exhausting battle. I have heard that Lincoln was dismayed but I am not sure Lincoln could understand how close the battle really was. It was by far the largest and most important battle of the Civil War. We clearly did not crush Lee's Army, but perhaps most importantly Lee did not destroy our army.

After three days of fighting our army was exhausted. Healthy young soldiers could barely rise from the ground. Many soldiers were led away in total shock their eyes glazed over. Had we attacked we would have made the same mistake that Lee made.

We would have attacked entrenched soldiers and that is always a mistake. After the battle, the heavens opened, and the rain came down in sheets. I feel Meade's decision to be cautious was the correct one.

Joe and I were entrenched near the center of the line. In this battle it was impossible to get any higher. We were already on the crest. We did not do great in this battle, but the line was long, and the action was so spread out. It was only on the last day did Joe and I really saw action.

Since the enemy was marching straight toward us it was much easier to make a killing shot. Quartering shots are more difficult. In that final charge of Pickett's, I killed 4 rebels. One enlisted and three officers. A total of 4 kills.

We did not have to move between shots because the entire line was firing at those fearless Rebels who had to climb such a long open slope. I started killing men at 600 yards and I reloaded and fired as fast as I could. We were just part of the general confusion. This allowed much faster shooting with rather more safety than normal. As always this killing is not like playing a child's game.

I well remember the first officer I killed during this battle. He was a handsome young man. He was probably 22 years of age. His hair was flowing, and its color was bright chestnut brown, he rode with such poise he seemed a god upon the battlefield. His uniform was spotless. Every button was polished and not one thread out of place. He used his saber to point at the lapses of the soldiers to close ranks and attack in such neat rows.

His men clearly admired him. In the heat of battle, they responded to his every directive. His mount was a rich bay with four white socks. This fine animal responded to the slightest wish of his rider. The mount was so spirited it seemed to float on the air. My crosshairs were on his master's heart.

When Joe said fire, I fired. I watched the death blow strike his chest. He wavered slightly in the saddle as if to correct for a minor loss of balance. Then he tumbled to the ground as lifeless as a stone. I killed him at 600 yards.

I could not pause another second. I loaded and fired as fast as possible. If I could not see an officer I killed enlisted men. I fear I will remember these shots until the day I die. The second man I killed was an officer. He was a much older man. He must have been in his sixties.

His face was lined with the marks of age. His eyes were direct. He was as trim and slender as a piece of rawhide. He looked to the right and left of his command as an eagle might from its lofty height.

His uniform was worn and torn from the clear signs of hand-to-hand combat. He was a courageous man and was completely indifferent to fear. He carried his saber as if on the parade grounds. His mount was an old beat-up bay. But his horse mustered up the strength to walk with dignity. Like his rider he seemed to be tired. Its shoulders were coated with the foam of exhaustion.

I watched as the rider patted his mounts sweat marked neck. When I fired I had the feeling he was looking right into my eyes. I saw the faint smile and he slid lifeless from his mount. His mount did not run away but merely nudged his fallen master and stood waiting. I suspected the horse was still standing faithfully when the battle was over. Again, I had to move on.

Then I took an officer who replaced the fallen officer. He was on the ground, and he was harder to take because of more constant movement. He paused to encourage an enlisted man and in that second I stuck him down. Killing men who support slavery is necessary. I have steeled myself against grief.

To stop slavery is worth nearly anything. Never have I regretted a shot. If the enemy want to place their life on the line to support such an inhuman belief such as slavery they forfeit the right to live.

I believe I can remember most of my kills. Some I may have lost in the heat of the conflict. I took them one at a time. It mattered not whether they were young or old. The horrid task must be done, and I hardened my soul and did the killing work. All humans who have aligned with slavery must die.

I do remember an older man in this battle. Men who carry the flag have an important duty. The flag goes to the most desperate spot and gives the troops something to keep aligned upon. I had just shot an old man that was carrying the flag. When he went down I saw a young boy run over to reach for the flag. I said to myself 'leave it down boy." But he picked up the flag and I shot him dead.

The raw numbers seem to be well confirmed. The Union Army numbered about 105,000 soldiers and the Rebels had around 75,000. Losses were 23,000 for the North and about 23,000 for the South. We are already hearing that this battle was the turning point of the war. I pray God that it is.

The Western Army under Grant took Vicksburg on July 4, 1863. This closes the massive river to the rebellion. Thank God that I have been allowed to see this day. I know there will be hard battles to be fought but I see a spark of light at the end of a bloody and long tunnel.

As is normal, it took several days for the Army to establish its normal formations. Religiously I tend to my rifle before I tend to my needs. As ordered I reported to Colonel Hunt and told him my kills numbered 64 kills and I had been ordered to report if my kill list exceeded 60 and as ordered I reported to him.

He appeared to be tired but happy to see me. I left his office as a First Lieutenant in the Union Army. I am exhausted but as happy as is possible in this horrible war.

Mary my love, please be there when I come home. Help me bind the wounds on my soul and in my mind. I miss your arms and the softness of your lips. I miss your breasts. I miss touching you in your most sensitive spots. I am not a hero nor am I a murderer. I am just a soldier who must do my part to stop slavery and maintain the Union. I do not feel young anymore.

My allotted task attacks every fiber of my humanness. I miss you so much. I have seen several young men whose girlfriends have drifted away. It killed them as surely as an enemy bullet.

Please stay with me. The only reason I can go on a single day is to retain the hope that I will eventually return to you. I have lost all patience with those who might object to our love. I have killed and killed again. I have paid my price, and I will love whom I choose. Woe be to the man or woman who places scorn upon me. My love for you is all that is important, and you are who I live for.

Love,

Ray

CHAPTER SEVENTY-NINE

July30,1863

Dearest Ray

The entire North is rejoicing over the important battle Gettysburg. It has been rumored that Lincoln felt General Meade should have destroyed Lee's army. As you noted it is not reasonable to expect Meade to destroy Lee's Army when the North's victory was so thin. Winning was the most important thing.

The fact that Lee did not destroy our Army is reason to celebrate. Lee's hopes of a massive victory were thwarted, and international recognition was denied the South. Fortunately, a long war does not favor the South.

As we predicted, Union Colored Troops have entered South Carolina. How this must put a dagger into proud Southern hearts! Suddenly colored troops are campaigning in South Carolina. The days of the South claiming that colored people cannot fight is now shown to be another Southern vanity.

Given rifles and proper training the colored soldier has proven himself to be equal to anyone. The idea of a stupid and menial Negro is shown to be one of the many Southern myths. That Negro soldiers should be in South Carolina is an irony too sweet to pass by. This is the very state which started this entire war and now they do not have the strength to push the "so called menial" black troops out.

It is my feeling that every structure owned by a white person in the entire state should be burned to the ground. This of course will not happen. However, it should happen. In their pride they rejected the Union and now their rejection should have a penalty. I feel every member of the Confederate State Government should go to the gallows. That includes Lee and well as Jefferson Davis.

How is it that thousands of Union boys lie in early graves and the instigators of this crime should be allowed to age well and walk free? Lee extended the war by at least two years because of his treason. The blood of thousands of Union boys is on his hands. He should die for his crimes. Why should he be allowed to rest in his old age? Every officer above Colonel in the Rebel Army should swing in the air.

Treason is the name for their crimes. Why should we show mercy when these Southern states have brought on this war with their vain statements of White Supremacy? The day they touted "States Rights" is the day they marked their own death. Now the Union is there and woe to the state.

Where is their vaulted supremacy now? What of their vain boasts now? I have heard it said that revenge is not "reasonable." These racist traitors have covered fields with innocent blood and somehow they deserve "reconciliation?" They deserve death.

I have received news that the Confederate strong point of Battery Wagner in Charleston was attacked by our Union forces on July 19. The charge was led by the 54th Massachusetts a colored infantry regiment, which had volunteered to do this attack. Although the extremely strong site was not seized all who saw the attack swore that the bravery of the colored soldiers was incredible.

Union soldiers who watched the charge stated that they would be happy to have such soldiers fight with them any day.

The myth of the useless Negro soldier is fading away. The Union soldier is a practical man, he knows that every Rebel a colored soldier kills is one less he might have to face. No-one has better reasons to fight than our Negros.

They have been berated and scorned for over two hundred years. With a rifle in their hands, properly trained and bravely led they are as good a soldier as any in the Army of the Potomac.

Our President Lincoln was wise to form Negro troops. It is impossible to withhold the vote from a man who has fought for his country. Since we need troops the country is learning that every Negro soldier is one less draftee from a white home.

The Negro soldier knows that his behavior is reflected in the welfare of the black race in general.

Union officers note that there are less discipline problems with colored troops than with white troops. The colored troops not only have a score to settle with the South they are eager to do so. Remembering our violent riots against the draft the government should breathe easier taking Negro volunteers. I hope the colored soldiers burn the entire South to the ground for the crimes against humanity they have performed for over 250 years.

I have also heard that a thuggish killer named Quantrill raided Lawrence Kansas and murdered over 100 men and boys. I don't know the exact date. I have heard that Quantrill is not an official officer of the South. This means they were not under normal military discipline.

When the war is over how does one bring such brutes to justice? The murdered men were unarmed civilians and not a military force. We can pray that such murderous animals will meet God's bar of judgment someday.

Love

Mary

CHAPTER EIGHTY

Dear Mary

The Union Army lost a major battle at Chattanooga Georgia. The Union Army under Rosecrans was nearly routed by General Bragg. Rosecrans retreated to Chattanooga Tenn. Rosecrans was under siege until Grant busted him out during The Battle of Chattanooga. This occurred November 23-25 of 1863.

These events of the Civil War did not raise much discussion in the Army of the Potomac or the feelings of Northern progress. There seems to be less backbiting. Apparently nothing sells like a firm belief in coming success.

Gradually there seems to be a feeling of impending victory for the Union cause. Slowly there is a sense that the forces of the Rebellion are waning. The numbers for each side seem to be stable but there is a vague but growing feeling that the Union Army is getting the edge on the South.

There is clear resentment that Grant is getting too much press and that his fame is growing faster than the eastern command would like. Yet the facts show that General Grant will fight and that his victories have bolstered the opinion of the North. I have learned during my stay in the Union Army that politics is not far from the battlefield.

It is essential that the Army is making military progress. With enough victories the politics remains benign. If there are setbacks in the field the political side will devour the Army and the President. President Lincoln expresses more interest in General Grant as time passes. The President likes Grant because Grant does not ask advice of the President unlike earlier commanders.

Grant simply takes charge and does the job. If Grant is advanced he has made it clear he will not be asking the White House for military advice. The only relationship between Grant and the government is getting supplies and manpower. Grant asks for supplies and Lincoln makes sure he gets them. This is the exact kind of relationship that suits both Grant and Lincoln.

Small things raise resentment between the Eastern Army and Grant. Grant is not too impressed with clothes. In fact, he is rather tacky. Nor does Grant like huge reviews that are so popular with officers that enjoy popular acclaim. There is the shadow of suspicion over Grant that he drinks too much and in fact is a drunk. The actual evidence of this shortcoming is sparse. These vague rumors do not seem to be grounded in fact. Grant has been most careful around festivities of the political sort.

In public, Grant avoids the limelight. He does not make speeches at social gatherings, and he avoids politics with great vigor. He has made several statements that he has no interest in a political career. The only issue that Grant is interested in is military victory.

He has written several letters to the President assuring him that he has no plans to challenge him in the political sense. Of course, this raises the Presidents interest in Grant ever higher.

There are rumors that Grant will be given overall command of the entire army. Naturally, this raises resentments among the Potomac Army group. To the Eastern Establishment Grant is country bumpkin. Grant is nearly unflappable in combat. He puffs away at his cigars while running his Army with great skill. I personally think the future is bright for Grant.

I have listened to headquarters, and it is clear they do not want to be working for Grant. I feel these are public statements that Grant must endure. It is certain that Grant will win over his critics even if that means sending a critic or two to Texas.

So far Grant has not revealed how he would run the Army as a whole. It appears that Grant will retain his common soldier attire. Yet those who have looked Grant carefully in the eye say they see great determination. General Lee has not been flippant toward Grant as he has with past commanders of the Army of the Potomac.

He has warned his staff that Grant is a man to be concerned about. Lee said here was a man who would batter his head against a wall until the wall is conquered. High testimony from Lee. It seems we will be going into winter quarters soon.

Love,

Ray

CHAPTER EIGHTY-ONE

December 17, 1863

Dear Ray

The year is gradually ending. There have been many terrible battles during this war and undoubtedly there will be more to come. We have no choice but to fight it out until we win.

On the 8th of December Lincoln issued his "Proclamation of Amnesty and Reconstruction." This would pardon anyone who is willing to take an oath to the Union. I am curious as to how many people avail themselves of this offer. Father is still very conservative.

He feels the Union is still venerable to the loss of a huge battle that goes against the Union. He does agree that piece by piece the Confederacy is weakening. There is a great weariness throughout the land. The costs have been so high and the loss of blood so deep.

When people get to a certain point of weariness they lose insight into the larger issues. The Democrats are certainly willing to allow slavery to exist as well as allow the South to form its own nation.

This would condemn the New World to become all slave, and God only knows how many centuries of that evil the world would have to endure. No, it is far better to finish the job at hand so that future generations will not have to do this over again at even greater cost.

Father and Mother are doing well at our hospital. Father serves as the general administrator, and he is unmatched in this task. Sometimes he must balance conflicting needs, and he does his best to make the hospital better in every way. The Federal government has sent inspectors to overlook our facility, and their words have been glowing

Mother is far stronger than many people have thought. She goes through the wards and comforts as many as possible during the day. She has held many hands of dying men and helped guide them through the portals to the next world. She has shed many tears during this heartbreaking task, but she has carried her load bravely. The men adore her and call her their angel. Daily she has shown by example what a woman can do when allowed to put her hand to the plow.

There are still close to 300 men in our urgent care ward and nearly 200 in our recuperation wards. We have also had the reward of men leaving our hospital mended and well.

To have seen the wounded with their untended wounds arrive at our hospital and to see that same person leave healthily is a reward that is impossible to put a price upon. Our death rate is the lowest in the entire Union hospital services. We lose slightly below ten percent.

Our English trained doctors have more advanced theories on sanitation then the Americans. We are scrupulous in the disposal of human waste/foul dressings, and we strictly quarantine any patient who has a disease.

We feed food of the highest nutrition, and we make sure all food is strictly fresh. Everyone tries every day to reduce our death rate, and our parents never stand on their laurels. Our parents deserve the highest praise for this humane hospital.

I am complying with father and mother dictates on my schoolwork. I am assigned to do the reading/writing to the patients in greatest need and I feel honored to do so. That said, I approach my studies with the fanaticism of a zealot. I work hard to excel in all my subjects. Mother says I speak French like a native.

There have been several French natives in the Union Army. These fine young men believe our cause is just. Mother had me converse with a young man for nearly two hours. The soldier was astonished to find out that I am not a native speaker. I love French and I give that language the highest marks as a language of love.

Father has retained a new teacher of the higher mathematics. I have outstripped my early tutors and with their blessing I am using my new tutor. I am advancing in trigonometry and the calculus. Father and Mother say they are quite pleased with my progress. All that I am and all I will ever be is due to this family. I know that I am not as strong as you, but my greatest hope is that you will find me worthy of love.

I don't know what the results of my studies will be but for now I realize that knowledge is its own reward. It seems so long ago to those tender years when you lent me books and I attended the free school. How I miss those warm dog days that we shared on a blanket in our hidden spot in the willows. Why would some denigrate passion is beyond me?

What a wonderful gift our Creator has given us. I long to bring back some of those golden hours when you return from this horrible war. To know that I can give you pleasure fills me with depthless happiness. I am yours and I want to live my life with you.

Your happiness is what I want most in the entire world. Someday the madness of this war must end and with effort we can put it behind us. I hold on to those memories with an iron grip. How dare society condemn love between two women! Is our love not as deep as any enamored couple?

In fact, it must be deeper because we hold our love in the face of a hostile society that wants to punish us and rip us apart. If God in his mercy has granted us love than who has the right to judge our commitment? I am waiting here for you to return to me. I have no other goal than to hold you in my arms and share the rest of our lives together.

Love Without End

Mary

Chapter Eighty-Two

February 14.1864

Dear Ray

I have just received news of a great breakout of captured Union soldiers from the horrible Libby Prison in Richmond. Apparently over 100 men tunneled their way under a street into an empty building. It appears around half were recaptured but the rest reached Union lines.

Father tells me that there are many Union spies in Richmond and throughout the South. It is believed that Union patriots may have helped in this great escape. These extremely brave Union civilians have risked their freedoms and lives to help defeat the Rebels.

I pray that God will reward them in the final judgment. Of course, the fate for captured Union spies is death. Think how much these brave individuals are helping to save the lives of our soldiers and the lives of those on the main battle lines! Father says that even minor details can promote victory for our troops.

I sincerely hope that the Union does not forget those brave souls who have been at risk for several years. Their help can shorten the war and save our soldiers. God's blessing on all of them.

Secret messages from Richmond say that the Rebels are building another prison camp in Georgia. Apparently some people call this horrid place Andersonville Prison. I fear for the sad captives. All evidence shows our prisoners are being treated horribly.

Shelter is non-existent and the food is of starvation quality. All this evil is because of slavery. No matter what it takes and no matter what the cost we must end slavery in America. Anything less will curse us all.

Love,

Mary

CHAPTER EIGHTY-THREE

March 2, 1864

Dear Mary

We are still in winter quarters, and everyone is on edge. We are pulling out and going to battle is just a day or two. The enlisted men have gone nearly insane with endless drilling. The drill Sergeants would rather go to battle than teach more drill. We will move soon. Everyone is looking forward to the summer campaigns.

There is friction between the officer's ranks. There is a never-ending debate as to what the Army is to do next. Lincoln and his staff debate on what is needed. Then that vagueness comes down to the General Staff which must give some answers to the President.

Eventually some plan must be hammered out. For example, part of the General Staff wants to conquer Richmond. Others say that is foolish. They want to destroy Lee's Army. Nearly everyone agrees that the Army cannot do both. Then you have the faction who believes that Lee has hundreds of thousands of troops and thus cannot be attacked directly. Others say this is false, they feel we have always outnumbered Lee by at least two to one.

As with any war there are new developments as to how one wages war. This war has seen extensive use of trenches. Those who favor frontal attacks have had to face the high losses that this entails. It is becoming clearer that 500 defenders in a trench can easily hold off 1000 attackers.

This is a new development. I have learned by being an attentive mouse that military men hate change. They want to fight their last war rather than fight this one with new methods. Any farm boy soldier knows that attacks against fortified positions are simply suicide.

However, the greatest change is the elevation of Grant to the overall command of the entire Army. The Army brass spends more time debating Grant than they do on General Lee. Feathers are being ruffled and egos are becoming clearer. Those in current command feel offended that a Western General was selected rather than an Eastern General. There is a great deal of worry as to how many heads will roll and in what direction. Grant was awarded the title of Lieutenant General a rank only held by George Washington.

Love,

Ray

CHAPTER EIGHTY-FOUR

March 28,1864

Dear Ray

Yes, the entire country is wondering what Grant will do. Lee does not downplay Grant as he did with past Generals. Lee views Grant as a man who cannot be bluffed. Lee has openly said that Grant will not be afraid to attack and even worse to keep attacking. The old pattern of beating the Union Army and then it retreats will not work with Grant. Grant will keep coming and this type of war will be costly to Lee.

There have been rumors that Grant is going to use his far-flung armies as pieces of a whole. In this method every movement of one adds to the other. Grant has said the Lee doesn't have enough army to fight all these armies coming against him. Father has said that he expects deep thrusts in various parts of the South. This will prevent Lee from shifting armies here and there. Each army will be fully engaged and cannot lend itself to the aid of others. Father says this will hurt Lee because in truth Lee does not have enough armies to resist all this everywhere.

What seems attractive about Grant is that he plans on the big stage. For the first time in this war there is a sense of overall strategy. There is a rumor that a big thrust will be made in the Red River Country in Louisiana. This would be the first true advance into the Deep South. Father has allowed himself a small amount of hope based entirely on Grant.

He feels that Grant understands the concept of total war. To father this means destroying civilian property as well as military property. This brings the pain of war upon everyone. It also means that civilian resources will not be available for military purposes because they won't be there to use. Potential supplies will be turned to ashes.

Your Love

Mary

CHAPTER EIGHTY-FIVE

April 21,1864

Dear Mary

There has been news of fighting in the Red River country. Apparently there has been conflict around April 8 to April 10. I have no conclusive news. What I have heard little is that the results have been vague.

Of greater importance is that the Union has lost Fort Pillow in Tennessee. The fort was taken by Nathan Forrest a well-known hater of the Union. The evidence clearly supports that Forrest murdered in cold blood many black soldiers who surrendered. If further events prove this out then Forrest deserves to hang from the gallows.

The Army of the Potomac is massing its forces and clearly is going to move soon. Its readiness is far beyond anything done in the former years of the war. Spirits are high. Everyone knows the cost will be high but there is a strong feeling that this will be the year when the South will be pressed against the cliff. There is a strong feeling that this will be the last campaign.

Grant will stay engaged until Lee is defeated. There will be no running back to Washington to be re-fitted. Grant will keep pressing

Lee until Lee has nothing to fight with. No-one is saying that 1864 will be the last year of war but many are saying by the end of 1864 there will be no doubt of a Union victory.

I am so very tired. The cycle of battle seems endless. I know that is not reasonable but that is how it feels. I wonder how many more battles I can survive. It seems likely that one's luck must run out. Joe and I are still a working team, and we have gotten closer every week. We can almost read each other's mind. When one serves shoulder to shoulder a bond forms. Joe and I are different in many ways.

Joe has not had the advantages of family and education. His sense of independence does not allow him to advance in rank in the Army. Yet he has fought side by side with me through it all. He taught me my first lessons and without him I would have died in my first battle. One can lose their life in so many ways in this war. It does not pay to think about it too much but of course I do think of it.

I want you so badly. I need you emotionally and I need you physically. We are young and this abstention is not healthy or normal. I want to be embraced by you. I want what any normal lover wants. In short I want you in every sense of the word. I want to kiss you.

I am young and I burn in passion for you and your body. In short I want to live and love. I want so much to be with you. The only reason I am here is to protect the Union and to free the slaves. When that duty is done I want to return to you.

Love

Ray

CHAPTER EIGHTY-SIX

May 9,1864

Dear Ray

Iknow nothing. The country is awash with rumors. The newspapers suggest Grant is on the march to Richmond. Others say he is still refitting outside of Washington. Father feels Grant will move shortly because the roads are dry and that is the usual requirement for fighting. Many armchair generals have no faith in him.

I read every day to keep aware of what is going on. Both North and South newspapers claim that Grant is a hopeless drunk. It is said the Lincoln went against the advice of his Cabinet members and against the advice of his military men to get Grant. Rumor has it that Lincoln said "I can't lose that man. He fights."

The papers also say that Lee will eat Grant for breakfast. Father feels quite different. He says Grant will fight to the last man and then he will fight by himself. There will be no more "one battle then retreat to refit" as was standard with earlier commanders. Grant will press on and let his reinforcements and supplies catch up with him.

Father says that many people will be surprised at the talent Grant has to shift, feint, and attack. Grant will pay the butcher's bill, but father feels certain of ultimate victory. Father said that Grant is roughhewn, but Father said his money is on Grant. Everyone else seems to be on pins and needles. All eyes are on Grant.

Ray, I am so afraid. I can't bear the thought of losing you. Please keep me abreast if possible.

Love

Mary

CHAPTER EIGHTY-SEVEN

May 13, 1864

Dear Mary

There has been two days of desperate fighting in an area called the Wilderness. It occurred between May-4-5. This is the first step of what some call the Overland Campaign. Grant intends to force Lee to fight by driving toward Richmond. Lee elected to attack in the terrain which is so thick that it nearly impossible to penetrate.

The size of the so-called Wilderness is about 80 square miles. In that confined space nearly 190,000 men fought. About 120,000 for the Union and the balance for the Rebels.

With the smoke of battle and the thickness of the terrain establishing battle lines was impossible. All chains of command were lost because the fighting men could not see nor even hear their officers. Men fought on their own.

They would answer shot for shot and advance toward the heaviest shooting. The cover is so thick that soldiers often cannot see their companions. They simply press on until they can go no further.

To add to the horror there were many fires that started in these woods which burned without check. Thousands of wounded men who could not move were burned to death by the fires. The men had nothing to shoot at, so they merely fired in the direction of the suspected enemy. Doubtless there were hundreds of soldiers hit by fire from their own side.

Some wounded soldiers were killed out of mercy because the fires were creeping toward them and the musket fire was so heavy the wounded could not be reached and extracted. It was impossible to use artillery. The artillery could not maneuver in the brush and had no clear field of fire.

As a result, artillery remained on the sidelines next to the hastily located headquarters. Joe and I were as blind as the rest. For the first time I shot from an elevated position. Joe and I climbed a tree. To kill the enemy this was forced upon us.

The ground was so covered with smoke that one could only wait for a slight opening in the dense smoke. This was the only way we could see to shoot. Our smoke just blended in with the rest.

Between the musket smoke and the smoke from the burning woods we were able to ply our deadly trade. We waited for a slight moment of clarity, and we fired at any Rebel we could see. This was a very dangerous fight for us because we were in the eye of the battle and not on the edges. Counter shooters were not likely.

Joe spotted and I killed six soldiers on the first day and five on the second day. This is the first time that Joe and I shot at regular line troops rather than higher value targets.

We saw our unit retreating and flanking to the left. We were happy to get on the ground. We doubled time to find our headquarters. Like everyone we were shifting to the left. There was a cheer when the Army realized we were not retreating. Grant intended to win this war.

I overheard at the staff meeting that evening the Union lost about 17,000 and the Rebels lost about 11,000 in the Wilderness. I must doubt these numbers because of the confusion. Grant elected to continue his flanking movement and thus forced Lee to come out of the brush forest.

The battle was probably a draw, but the huge difference was that Grant did not fall back toward Washington to regroup. He continued to press on toward Richmond using flanking movements.

This surely put fear in Lee's heart because the Union could replace Grant's losses and Lee was scraping the bottom of the manpower barrel. Grant is here and he clearly has a plan. I believe that plan is to win the war by attrition. Lee should run out of men before we do.

This is the horrible mathematics of this war. Despite this horror, one could feel the extra energy of the Grand Old Army. For the first time Lee battled against Grant and between the two of them I fear war is to be redefined.

I also learned during the evening staff meeting that General Sherman is marching south with his forces with the object being Atlanta. I think he started around March 7, 1864. He is facing Johnston who is apparently undermanned. The South is bleeding hard now. There are almost no men the South can call up to fill their losses.

Apparently Sherman also likes flanking movements and rather than lose his army Johnston must keep withdrawing toward Atlanta.

At this moment it appears likely that in time Sherman will place Atlanta under siege conditions. All of this will force Lee to do his own fighting. The units that normally might have been available to Lee are fighting their own battles to survive. Grant is not McClellan.

Love,

Ray

CHAPTER EIGHTY-EIGHT

May 24,1864

Dear Ray

We hear the results of the fighting quickly because of the telegraph. Where are these horrible places? Who ever heard of "Spotsylvania, Cold Harbor, or North Anna? All we have heard is massive deaths on both sides.

Can it be possible that 30,000 more men have died because of slavery? What was this "bloody Angle? What was the "Mule Shoe?" Of course, I have heard of Petersburg. Apparently Grant is in siege or will be in a siege soon? I don't even know if you are getting my letters.

I am such a weak reed. I know that more hospital work would kill me. Mother tells me to keep up with my schoolwork. She says educational service will be needed after this ghastly war is over. Thus, I apply myself harder and harder. My teacher is pleased with my progress.

He has suggested that I don't study quite so hard. I tell him that this intense intellectual focus is literally my only mental escape from my over-taxed world. So, I try to be strong and press on.

I am so lost. I have not heard from you recently. The family is so worried. I pray every waking hour. Your mother is in bed. She is ill and exhausted. There is a trained nurse with mother at all times of day or night. Father is so silent. He takes long walks at night, and I fear for his safety.

Grandfather damns the Confederacy to the deepest depths of hell every waking hour. He wants to fight but because of his age and family name the recruiters kindly turned him away. He volunteers to be a lowly soldier on the firing line. A military doctor spoke with him and gently explained that the rigor would just be too much for him. The doctor kindly suggested some other way to serve. They were so gentle with Grandfather, but he is still angry.

Our hospital is over-flowing. Many large tents are being used for the overflow and large construction gangs are building a hospital day and night that will hold a thousand soldiers. Lincoln has sent the permits and says he is thankful for the Summerfield kindness.

Father must be spending hundreds of thousands of dollars. He now spends so much time in Washington D.C. I see him less and less. When he returns he is pale and seldom speaks to anyone.

When he does speak he says he talks with Lincoln nearly every day. Father says that Lincoln's chances of re-election are slim and the President himself does not feel he has a political future.

If Lincoln is not elected then Democrat turncoats will elect someone that will bend their knees to the slave holding South. This political scum will curse the western hemisphere with slavery for hundreds of years. Our glorious Union will perish, and its bones will be picked gleefully by the European and Southern oligarchs who will ravish our lands.

All these fine Union soldiers had to die to crush a rebellion started by slave holding traitors. It is no secret that the rich Planters control all state governments of the South. It is also no secret that it is the common man who is fighting their fight.

The reframe "Rich man's war, poor man's fight" is totally true. We have learned that if a slave holder owns 20 slaves they are exempt from the fighting. If that inequality is not clear enough the common Southerner is truly blind.

The South is praising Lee to the high heavens. Lee is a traitor. By using his evil talents, he has probably prolonged this war for over two years. He has the blood of thousands of innocent soldiers on both sides on his hands.

He helped murder thousands of soldiers who were not even related to slavery. They were murdered because evil wealthy Southern men like Lee want to enslave Negro human beings. Every rebel soldier over the rank of Colonel should be hanged. The blood of 250,000 Union soldiers demands it.

Davis is just another Planter who started this war to protect his investment in human flesh. The common Rebel solder is just an uneducated dirt scratcher. Most cannot read a word. Most have never been twenty miles from home in their life. That is the reason that the South lags on so many fronts. The worst crime beyond slavery is the Southern elite depriving their citizens of a basic education. But a Planter only cares for himself and his family. Those dependents are to have every advantage.

I am becoming so hateful. At times I hate myself. What is this war doing to us?

Love

Mary

CHAPTER EIGHTY-NINE

June 1,1864

Dear Mary

The names you wondered about are just name locations on a map. They are places where soldiers died by the thousands at various places. The combined conflicts are called the Battles of Spotsylvania. The place called Cold Harbor will be the topic of my next letter.

We were engaged with Lee until the 21st of May. Grant forces engaged in repeated battles which were expensive for both sides. Grant does not remain static. He is capable of striking both flanks and the center if he feels it might be a military necessity.

Like Lee he wants to attack at any chance. The Union has lost somewhere around 18,000 and the Rebels somewhere around 12,000. That is the 30,000 losses you mentioned. Again, the horrible mathematics means that Grant can replace his losses and Lee cannot.

Grant merely began flanking movements forcing Lee to move as well. Every time Grant flanks Lee the closer he is to Richmond and the railroad lines that feed Lee and Richmond. Grant knows Lee must stretch his troops thinner and thinner to cover the trenches that are getting longer and longer. Soon that line will crack and be over-run. Once again the mathematics of war are simple and deadly.

Do not be hard on yourself. In this war all of us hate and are angry. War brings out the worst of us and if we control ourselves the emotions will pass in time. The urge for revenge is deep within every heart. Nevertheless, we want Union, peace and the end of Slavery. Revenge will not work.

Revenge would haunt our future Union and would make a lasting peace impossible. Revenge feeds itself. One act of revenge leads to another and that is only war by another name. Thank God I do not have to make the big decisions as to what will happen after the war. Let the big wheels do their job. I just want to go home and enjoy you for the rest of my life.

There is now no doubt that Lee's days are numbered. If our country does not falter the victory over the South is certain. Lee's army is starving. Desertions from his army are by the dozens every day. He has no offensive ability. He does not have the incentive any longer. Most of his troops are bare foot. Grant controls the direction of the war. Grant acts and Lee can only react.

Again, I must state, the heinous mathematics of war means that Lee will run out of troops. Sooner or later Lee will have to abandon Richmond, and he will become a rabbit fleeing from the hounds. Grant is the hell hound of bad dreams. He will not stop until he wins.

Grant cares for the troops only so far as they are a means to victory. He is perfectly happy to spill Union blood so long as he can make Lee lose a lot of blood as well. However, it is just that ruthlessness that will win this war. Of course, Lee is dangerous, but he just does not have army enough to win.

Civilians think of war as great strategy and brilliant tactics. In truth, most battles are decided by the number of troops in the right spot and how to feed them. I have heard it said whoever gets to the objective first with the most troops usually wins. This is a solid truth.

Watching the staff meetings has shown me there have been several times that victory was lost because we just did not get to the objective first with the most. Grant is not brilliant. He has made mistakes. Yet Grant knows the most important word: Attrition.

As sure as gravity Lee will be destroyed. With the defeat of Lee, the South will fall in a few days. However, I have no idea whether I will survive the war.

Were you aware of the battle at Yellow Tavern? Sheridan's Cavalry met Stuart troops at this place and beat them. Stuart himself was killed. Stuart is now another skillful traitor dead. Stuart had it his way at the start of the war. Northern Cavalry did not have equal skills compared to the South. However, those learning days are past. Our Cavalry has fresh horses and the skilled men to ride them. This was a large battle with nearly 18,000 men fighting hard.

Our Cavalry now has the repeating seven shot Spencer rifle. This is a tremendous increase in firepower over the single shot carbine. Sheridan has developed a strong tactic. The Cavalry now dismounts to engage the enemy. That means large numbers of men can shift very rapidly in battle and this is a new factor.

Sheridan now has 10,000 troops under his command. That can shape the battle in many ways. Speed can be decisive. Yet, one must always remember that in a war no-one is immune. We have lost many generals and many brave soldiers. With the massive amounts of bullets in the air it is a miracle that anyone survives.

Due to the close nature of the battles Joe and I have been exposed to a high degree of enemy fire and we are unable to get enough stand-off range to operate with our standard methods. This raises frightful odds against our survival. On the plus side our musket smoke is just part of the whole. Counter sharpshooters were not a problem. They cannot see us. Over the 13 days of battle Joe and I killed 9 men. Nearly all enlisted men.

Mary, please pray for me. I believe we are in the last year of this war. Joe and I are in extreme danger. If only I can survive long enough to get home to you.

Love,

Rachel

CHAPTER NINETY

June 15, 1864

Dear Ray

I am so frightened for you. These battles and many more are swarming around the home fronts. Things are happening so fast we do not know what is real and what is rumor. Grant's armies seem to be advancing in so many directions.

Your letters are the only clear light that we have. We have information of a battle called Cold Harbor in Virginia All we know is the Union took heavy losses trying to assault Lee's defenses.

Why are frontal assaults used when they have such a horrible price and seldom any fruits for our blood? I am just a farm girl. I don't know anything about fighting. All I can do is to watch in horror as tens of thousands of young men drown in their own blood.

We have heard that Nathan Forrest inflicted a huge loss again General Sturgis of the Union. What this consists of and what are its implications I do not have a clue. The increasing pace of battles large and small seems to indicate that Grant has an overall plan.

I hope to God he does. We have just had a rumor that Grant is assaulting the Petersburg defenses. We have been told that these defenses are formidable, so my hopes are not high.

Your brothers show exceptional talent at administrating and thank God for them. We have been told by the Lincoln administration that their service at the hospital is critical and they are exempt from the draft. The entire family feels this is just. Our brothers are putting in 18-hour days and were it not for their youth I believe they would die of overwork. Please write.

Love,

Mary

CHAPTER NINETY-ONE

July 15, 1864

Dear Mary

It is possible that our mail is crossing somewhat in the system. I will just write. If I repeat some information don't be surprised. It has been a month of intense combat. Grant is using his armies as one weapon. On June 15-18 as you noted Grant has made several costly frontal assaults. The Battle of Cold Harbor was a blood bath for the Union. Grant lost over 13,000 soldiers to Lee's 3.000. Grant got few returns for this effort.

Yet Grant presses on. It is rumored that Grant never visits the dead and wounded because he cannot take in the horrible sights and mental pain. Grant is willing to spend his soldier's lives freely. God save us from war. Grant decided to change his goal to Petersburg.

The Union Army quietly crossed the James River. Petersburg has key railroad works that supply Richmond and Lee himself. It appears there was a brief window that Petersburg was weakly defended. He chose Butler to take the goal, but Butler again moved too slowly, and Lee quickly filled the gap. Grant has been cursed by slow generals. Grant decides he must reduce Petersburg by siege methods. Lee is aware he cannot win a siege battle. His supply line is weak and is exposed to nearly constant attack.

Joe and I have been able to do only fair work in these conditions. We have gotten 600-yard standoff distance, and we are again in a shoot and move routine. The problem is that targets in trenches are small and fleeting. They are not walking around as is the case with an open battle line.

Often we must wait for the same head to poke out for a couple of seconds. We were only able to get four kills. In all cases the targets were enlisted men. Our own lines are also a target for enemy sharpshooters. With so many trenches and debris the enemy shooter can be well hidden and difficult to find

There was also a battle on Kennesaw Mountain Georgia. This was part of General Sherman's march to Atlanta. Sherman attempted to charge a strong defense system. His attack was poorly thought out. Sherman took a 3000 man loss for no gain. He then resumed a flanking movement, and the enemy had to again retreat toward Atlanta.

The Battle of Monocacy was fought approximately July 9-12-1864. Jubal Early tried to take pressure off Lee by marching on Washington itself. He briefly fired at Washington defenses but was delayed by Lew Wallace with his 6000 men.

Even though Wallace suffered a loss it delayed Early long enough that Federal troops reinforced Washington defenses. This was not a serious action, and it was barely discussed at the general staff meeting. It is said that Lincoln himself briefly viewed the battle.

For the first time during my service in the Union Army I firmly believe we are within one year of victory. Lee is no longer able to set the pace or choose the ground of battle. He is forced to react to Grants actions not the other way around. In my opinion Sherman will take Atlanta soon.

I also believe the Shenandoah Valley will soon be removed from the Rebel cause. All food will be destroyed or removed from the Shenandoah Valley. The destruction of Lee's Army is the key to the entire war. How easy it is to put these thoughts on paper and how many tens of thousands of Union men will die to make it a reality.

I am so tired. Yet, I must focus and concentrate on my duty. It is critical that one never takes his mind off the task. During that moment of lapse the enemy can kill one. I have killed many men, and I will have to take that to my grave. I have no regrets, but I wish it never had to be done.

I confess that in the beginning there is a certain excitement to combat. Then over time the mind grows numb to its daily reality. Then that reality turns dark, and depression starts to sink deeply into one's heart.

Once depression enters the heart it becomes much more difficult to make it through the day. I know that Joe feels it as well. We know each other so well we can go for hours and never speak a word. The slightest touch or the smallest inclining of the head tells me where my next target is.

When the shot is taken we each know our next actions so well that not a word needs to be spoken. When Joe looks at the sunset I know the war is exacting its costs on his mind as well. I wonder what Joe can be or do if he survives this war?

Will he drift into heavy drinking and end his days on the trash heap of wasted lives? Will he or could he take a wife and live the daily routine of making a living? Will he become one of the thousands that will leave this war violent, ruthless, and ruined like a rabid dog?

The difference between Joe and me is that I have hope and the capacity to love. In short, I have you. In all the time I have known Joe he has never received a letter. I don't even know if he can read. Men in this business do not ask questions. It does no good to ask how a man became a daily killer.

Joe has never discussed the cause of this war. He has never spoken about slavery one way or another. He has never given me any of his ideas on the need for the Union. Something deep inside him made him what he is. Did he lose a loved one to this war? Did he lose the love of a simple girl who chose another? Did he lose a son in this caldron of boiling blood? Did he commit a crime so serious that his only escape was a military that asked few questions?

I have been as close to Joe as a man could possibly be and I don't really know him at all. Perhaps if I survive this war I can do something for Joe. Soldiers do not like to discuss what one will do when the war is over. It seems to be flaunting fate to believe that such a thing is possible.

With you I ask only the simplest of things. Will you love me when I get home? Will you help me heal my wounds and hold my head to your bosom? Can we be young lovers again and make love to each other in wonder and awe? Is it possible you will hold my hand as we walk together?

I have no idea whether I will be alive for another hour. The enemy is less than one mile away. Sixty thousand loaded muskets seeking to kill all of us. God only knows how many cannons. Mary my love, support me with words of love and passion.

Will you give me a chance to become your lover again? I am immersed by words of hatred, words of revenge and even words of total extermination of the South. We have many men who have lost their humanity and love killing. Good decent men that the war destroyed. How will they rejoin civil society?

Love,

Ray

CHAPTER NINETY-TWO

August 1,1864

My Dearest Ray

You must keep your spirits up. As to the when and how of grand strategy I know nothing. I depend on you and you alone. We have heard of battles near Tupelo Mississippi. Apparently the monster Forrest was finally whipped. This prevented him from cutting Sherman's supplies for Sherman's continued march toward Atlanta.

We have also heard that the Confederate General Johnston was replaced by General Hood. Jeff Davis apparently wanted more fighting and less retreating. Hood attacked around July 24th and was badly defeated with horrible losses. Hood attacked the next day with more horrible losses. It appears that the golden goal of Atlanta is within Union reach. God let it be so!

Mother is doing much better. She is kept so busy with the hospital. I wonder why she works so many hours, but her help is needed if she can stand the carnage. I think she has found some spiritual relief and that is giving her some comfort. I know you are on her mind constantly.

I have found her weeping in quiet places, and I know her concern is for you. We hug each other and we promise to help each other to go forward. We both love you so much as we are so afraid that the Lord will call you to His home.

As far as her concern about our sexuality I can happily tell you that it is in the past. She has told me that she is so happy for us, and she has told me she will never criticize our love for each other. She said this war with all its hate and tragedies has made her believe that love is holy and if two people can love each other that is God greatest gift regardless of gender.

She told me that any couple that can find happiness together must be approved by God because they were made by God. Mother now feels that committed love is a gift not to be questioned by anyone. I am so grateful to our family and to you.

Many times, your mother will tell me what a blessing I am to her. She says she is so happy that I am part of the family. This kind of talk makes me weep. I feel so unworthy of this family and even at times I feel unworthy of you. All I can say is that I love you and our family completely and all I want is for all of us to be together in peace.

After so much war I can barely remember peace. When this happens, I remember all the hours we spent together near the river. Our lovemaking was the closest to heaven I will ever have on earth. Our gentle passions will never be forgotten.

I know that many people question the existence of God, and I understand that. At times I question that existence as well. Then I am confronted with the reality of love. It must be the gift of a loving God who exists in holy splendor.

If we were just animals we would just couple and go our separate ways. To prove that we are not animals we are given love and passion by our Creator.

I know we are not animals, and I believe in love and the source can only be God. If only you could be here. I would shower you with kisses and help you reach that holy moment after which we feel so sated and so in love with each other. Slavery is the opposite of love. To steal a living life is so wrong and so hateful.

Why can't the South realize this? Yet we both know slavery exists because evil people have the power to force it to exist. Slavery must end. I just pray that I can endure the cost of this great quest. Please come back to me alive. You will find love, joy and passion waiting here for you.

Love Forever

Mary

CHAPTER NINETY-THREE

August 14,1864

To Mary

Your love gives me the strength to go on. No-one can go through a war without damage. Our minds were never made for this madness. One must work at keeping one's humanity. This is not easy. One sees one man die and right next to him is a soldier unwounded in any way. Why did one die and not the other? The answers to this are not given to us.

During these battles it seems the very sky turns red. The noise is utterly crushing. The cannons roar and thousands of rifles add to this deadly harmony. My ears often ring for hours after action. Yet one must force himself to be calm and to think clearly and rationally.

I depend on Joe totally. Nearly always Joe will select the target, and he has an uncanny way of finding the right man to kill. He tells me the range and the wind conditions. I make the adjustments and take the shot. Joe has never made a mistake on the range and only rarely on the wind. In this trade there is not a second chance.

If one makes a mistake it can easily be his last mistake. Joe has forged me into a human killing machine. He selects and I kill with no remorse. If I survive will I ever be normal again?

Joe also has great ability to spot enemy sharpshooters. These are the most important targets in any action. That enemy is doing exactly what I do and that is killing the most important soldiers. These enemy sharpshooters have great talent, and it is not easy to find one. The enemy sharpshooters are dangerous.

All the stupid sharpshooters have died long ago. It is survival of the fittest and the luckiest on the battlefield. I have only killed four sharpshooters in the war, and I feel a special relief each time because I know I have saved some unknown officer on our side.

You were correct about the defeat of Nathan Forrest at Tupelo Miss. He was defeated by an army group of Cavalry under General Sherman. General Sherman fought him at a place called Tupelo Miss. and whipped him badly. The days of Southern cavalry superiority are over. The Union has learned this trade, and they are as good as any cavalry in the world. We have a huge edge in the quantity and quality of our horses.

We buy the best and the freshest horses available. The Southern trooper owns his mount, and their mounts are wearing out. It appears that the horses are as exhausted as the common soldier. On some occasions the enemy's horse can barely run.

This defeat of that bastard Forrest is wonderful news to the North. This defeat will secure Sherman's supply lines as he continues toward Atlanta.

Rumor has it that Forrest has murdered some Negro army soldiers who had surrendered.. There is enough killing between the armies to sate any madman. The flat murder of the surrendered Union troops is a violation of all rules of warfare. If this is true then Forrest must hang.

We learned that Hood replaced Johnston in the Tennessee/Atlanta sector around July 20-21. Hood in turn came out of the Atlanta works to attack Union General Thomas. Hood took large losses. When will these fool Generals learn that charging an entrenched line is not successful in modern war? Some of our generals have visions of saber charges on white horses.

Most of our generals are utter fools who have no ability to change tactics to wage a modern war. They learned how to fight old historical battles with old weapons and old tactics. The battlefield has changed dramatically. This is literally an adapt or die situation.

The day of white horses is gone. Modern war is a vast inhuman killing machine. All we do is run the war machines and keep inventing more machines that will kill with ever more efficiency. Some days I am so angry. They send men to West Point, and they cannot do better than this? Telling young men to charge impossible positions is an utter disgrace. Usually, the brave men do not make it within 200 yards of the objective. They are cut down like a razor-sharp scythe goes through ripe wheat.

There is much hope that Atlanta will fall soon. There have been small attacks on small locations. Sherman is fighting for control of the vital railroads around Atlanta. Through these small actions we know very little.

Love,

Rachel

CHAPTER NINETY-FOUR

July 30,1864

Dear Mary

A crazy idea came up from that fool General Burnside. Burnside's idea was to tunnel beneath enemy breastworks and blow the line up with a massive number of explosives. All that happened was a massive loss of Union life. Joe and I had some set-back range. During the din we were able to shoot repeatedly. We did not need to move. I killed several men who were shooting at our helpless men trapped in the crater. Joe gave me the range and I shot as fast as I could.

I must have seemed like an insane man. Even in these conditions I still remember every shot. I still see and remember every Rebel I cut down. I wonder if I will be able to forget these shots if I live through this horror. Joe and I killed four enlisted men and one officer. In less than 30 minutes our Union defeat was total. I have no idea of our losses, but it must have been in the hundreds.

It was said that General Grant was furious. He paced back and forth chewing on his famous black cigars. Yet even at this strained time he never lost his composure and never dodged the responsibly.

Grant has such a will. He will not leave the field, and he is constantly pressing on. He always moves the Potomac Army to the left. In time he will cut the last railroads who feed both Richmond and the Confederate Army.

Soon the Confederate Army must flee or be trapped in Richmond. Lee knows being trapped in Richmond would allow Grant to starve him out like he did at Vicksburg. Deserters who enter our lines tell us that General Lee knows he is losing. Even though some of Lee's staff officers are certain Grant's losses will force the Union to retreat. Allegedly Lee said "No, Grant will never retreat if he has an Army. Our only hope is to bleed him dry and pray the political situation this fall gives us a President that wants to quit"

Morale is high in this Army despite serious losses. There is only one reason for that, and it is the name General Grant. Finally, one feels the war is being fought using a plan. One can sense the tide slowly turning. General Lee is unable to take the incentive anymore. He just does not have enough men. His men fight viciously but one can feel despair on the part of the Rebels.

General Lee is a great general, but his army is just not numerous enough to face Grants Army. Lee cannot summon other rebel armies because they are already engaged with Union troops at their heels. Grant's tactic of flanking to the left means that we are getting closer to Richmond and closer to the railroads that are the life blood of Lee's Army as well as Richmond.

Lee cannot allow himself to be trapped in Richmond. If this should happen Grant would just starve him out. Lee's only chance is to be able to maneuver in the open fields. However, Lee does not have enough troops to defeat Grant in the open.

I am certain of Union victory but few people besides the general staff seem to know it. The papers do not really understand military tactics. They certainly know defeat or victory but beyond that they are limited.

Relations between officers on the general staff are improving. These sharks smell blood in the water and all are maneuvering to claim an oversized bite from Lee's defeat. I would like to emphasize that the war will probably go on for months. I have no doubt that tens of thousands of more men will die. Despite all this tragedy the Union is going to win.

This does not mean I will be alive to see this victory. War is fickle, and oddities abound. Millions of bullets will fly though the air before Lee's army stacks its muskets. Many of those bullets are going to hit Union troops and many of those victims will die.

I hope to God I am not one of them.

Love,

Ray

CHAPTER NINETY-FIVE

September 21,1864

Dearest Ray

I hope my letters are reaching you. It does seem some of our mail is lost in transit. I will just write on. I am so glad that you fully understand my commitment to you. You are everything to me. You are the person I want to live with for the rest of my life. We are young. I want all of you. Just come home.

We know on August 21-September 1 was the battle of Jonesborough in Georgia. Probably a last gasp effort to defend Atlanta. This was a Union victory and praise God to the highest Atlanta fell on Sept 1. The falling of Atlanta is the death rattle of the Confederacy. The most beautiful city in the South is now in the hands of the Federals.

Everyone in the North and South knows this is the end of the Southern cause. Yes, there will be more battles and thousands more will die but the end cannot be stopped. Lee will be hunted down and perhaps some rag tag Southern troops will extend the war for a few days. However, the Rebels will soon be finished.

Much of Atlanta is burned to the ground. How much by war damage or intentional arson I don't know, and I don't care. The result is the same: A completely defeated city. General Sherman has burned a path of destruction during his journey and perhaps he burned Atlanta as well. It doesn't matter. The pride of the South is now crushed in mud and ashes.

It is said that Sherman burned a 100-mile-wide strip on his way to Atlanta. All of value, all eatable, and every structure burned to the ground. I am told that the finery of Southern ladies went up in smoke with their vast Planter mansions. I hope the ladies and the entire Planter class will be left naked, starving and without shelter.

I hope our Army will burn everything in the entire Confederacy states. I wish everything would turn to ashes. I want the South to be destitute in all that supports life. They must pay for the lost lives of 250,000 of our finest Union soldiers and all their lost dreams, wives, lovers, and children.

They must pay for the two hundred and fifty years of slavery the South inflicted on millions of innocent people. The South fully deserves this fate. I have no mercy. If the Planter class is allowed to live they will return to power and they will create de facto slavery once again.

How vengeful I have become. God forgive me. I have also heard that Sherman may march to the sea. He threatens to continue leaving a trail of ashes 100 miles wide. He has shown the proud Southern racists that the Union Army can travel at will and no southern force can stop him. This will cut the heart out of the South. Thank God this day has come.

We have heard rumors that the entire Shenandoah Valley is to be destroyed. All barns, fields, homes, outbuildings and storage are to be destroyed by fire. If this is true then Lee's Army will be deprived of its food stuffs. The Shenandoah Valley has been the breadbasket of the Southern cause.

If what we have heard is correct, we finally have Generals that understand war. Unfortunately, there will be no separation between the hunger of the soldier and the hunger of the civilian. However, that is the purpose of total war. Bring the hardships to the soldier's family, and the war will end much sooner. What a horrible means to end a horrible war.

Love,

Mary

CHAPTER NINETY-SIX

September 29, 1864

Dear Mary

On September 30,1864 General Sheridan defeated Jubal Early near Fishers Hill in the Shenandoah Valley. The enemy is driven out of the valley. This means Sheridan will destroy everything that supports life in the entire Valley. This means thousands of barns will be burned, countless homes will go to the flames, and any food stuff will be burned or removed. The Valley will starve. No-one will be able to survive the winter there.

All the families are fleeing the ravishing hordes of Sheridan and his hungry torches of fire. It is said the entire valley is covered with smoke and ashes. This is horrible but this is total war, and it is the only way to deprive the South of their main food reserve.

It is well known that Lee's troops are starving. Our spies in Richmond all confirm that fact. This in-depth information is due to my mouse-like attention to the generals who debate the next move. No-one seems to know the losses in the Battle of Fishers Hill.

Love

Ray

CHAPTER NINETY-SEVEN

November 9,1864

Dear Ray

Thanks to our glorious Union Army our President Lincoln was re-elected. The Democrats with their treasonous hearts will not regain the government and betray our cause. Sherman's victory in Atlanta put one stake in the Southern monster and Sheridan's victory in the Shenandoah Valley placed another sharp stake in the monster.

Grant showed his personal greatness by giving all the credit to his wonderful generals Sheridan and Sherman. Praise God to the Highest! Grant has Lee pinned down and sooner or later victory will be ours.

There are many rumors as to where General Sherman is going now that Atlanta has fallen. There is some thought that Grant wants Sherman to pursue Hood's army into Tennessee and after Hoods destruction to rejoin with Grant to run Lee into the ground. Another rumor suggests Sherman wants to go through the Carolinas.

One of the difficulties about understanding this war is how to separate rumor from reality. Since the fall of Atlanta and the destruction of the Shenandoah Valley all objective people can see that Union victory is only a matter of time.

I know for certain that Sheridan has scoured the very earth of Shenandoah Valley with fire and destruction. There is not one speck of food in the entire valley. The food basket of the Confederacy is destroyed. The morale of the North is one of optimism.

Indeed, the main challenge is convincing the public that many hard battles are ahead and that the war will not be over soon. Yet everyone is beginning to see glimmers of hope that the end of the war is in the distant future.

Everyone is on pins and needles wondering what Sherman will do. Father has good sources, and the underground news says that nothing that could burn is still standing. Sherman's soldiers have killed, burned or taken everything of military value. The troops have stripped every one of their valuables. Everything went into the pockets of the troops. Everyone great or small has lost everything of value including the silverware.

The Planter's families will have nothing to trade for food. Father says this is total war and Sherman is bringing the real costs of war to those who felt they were safe. It is said that every great house of the Planters is burned to the ground and all that stands are chimneys.

The pampered wives and children who have never known want are starving and without shelter. Their slaves are thronging to Sherman's Army and freedom.

The destruction is total. Everything of value is gone. All the cotton gins are ashes. All the bales of cotton are burned. Every mile of railroad rails are heated up on a pile of railroad ties and then the rails themselves are bent around trees so that they cannot ever be used. These twisted rails are called "Sherman's neck ties." Yet all of this was at a great cost. It appears the Union lost nearly 4000 troops and the South around 9000.

Love,

Mary

CHAPTER NINETY-EIGHT

November 15,1864

Dear Mary

Rumors fly around this Army as well. Due to my unique position as the aide to Colonel Hunt I can hear the debates firsthand. I always stand in a dark corner, and it seems no-one cares a thing about me. Sherman wants to march to the Sea and depend on the rich countryside to feed his army.

Grant is dubious about the idea. The risk is high, Sherman's army could be trapped and destroyed in the Eastern swamps. The President himself leans toward not approving the bold plan. The War Cabinet of the Union is fully against it.

Sherman argues against all of them. He feels he can do the job and show the entire South that nothing can prevent the Union Army from going anywhere they want. Sherman claims this campaign will shorten the war. The Generals in our Army are all against it. Only my direct superior Colonel Hunt is for it.

He said if we want to win this war we must ravish the South and break their proud spirit. This takes real courage from my Colonel to buck the idea against the main generals. Lesser things have ruined the career of many bold officers.

The big shots ignore Colonel Hunt. They want Sherman to follow Hood and destroy his army. In truth, the Eastern Army is humiliated that this huge victory was won by a Western officer. The do not want to see another victory going to this rough and ready army that openly despises the polish and the flourish of the Eastern Command. Grant is in direct commutation with Sherman through the telegraph.

I have breaking news. Grant has decided to allow Sherman to go to the sea. Sherman will leave tomorrow and be unheard from until he reaches the sea. Grant says Sherman and him have trusted each other for a long time. It is said that Lincoln simply stated, "If Grant says go then I will support him." Mary, please pray for Sherman's Army. If Sherman fails all our gains against the South might be lost.

I overlooked a detail that I missed. A surprise happened in the Shenandoah Valley. Apparently on October 19,1864 Early re-attacked and gained some ground.

However, Sheridan rallied the troops and swept the Rebels from the field. Early's army is truly destroyed. His remnants are fleeing to Lee's army. Everyone from the lowest private to the greatest general knows that Lee and his evil cause are in serious trouble.

With All My Love,

Ray

CHAPTER NINETY-NINE

December 3,1864

Dear Ray

I am so frightened that I will lose you. I know it is silly to ask you to be careful. Yet there is nothing I can do or say to help you. Return to me. I hunger for you. I pray every waking hour. Sometimes I am so frightened that I must sit down on a chair. I become so weak.

We are getting news of a great Union victory somewhere around Franklin Tennessee. General Hood of the Southern Tennessee Army attacked General John Schofield's Union Army strong line. Hood's Army took large losses and was nearly destroyed. It is said the Hood lost all his generals in the frontal attack.

Are all Generals stupid? Nearly every frontal attack on reinforced positions is a failure. The Rebels are our enemy but think of the thousands of simple farm boys that were lost because of a stupid General like Hood. Union losses were 2000 and Hood lost 8000. How simply do we say these words. 10,000 men are lost, and we think little of it. Will we ever regain our humanity?

Love

Mary

CHAPTER ONE HUNDRED

December 18, 1864

Dear Mary

P raise the God of all battles! Sherman has arrived at Savannah on the sea! Sherman has taken Fort McAllister and the enemy has fled from the town. The cannon all along our line and in Washington are firing 100 cannon salutes to celebrate this victory. The nation wonders where General Sherman will go next.

Events are happening rapidly. At the Staff Meeting all discussion turned to the major Union victory at Nashville, Tennessee. All agree that the Southern Army of Tennessee is destroyed as a combat army. Southern General Hood and his army were crushed. This outcome was under the hands of General Thomas with a strong supporting role played by General Schofield. I know nothing about Thomas or Schofield.

This victory was another big step to winning this war. The walls are closing in on the Confederacy in general and on Lee specifically.

Love

Ray

CHAPTER ONE HUNDRED-ONE

January 7, 1865

Dear Mary

This is a long letter since I have time to write it. I am wounded. It was during the so-called Siege of Petersburg. We were very near to Richmond, and it was just another day in hell. Joe and I had good standoff range, but this battle of trenches is so dangerous. I was hit by an artillery airburst. I was hit in the upper right arm with a large piece of shrapnel.

It is a nasty wound, but I thought I would be patched up to reenter the fray. Or so I thought. Unfortunately, there is more to this incident that I must share with you. The shock of the hit caused me to lose consciousness.

When I regained consciousness I was lying in a line of wounded soldiers waiting for the doctors to get to me. Thank God I had Joe with me. He carried me and my rifle back to the rear. I told him to take the rifle, use it and take care of it. If I didn't make it I would want him to have the rifle. I swear to God that Joe had tears in his eyes.

I tried to smile and told him to shoot straight. Joe kept the rifle and returned to the line to carry out his deadly trade. When the doctor got to me he took large shears and cut my jacket wide open to get at the wound. He immediately saw my bound breasts. Without a word he cut my wrapping, and both my breasts were exposed. I will try to tell what happened to the best of my memory.

Without giving me away the doctor quietly said, "Soldier you are a woman. What the hell am I supposed to do for you?

My thoughts were still fuzzy. Then I asked, "Please patch me up and let me go back to the line. Please do not give me away. I am a patriot, and I want to serve my country. I have been with the Army as a sharpshooter through many battles and I have killed over 66 enemy soldiers. Mostly officers. Please can you get me back to my partner? I swear to God I will never mention you to anyone."

"Don't you think the war should be over for you?" He spoke very quietly and asked with concern. All the while he was cleaning my wound and picking pieces of bone, shell and imbedded cloth from its depths.

"Sir, I came this far, and I want to see it through. I am begging you to patch me up and send me back to the line. I am an aide to Colonel Hunt. Perhaps he would agree to light duty. I want to see this war through."

The Doctor was a short intense man in his fifties. I remember how blue his eyes were and his clear concern for me. He looked deeply into my eyes and said, "This is not right but I can't bring myself to turn you in. God knows what the Army would do. I may dread this decision until the day I die." He bound my breasts in a cross pattern so that the wound could be accessed with a good possibility my gender would not be noticed. For the first time in my life, I was happy with my small breasts.

He went on to say "I will not give any kind of release. You are hurt badly. Your arm must be immobilized for three months at the very least. I absolutely will not release you to go back in the line. You could not ward off infection in front line conditions. You would be dead in two weeks.

Your right arm is damaged badly. This wound must be watched with great care. Infection is the short-term danger. If you can survive that stage of treatment it will take you months to fully heal. You will have some limitations with your injured arm. I am not sure of the extent. I can tell you that you will never fire a rifle again with that arm.

All this conversation was done at a whisper and very rapidly.

I said, "Thank you doctor. I wish it was better news."

All he said, "go to that wagon and the orderly will make you as comfortable as possible." "You will be taken on the next ambulance to the rear. I will be sure your case file reaches the right hospital. My name is Dr. Franklin Rosenburg. Harrisburg Pennsylvania. Let me know if you survive the wound."

The doctor dressed my wound very rapidly. "Soldier it is time for you to be treated in a hospital and in time you should be able to go home. You will be out of here in an hour."

"That is that. I didn't have any chance for long romantic good-byes to the Colonel or to Joe. No last sunsets and no glory. No emotional handshakes and no sad hugs. I never got to make wise statements to those I left behind. There was no pathos for me or anyone else. Instead, I was loaded up with other wounded like a side of beef taken to market.

The worst part was not to be there at the end of the war. It was what I had been fighting for and it would have been nice to be there. Kind of like a period at the end of a sentence. I have not the slightest doubt Grant will finish the job soon. I thought about all the fighting and the killing. I remembered all the nights of pouring rain under a battered overcoat. I remembered how close to death I had been for so many months.

I felt a growing warming spark inside me, and I decided I wanted to live.

I thought of you. How faithfully you wrote to me. How you reminded me of our love. I thought of all those times enjoying our love and sating our passions. No-one on earth has the right to judge our private hours. During my worst hours I would re-read your letters many times. In fact, those letters gave me the only hope I had in this war.

I am battered up, but I am alive unlike hundreds of thousands of our fellow soldiers. I let myself think of holding you in my arms and in a flash I wanted to go home and be with you for the rest of my life. I have done my part, and I have seen enough of this war. Seeing you again would be far better than watching General Lee surrender to General Grant. All my concerns about this war just dropped away. I knew the end of the story and I did not need to be there. All I want is you.

The first part of the trip was extremely painful. Then someone gave me morphine pills. Then I felt no pain at all. Whoever discovered the benefits of morphine should be in heaven. Now I seem to spend most of my time asleep. I was finally transported by water, but I have no idea of the vessel. With hindsight I must have been taken down the James River. I seemed to fade in and out. I slept a great deal. There must have been at least 250 patients. There were some nurses and many volunteers.

The same female volunteer on the ship treated my wounds. She had told me she was from France. She gave me great care. I think she was ecstatic to converse in French. I was given morphine several times in my travels. I could not believe how the chemical could stop pain so quickly.

Mary, my love, I am in the Grosvenor Hospital in Alexandria Va. They insisted I go there because it was the best. Please send me a letter.

All my Love,

Ray

CHAPTER ONE HUNDRED-TWO

January 11, 1865

Dearest Ray

By the time you get this letter I will be at your side. It is possible you may be able to be transferred to our home hospital in time. I pray to God I will be able to help.

Love,

Mary

CHAPTER ONE HUNDRED-THREE

January 16, 1865

Grosvenor Hospital

Alexandria Va.

Thank God in Heaven Mary is here with me. We held hands. Mary and I wept. I never hoped I would see her again. After all the battles and all the death, I never truly believed I would survive. My wound healed very slowly with many complications. I lost part of my movement in my right arm. My battlefield doctor was right; I would never be able to shoot a rifle again. This did not present any problem. After all my shooting in the war I was happy to lay my rifle down for good.

Despite my efforts to conceal my gender it was discovered at the Grosvenor Hospital on the first day. I was an object of curiosity for a while. Many people came to my bed and asked questions. People were astonished that a woman could serve as a man and keep her gender a secret. I never talked about gender equality. In fact, I hardly talked at all. Curious people apparently believed I was a deaf-mute and eventually they drifted away.

I felt the interest would die down if I did not feed it. After all there was a war going on. However, my identity with my powerful Summerfield family could not be kept out of the papers. Colonel Hunt attested to my war record and insisted on asking the government for promotion, war medals, lifetime health care and a pension. President Lincoln rapidly intervened and I was awarded these benefits on March 16,1865.

However, President Lincoln formally and personally declined my request to return to active duty based on my injury and my gender. The president added a small personal note.

It stated:

> To First Lieutenant Rachel Summerfield
>
> "If I had known that women could fight like you I would have never bothered with men."
>
> With All Due Respect and Many Thanks,
>
> President
>
> Abraham Lincoln

I was in this hospital for seven months. At last, the doctors decided I would be able to travel and return to my family. The war has been over since Appomattox April 9,1865. The family hospital gradually closed as the Civil War patient's needs faded away. The Union was saved, and slavery was abolished. The total price of this war will never be known. Lincoln was assassinated on April 14, 1865, less than a week after the general surrender. It will take decades for the nation to heal its wounds.

After I was out of the Army Father explained his sadness over the death of General Branch whom I had killed. Father and Mr. Branch were close friends in Congress before the war. However, father felt that anyone who would support slavery and commit treason deserves his own fate. I felt nothing with General Branch's death. After all I had killed many men, and I did not mourn any of them.

I was able to locate Dr. Franklin Rosenburg after the war. It was he who concealed my gender and we had close correspondence for many years. He was one of many who were responsible for bringing medicine into the modern world. We became close friends. We wrote to each other for many years before he passed away.

We asked Dr. Rosenburg if he knew of any quiet rural place that Mary and I could vacation without too much attention. He suggested Red Cloud Nebraska. His parents were still living, and we visited the area. The Elderly Mr. and Mrs. Rosenburg were delightful people. We found a large twelve-section farm that we thought would meet our needs and purchased it.

My war partner Joe was seriously wounded by an airburst three days before the surrender at Appomattox. He was not present when Lee surrendered to Grant. My family saw to it that he received the finest care. His deeds were finally noted by the Union Army, and he received promotion and many awards that he fully earned. He was awarded a full pension and lifetime healthcare. Nevertheless, Joe left the military. He easily found me and insisted on returning my rifle.

The family knew that Joe had kept me alive many times during the war, and he is an honored friend of my family. He accepted a good position working for my father. When our parents died they left

Joe a great deal of money. The sum was more than enough money to live comfortably for the rest of his days.

Mary became very close to Joe. She was able to draw from Joe that his dark-skinned daughter was kidnapped by slave agents and sold to the cane fields. Joe sought her for months before he discovered she had died in the cane fields and her unburied body was thrown to the alligators in a swamp. This was the common fate of hundreds of slaves who died in the sugar cane fields. For this reason, he joined the Union Army and fought against slavery.

Unknown to me, Joe could speak French with complete fluency. He and Mary spent hours conversing in that beautiful language. It took many months, but Joe was finally able to laugh when he visited Mary. He eventually courted and married a Negro woman who escaped slavery during Sherman's march to Atlanta.

Colonel Hunt served his country for many years after the Civil War. He retired a Major General in the United States Army. He authored a book on Military Artillery that became the standard text on the subject for many years. We often corresponded until his health failed. He had a good sense of humor and claimed he knew I was a woman from the very start. I doubt this statement.

Immediately after the war Mary sought a formal education in Pennsylvania and received master's Degrees in French, English and Mathematics. Her home preparation provided by our parents made obtaining formal education quite easy for her. She opened and supported a private school for gifted girls near Titusville which she was able to expand into a highly rated private women's college in Western Pa. Later that school was gifted to the state.

As mentioned, Mary and I bought a large farm near Red Cloud Nebraska. We built a small house in the middle of our twelve sections. We wanted no people closer than one mile in any direction. We wanted a quiet place where we could spend 2 to 3 months every summer. In Nebraska I was able to indulge in my love of books, book collecting and sharing quiet times with Mary. Here we had as much privacy as we wanted.

Mary and I helped support the small local school. Many of the students were grandchildren of original settlers in this raw land during the frontier days. Mary and I provided full scholarships to any local student who wished to go to college. I focused on Mary, my books and my growing book collection. Beyond this Mary and I resided at home in Pennsylvania. Mary and I treasured being with our wonderful parents until their passing.

Mary left her timid childhood behind and developed into a strong woman writer and speaker. She became a leading author in the women's right movement. In addition to standard works on woman's equality she wrote well received seminal works on lesbian love that made great progress in legitimizing these relationships.

She spoke to many audiences on women's issues, and she had the talent to charm and educate her audiences. She was liked and well received by most groups.

I was able to escape my Civil War notoriety by silence and time. Mary and I never hid our relationship, nor did we flaunt it. All we ever wanted was freedom with peace and that is what we got. The community has been kind to both of us.

Rachel Summerfield

EPILOGUE

August 24, 2017

I and Ann retired within the next year. The letters between Rachel and Mary formed a remarkable story. A simple story of two lovers named Rachel and Mary. The story would never be a literary classic or a bestseller. It was a simple collection of correspondence between two young lesbian lovers who lived through the Civil War Era.

How these young lesbian women survived during that terrible and tumultuous time is inspirational. We diligently did our research on Rachel and Mary.

Frankly as far as the background of Rachel Summerfield and Mary everything was open to any human who wanted to put in the time and research. The only thing that remained hidden was Rachel and Mary's lesbianism and their passionate love for each other.

Beyond that there was no secret about their lives. This was a story of two young lesbian lovers in a difficult time. Ann and I cast our nets far and wide; we retained experts in the field of investigation. We ourselves sent many letters of inquiry and we placed advertisements in all relevant places.

What we ended up with were two ordinary people who lived visible lives. Every fact that Rachel said or stated was easily verified by public and war records. She was born in Titusville PA. Her father and Mother were rich almost beyond reality. Rachel lied about her gender to fight for Union and against slavery.

Military records show she served as she stated for the period she stated. Rachel was an excellent marksman who won many long-range matches prior to her military service. This ability was well recorded in the rifle club records of that time.

President Lincoln did recognize Rachel's war service, and she received the benefits she stated. Lincoln formally declined her petition to rejoin the war due to gender and injury.

She was wounded as she described. Dr. Franklin Rosenburg did in fact serve and lived where he had stated. The correspondence between Rachel and Dr. Rosenburg was preserved. The Doctor kept all correspondence, and it was found in his estate when he passed on.

These letters were invaluable in our research of these remarkable women. Her treatment and recovery were as she stated. Colonel Hunt attested to her service, and he touted her achievements to those with higher powers. Colonel Hunt was successful in getting her records in front of the right people.

Unknown to Rachel her superior officer Colonel Hunt kept a diary. His diary was a precious jewel to our modern-day research. His diary of his experiences in the war created a clear record of those events. He also kept a record of "Ray" who was of much interest to Colonel Hunt. He recorded all her kills. With 66 kills she was the most successful sharpshooter in the Union Army.

He claimed that he knew "Ray" was really a girl from the beginning. This claim is highly doubtful and in any event impossible to verify since his diary only mentions "Ray" toward the end of his memoirs. She did obtain the rank of First Lieutenant and was given an honorable discharge. The weapon kept in Mr. Hansel safe was the Sharps rifle Rachel/Ray used in the Civil War. As Rachel wished we donated the rifle to the United States Army Museum.

Rachel's letters were remarkably factual and accurate as far as she could have possibly known about the battles and thoughts of the war. Her unique position with access to General Staff meetings yielded priceless information on the conflicts within the Union Army leadership. She made some minor mistakes but all in all the letters are remarkably accurate.

Her heavily edited letters were published by a Civil War History publisher. This small history book with scholarly notes has shown remarkable sales to the many people who have an interest in the Civil War and that time frame.

We retained the right to sell the unedited manuscript to a lesbian publisher where it received very good sales. Accounts of lesbian Civil War soldiers were non-existent up to this point.

What about Mary Sheldon? Again, everything was straight forward, and all records were verified. She was also born in Titusville Pa. Records show that she was born in a poor family and attended a free school. Her letters provided the link between Rachel and Mary. Rachel's parents took many photographs that also showed Rachel and Mary together.

Many photographs showed them hand and hand. As the letters stated, Mary was formally adopted by the Summerfield family during the time frame described in the letters and is verified by court records. Local and State records also showed these basic facts.

Mary did in fact obtain several master's Degrees from reputable schools in the areas of instruction as was noted. Mary matured into a strong woman. She became extremely active in women's right movements and was an author of early and well received books on Women's Rights and Lesbianism.

Strangely only one letter was found written to Rachel/Ray by her father. Likewise, only one letter has been found written to Rachel/Ray from her mother during the war years. An oddity between Rachel and Mary was their habit of writing short notes or poems to each other from time to time. This habit continued throughout their lives.

Some were found in the chest but many alluded to more letters that have apparently been lost. The subjects of this correspondence were mostly romantic poems or short letters mostly on the love they had for each other. Most were short notes of endearment for each other.

The Civil War beliefs and actions of the lovers were consistent with their background and times. Records show property was purchased in Nebraska in the names of Mary Summerfield/Sheldon and Rachel Summerfield.

Rachel's father died in 1890, and her mother died in 1892. The very large estate was divided among the children share and share alike. Mary the adopted child was an equal part of that estate disbursement. Again, these records were easily found. The library that Rachel and Mary owned in Nebraska numbered over 2200 books. To be exact 2274 volumes.

Rachel kept a solitary lifestyle. She was not a joiner in anything. She was an avid reader and book collector. Many photographs and acquired letters showed that Rachel and Mary were deeply in love right to the end of their days. Mary passed away in 1925 after a long productive life. Invoices show that Rachel had a single red rose placed on Mary's grave every single day until her own death in 1927.

Mary and Rachel did contribute to their community in Nebraska. They did help support the local school in Red Cloud Nebraska. Rachel and Mary received many awards for their support of various charities and causes in both states.

Although Rachel and Mary were supportive of many churches there is no record of formal membership in any church. Legal records show no conflict or interaction with the legal system in their entire lives.

Rachel died in 1927 at age 84 after she survived Mary by two years who passed at 82. There was a family service without religious rites. I and Ann visited their modest graves in PA. Rachel and Mary were buried side by side in the family plot without fanfare. The stones recorded their names Rachel Summerfield and Mary Summerfield/Shelton followed by birth and death dates.

There were no emblements to indicate their private relationship.

~THE END~

Made in United States
Troutdale, OR
12/23/2024

25982506R00216